A Man with a Past

A Man with a Past

Mary Connealy

THORNDIKE PRESS
A part of Gale, a Cengage Company

LIBRARY OF CONGRESS CIP DATA ON FILE.
CATALOGUING IN PUBLICATION FOR THIS BOOK
IS AVAILABLE FROM THE LIBRARY OF CONGRESS.

ISBN-13: 978-1-4328-8987-6 (hardcover alk. paper)

Published in 2021 by arrangement with Bethany House Publishers, a division of Baker Publishing Group

Printed in Mexico
Print Number: 01   Print Year: 2022

This book is dedicated to a beautiful
new baby in our family.
Welcome, Adrian.
You make Grandma's heart just sing.

ONE

When a man grows up in wild country, huntin' food, eyes wide open for trouble, he knows when he's being watched.

And that stranger back'a him weren't out lookin' for a place to have a Sunday picnic.

Falcon had fought shy of a dozen towns and wanted no part of Independence, Missouri. 'Ceptin' he didn't know where in tarnation he was going, and to his understanding, this was his last chance to figure it out.

So he went ridin' right smack into that beehive of a town on his old rawboned mule to find out how to get to Wyoming. And a man commenced to following.

For a lot of people, it might be right hard to spot a single man on these crowded streets full of shops and freight wagons. Everywhere Falcon turned, people

7

swarmed.

But staying alive wasn't easy in the Blue Ridge Mountains of Tennessee, where a man could find a way to die near every time he turned around. And yet here Falcon stood, as tall and rawboned as his mule, proving he was a tough, savvy man, and he didn't intend to trust luck with that man on his tail.

He intended to trust skill.

He'd said a word or two here and there as he traveled — and more often just a word, not two — and found out how to go along the Oregon Trail. Funny how much a man could learn by listening. He didn't want to ask a lot of questions for fear that man a-doggin' him might come along wanting to know what Falcon had been talking about.

The same men who went to yammering about the Oregon Trail would be just as likely to shout out every word Falcon had said.

So he said mostly nuthin'.

But he'd learned enough to find which way the trail went. As he understood it, Wyoming was two or three states along it to the northwest — mighty big states. Bear Claw Pass was the town he was looking for, and it was right on the trail, too. If he just followed the path, well-marked so they said, he'd find what he was looking for.

But before he showed himself there, Falcon wanted some answers. A lawyer who held information for him about an inheritance was in Casper, the first town east of Bear Claw Pass.

The sun was setting on a long August day when Falcon headed out of Independence. He planned on sleeping at a campfire tonight, as he'd done every night. He'd heard tell of such as a hotel, but he couldn't figure why a man would pay for a roof when he could have the stars for free.

The crowd thinned as he edged out of that crazy, loud town. The closest he'd come to a town before, not counting the ones he'd avoided on his way out here, was Chickahoochi Cove back home, and he didn't go there 'cept if he had trading to do that the traveling peddler couldn't handle. That'd only happened a few times in his life.

As he left that wild herd of people behind, the man following him dropped back and back and back.

And when the town got really thinned out, that's when Falcon spotted the second man. The other lagged farther back. Falcon only spotted him because the buildings were sparse on the edge of town.

One man, on foot, Falcon might've just

braced him and told him to fight or run.

But two was a more concernin' business. And two men riding.

Checking his saddlebags, he was able to sneak a good look at both men. Well-armed. Not tenderfeet. Falcon would beat 'em. But it wouldn't be easy. And tough as he was, those two men could get lucky.

Leastways now he knew what he was up against.

There were bluffs outside of Independence. They weren't any match for the Blue Ridge Mountains back home but hills sure enough and fully wooded. And these humble Missouri woods and hills called to him as if they were his natural home.

Land he could vanish into.

A lot better to take these varmints on here than on the plains he'd ridden across coming west. Of course, he'd've done it if he had to, but these men had only taken up after him today.

He did himself some thinking as he rode toward those trees, doing his best not to alert the men that they'd been spotted. He wanted to vanish, and for that, he needed surprise.

Were they horse thieves? He was astride his mule, but Harvey wasn't worth much money. They'd passed dozens of riders with better stock than old Harvey.

He had every bit of money he owned tied into a leather pouch tucked inside the waist of his britches. His bedroll was tied on the back of his mule. And his saddlebags just had food, a few pans, and bullets and a bullet mold.

Falcon had sold what little he had when he headed west, but he hadn't flashed the few coins he carried. He wasn't a rich-lookin' man. Homespun clothes and moccasins and a fine broad-brimmed hat that he'd made himself. His family had never had themselves any cash money, and there was nuthin' about him that looked worth stealin'.

It must be they were after Harvey.

He'd let 'em have the saddlebags if they were only packed with food — he was a good shot and could get more of that — but he needed those bullets and the mold to make more.

There was a pistol holstered at his waist, a rifle slung across his back, and a razor-sharp Arkansas Toothpick tucked in a scabbard under the front of his shirt.

A man could live forever with those tools. Falcon Hunt was likely to have to prove that right soon.

He rode into the trees covering a bluff and

11

took off up a game trail climbing north. He considered every move he'd make because likely enough he was only going to get one chance to do this. He needed to use his woods savvy to hide, and he could do that a whole lot better alone. It burned him bad to realize he might have to let them take the mule. But he'd get him back.

He watched the woods, scouting out a spot where he wouldn't leave a track.

He heard hoofbeats picking up speed behind him and knew the men were closing in. Not much time to find just what he needed.

And then, right before him, a massive, fallen-down tree stretched from the edge of the trail into the woods.

Falcon leapt down, landing on the rough bark of the massive broken trunk. He stripped his saddlebags and bedroll from the mule in a few quick swipes and slapped Harvey hard on the rump. The old boy wasn't stubborn, as mules were often said to be. He took off up the trail, knowing that was what was asked of him. The coming riders would be on him in a minute. Falcon scampered along the trunk, glad he wore moccasins instead of boots.

A bullet cut through the trees, then another. A man shouted, "Stop or we'll kill you!"

Stupid thing to yell. Nothing about it to cause Falcon to stop. But the shooter must've caught a glimpse of Harvey or Falcon or both, or he wouldn't have opened fire.

The downed tree Falcon stood on wasn't long dead. An old oak. The branches spread before him, thick and a lot of 'em still hung with dead leaves and clusters of acorns. Ducking around limbs, he looked for a hiding place. He didn't want to be seen, but he wanted to be close.

One of the heavy branches had snapped off and wedged against another big tree, slanting up such that it formed a near cave.

He heard the riders coming and dropped down to the ground in the *V* between the tree trunk and the broken branch. He ducked low and waited, tensed up, his hand on his pistol.

Cheyenne had nightmares . . . and she wasn't always asleep.

Nightmares of digging up Clovis Hunt and strangling his rotting corpse with her bare hands.

She jerked awake, as she did nearly every night since they'd read the will.

Her ranch. Given away to strangers.

A ranch her pa, Nate Wild Eagle Brewster, had started before he'd married her ma. Pa was a long-time friend of Grandpa's. He had been the trail guide on the wagon train that brought Grandpa and Ma out west, and he decided to settle in the same area they did. After a while, he and her ma had gotten hitched.

Pa had died when Cheyenne was a wee thing. Before Ma's head had cleared from her grief — or at least that was Ma's story — she'd married up with a handsome mountain man by the name of Clovis Hunt. Clovis was Pa to Cheyenne's little brother, Wyatt.

Wyatt was her partner in the ranch and a fine man, but his pa was as worthless as perfume in a chicken coop.

Now Cheyenne lay awake fretting. Her mind chasing like a mad thing, trying to undo what had been done to her.

She rolled onto her shoulder and stared out the window. She'd propped it open to let in the warm summer night.

No more sleep tonight. Not after she'd gone round with Clovis in her nightmares. Studying the sky, she saw the moon was low and the stars were winking out.

Throwing back the covers, she decided to

get on with the day. Maybe she could make a big breakfast and have it ready when Wyatt rolled out of bed. Slipping silently into her clothes, she swung her door open to face Wyatt.

He was fully dressed and heading downstairs. "I thought you might be getting some sleep for once," he said.

Shaking her head, she said, "You want flapjacks and side pork? I can add biscuits and gravy." She threw her arms wide. "Oh, for heaven's sake, there's plenty of time if you're hungry for an apple pie."

His mouth turned up in a humorless smile.

"Flapjacks if there's plenty of 'em. I'll help. We can get a jump on the day."

They'd gotten a jump on the day every day since Clovis had turned up his toes. Died peacefully in his sleep like the lazy varmint he was. Cheyenne and Wyatt hadn't even noticed he was dead until the noon meal.

They walked downstairs together. She thought of Winona Hawkins asleep in her own room. No sense making her get up. They'd leave food for her.

She'd squawk. She was over here staying to help feed them during branding. But she sure didn't sign on for breakfast two hours

15

before sunrise.

While they worked silently together, Cheyenne fumed. She and Wyatt were a good team and had been since Ma died three years ago. And why not? They were equal owners in the ranch and had been raised for that.

And now two unheard-of brothers, no doubt sidewinders just like Clovis, were heading here to steal all of her ranch and a chunk of Wyatt's. Wyatt held on to a third, but Cheyenne was cut out of everything.

She couldn't strangle Clovis Hunt, but she kept the idea in reserve in the event she got a chance to use it on Wyatt's brothers.

16

TWO

The horses came into sight. The saddles were empty.

They knew Falcon had sent Harvey on ahead.

Dropping to his belly, Falcon listened with every bit of his wits.

Eyes sharp, smelling for anything out of place, listening for the slightest rustle of leaves while trying not to make a sound or a sudden move.

The huge, broken tree stretched into the woods. Falcon edged along it. He had to get over it to go downhill. If the men were on this side of the trail, he'd come upon them.

There were only the quiet sounds natural to the forest. An inch at a time, Falcon reached a tear in the earth that looked like water ran down it during heavy rains.

It allowed him passageway beneath the tree trunk. He scooted under. The gap was

17

skinny enough he thought for a second he might get stuck. Sucking his stomach in and shoving hard with his feet, he got through.

On he went, downward, listening. A soft crackle of shaking leaves drew his gaze up and to the left. Close to the trail. Up and up some more. Overhead, he saw one of the men climbing a hickory tree. Hoping for a lookout spot.

Easing to the side, under a thick stand of scrub cottonwoods, Falcon watched. He didn't want to shoot. It wasn't his way to go shootin' a man. He'd do it if there was no other way to stay alive, but he wasn't to that point yet.

But close maybe.

Besides, any gunfire would bring the other outlaw down on him. The man overhead was the one he'd spotted earlier. To his way of thinking, that made the other man more careful, more dangerous.

As alert as a jackrabbit in a wolf den, Falcon heard the other man. Focusing on the source of the sound, it took all he had to make this man out. He was motionless, nearly silent. His clothes blended into the dry leaves and bare trunks like part of the woods.

Falcon might never have noticed him if

the varmint hadn't blinked at just the right time.

With care to keep hidden from the man overhead, Falcon moved straight for the one on the ground, using dips in the dirt, stones, and scrub brush for cover. The outlaw was looking at the trail, as if he expected Falcon to come walking down it. Falcon was coming at him but from another direction.

The outlaw held an aimed gun. One wrong move, one snapped twig, one startled bird, and he'd see Falcon coming. All he had to do was turn his head.

Checking the man in the tree, who was facing the trail when he had oughta be looking around him, Falcon drew in a deep breath, then launched himself rattler fast at the man in front of him. Falcon slashed his gun butt across the man's head.

The only sound was that dull thud.

Falcon grabbed him before he collapsed. Eased him to the ground and tucked him out of sight behind the undergrowth.

Stripping him of his pistols, rifle, and knife, Falcon made quick work of hog-tying him. He had more sneaking around to do, and he didn't want this one coming around and getting back into the fight.

Mulling what to do about that varmint perched up in the tree, Falcon examined him through the heavy thicket of branches surrounding him.

Giving the man plenty of time to settle in, Falcon watched him study the trail, then after too long, look around. Content that he saw nothing, he looked at the trail again. The man must've figured his saddle partner was sneaking up on Falcon and this fool was keeping a lookout.

The Tree Climber gave his long look around, then went back to the trail. Falcon didn't think he could climb a tree without the idiot up there noticing him. But he didn't think he had to.

He worked his way around so he was downhill, the direction the man almost never studied. Pulling the knife he'd taken off his captive, Falcon gathered himself, and then in one smooth motion, he stood to get all the strength of his legs and back involved and hurled the knife straight at the man.

Falcon dropped back into hiding just as the man howled and clawed at the back of his leg where the knife sunk deep. In his desperate grab for whatever was biting him in the leg, he let loose of the tree and fell to the ground. Landing with a painful crack, the man started firing his weapon in all directions. Falcon kept moving, heading for a large tree just a bit on downhill. He ducked behind it and waited for the gunfire to stop.

When he heard the hammer click on an empty gun, he leapt up and charged the man, who was still yelling like a lunatic.

Falcon had a notion of what he looked like by the sheer horror on the man's face. He knew he had strange fiery golden-brown eyes. Eyes that he'd been told could go wild and mad.

Ma had called him a berserker. She had talked of such in her family history and said he had the blood of Viking warriors in his veins.

The man's screams dropped to whimpers. Falcon slammed a fist into his face to shut him up. He jerked the knife out of the man's leg and wiped it on the Tree Climber's pants. He added it to the saddlebag he still carried.

Then he stripped the man of his guns and knives. Tied him up and dragged him to where the other man lay, still out cold.

Studying the two, he had no idea what to do about them.

He could take them to the sheriff, but Falcon had bested them at every turn. If anything, *he'd* attacked *them.*

They'd followed him. They'd taken their shots. They'd threatened him.

But were they men a sheriff would hold? They'd done him no harm, despite making a good effort. And Falcon had done them plenty.

A chill ran down his spine as he thought of stories he'd heard of men who had the ear of a sheriff. Such things happened up in the Blue Ridge Mountains where he'd grown up. Family roots ran deep, and a lawman might turn against an honest man and fight for kinfolk. For certain he'd do it if it was a choice between kin and a stranger.

Grimly unsure, Falcon pondered it for a while, even sat on the ground and ate some jerky while he thought it over.

Neither of them showed any sign of waking up. He wasn't sure what he'd ask them if they did. The only real question he could come up with was, Why in tarnation did you pick me to rob?

They were breathing steadily, and he figured they'd live. He'd never killed a man before, but he'd fought plenty. He was known for fighting at the drop of a hat. And he'd been known to drop the hat himself.

Someone always needed a lickin' back home. He'd hoped the world outside his Blue Ridge Mountains were a sight more peaceable.

Just now he wasn't feeling particularly

hopeful.

The day was wearing on, and he wanted to get on down the trail. He figured when these two woke up, they might be right behind him again.

Finally, he decided to hand out his own kind of justice. He took the men's guns, nice ones. Frisked them more carefully and took a hideout knife that'd come in handy.

He even took one of their store-bought holsters. A sight better than Falcon's hand-made one.

He found a leather pouch full of coins in one of the men's pockets. The other man had a bit of cash money, too. And of course, they both had horses. They'd soon fight free of their bonds, but they'd be hard-pressed to ride after him without horses. There was a brand on the critters, not the same one on each. Falcon had no notion of what the brands might mean, who they'd be connected to. Well, he'd find out if the brands were trouble when he tried to sell them, but he wouldn't get to that until he'd put plenty of miles between him and these would-be killers.

About the time he scouted out their horses and gathered up the reins, figuring to search the saddlebags later and keep the leather along with the horses, Harvey came meandering down the trail. Falcon strung the two new horses end to end behind Harvey and rode on.

He usually set up camp before dark but not tonight. Falcon set out to put some miles between him and those two sleepy men. Maybe even a whole state.

He rode into the night a much richer man.

THREE

He kept the animals with him all the way to Omaha. There he'd gotten decent money for the horses and other things he'd taken from the men. Except he kept a six-gun and a rifle for himself and sold his own single-shot rifle and the ancient pistol that was a breechloader.

He couldn't shake the itch of concern between his shoulder blades ever since he'd snared those two men, so he decided to take the train west rather than ride Harvey. With some serious second thoughts, he sold Harvey to a nice family that pulled a cart delivering supplies from their general store. He expected that Harvey would be treated well.

He had money enough after his train ticket to buy a horse when he got where he was going.

He boarded the train, gritting his teeth

against the roaring engine and the blasting whistle.

Stowing his bedroll and satchel beside him, he sat down. They said he'd be in Casper, Wyoming, tomorrow or the next day. Train travel was a wonder.

He'd planned on taking most of the summer to get there.

As he relaxed onto the wooden bench, he thought of Patsy and how she would have enjoyed this train ride. She'd always been a curious girl, ready for adventure. Though in the Blue Ridge Mountains the closest they came to adventure was riding over the ridge to see her folks.

Back home, it was a twenty-mile ride on Harvey to reach a trading post. And since there wasn't much Falcon couldn't catch or build himself, he didn't make the ride any more'n he could help it.

A peddler came through pulling a brightly painted cart once or twice a year and carried more than anyone might need.

Falcon had had a good life. A sturdy cabin, plenty of food, and a pretty wife who was quick with a smile and seemed to love him.

And then Patsy had died.

And her folks blamed him.

Why wouldn't they? He blamed himself.

26

But havin' a baby was as natural a part of living as breathing, and no healthy, happily married man and wife were gonna do naught but bring young'uns into the world.

Patsy Sulky Hunt was the prettiest girl Falcon had ever seen. Blond and blue eyed. Smart too. That woman could find a possum in an apple tree, fetch the food home, and make everything up into a stew and a cobbler without hardly anyone knowin' she'd been gone.

She'd been the shinin' light of his life. And she'd died in his arms.

When Patsy died, the babe went with her. And Falcon's heart went right on along.

Then her menfolk came around, ragin' mad. Falcon figured they'd shoot him, and he wasn't much inclined to object. He was that sad. That weary of the thought of years stretching out before him without his Patsy.

It must've been why he just plumb turned himself over to the Sulkys. And his not fighting back had saved him.

After swingin' a fist or two . . . or twenty . . . they saw he was like to just stand there while they beat him to death, and that must've taken any satisfaction out of it for 'em.

Or maybe they could just see his broken heart — which matched their own.

They headed on home and told him not to come around ever again.

Falcon's ma had died years ago, and he'd lived in that dirt-floor cabin that clung to the side of the mountain alone. He'd lived the kind of life where a boy got tough or died, and Falcon got tough. He was strong as a herd of bulls and mean as a badger.

And then he'd met Patsy.

She'd tamed the mean out of him and liked the rest. A strong, savvy woman to match him.

A big strapping woman but not strong enough to bear his child, which meant he dare not ever have another, as no woman was going to be bigger and stronger than Patsy.

And he'd been taken into Patsy's family. When she died, he lost her family along with her.

Before he'd more than healed from the beating, before he'd figured out how to go on living alone again, a rider came to his cabin carrying a telegram — and the rider was good enough to read it to him. That telegram tore loose everything he'd thought he knew about his raisin'.

A telegram telling him he owned part of a ranch in Wyoming. Left to him by his pa.

His pa who'd been dead, as far as Falcon

knew, for twenty-some years. He'd sure enough been gone that long. A letter had come, back before Ma died, with the news of Pa's passing. Falcon was sure of it, but it was a vague memory, something his ma spoke of now and then.

But here was Pa newly dead again and owning a ranch. Part of it to go to his son Falcon. To share with his brother in Wyoming. Another family.

It was a stab to his already bruised heart to think Pa had gone off to find a family he liked more'n the one here in Tennessee. Had another son. Probably hoping to do better.

Well, Falcon wasn't in any frame of mind to hurt even more.

Instead of taking that stab like he'd taken the beating, he got mad.

The mad in Falcon overcame the broken heart over Patsy, or at least distracted him from it. He actually owned the cabin he'd grown up in and had a few fixin's. He sold what he could and scraped together a bit of money.

Without speaking to a soul beyond those he sold to — who else was there to speak to? — he decided to claim his land and start a new life far away from this place of sadness, all the while wondering what exactly a *ranch* was.

He made up a bedroll and packed all the food he could gather. He had a change of clothes besides the ones on his back. Then, because he knew he faced a long hard trail, he strapped his rifle gun on his shoulder, and his pistol on his hip and gathered every bullet he owned and the mold for making new ones. Finally, he saddled Harvey and set out for a place called Bear Claw Pass, Wyoming.

Mad as a rabid skunk, he rode across the country, aiming first for Independence, Missouri, and planning to follow the Oregon Trail to Wyoming. Once he got there, he could talk to the lawyer, some fella by the name of Randall Kingston, from Casper, who'd sent the telegram. He'd ask Kingston where the Rolling Hills Ranch was and get a few more details about his new life.

Now, instead of a long ride on Harvey, he'd bought a ticket. The train was going straight to Casper, and the conductor would let him know when it was time to get off.

He settled in to ride this rattling train across two states in two days.

FOUR

Falcon climbed off the train in Bear Claw Pass, glad to be on ground that wasn't rolling.

"Pa, is that you?"

Falcon's head snapped around. He raised his eyes to meet a brown-headed man an inch or so shorter than him, with eyes that were all too familiar. Even a man without a mirror knew his own eyes when he looked at 'em. They were a strange light brown with stripes of gold.

The man was mighty confused if he thought someone mostly his own age was his pa. "I ain't no one's pa, mister."

"Of course you're not. You must be Wyatt Hunt. I'm Kevin. Your . . . your . . . your b-brother from Kansas."

"I ain't Wyatt Hunt, neither." Kevin? A brother from Kansas? Falcon hadn't been told of any brother in Kansas in this mess. "I'm here to *meet* Wyatt Hunt."

31

Kevin stared blankly at him. Falcon narrowed his eyes and repeated, "I'm here to meet Wyatt Hunt, my brother."

"If Wyatt is your brother, and he's my brother, then . . ."

A young woman and a younger boy, both blond as sunlight, started talking at Kevin.

Clomping boots on the train station platform accompanied a new voice, one with a strange drawl. "I reckon we're all three brothers."

Falcon turned. So did the others.

They faced a tall, lean man with overlong brown hair clamped down with a Stetson.

No sign of Pa in this man — except those same eyes. Ma had called them hazel.

"I'm Wyatt Hunt." The man with the clomping boots tugged his Stetson as if in greeting, but nothing in his expression was welcoming.

Falcon wasn't an educated man. No school within walking distance of his cabin. But he wasn't stupid. He stood right now with the pure truth of his father being more than an abandoning liar. He was also a low-down cheat.

"So y'all need help buryin' Pa?" Falcon asked. "I'd be glad to tamp down the dirt hard enough to break both his legs."

No help needed for a burying, but Falcon got himself a ride out to the ranch he now owned. A ride with a bossy woman Wyatt had brought along to town, while Kevin got to ride his own horse, just like a real grown-up.

But that bossy woman, he'd heard her called Win. Odd name . . . of course his name was the same as a bird, so he'd probably best not judge. . . . Win had declared there were horses by the dozen at this ranch he'd inherited, and a third of them would be his, so it'd be dumb to buy a horse.

She liked to sass, but he took some satisfaction in seeing she tended to only do it with him when she was out of reach.

He'd never hurt no woman, but this one he didn't mind scaring a little.

He rode in the back end of the wagon, his satchel, bedroll, and rifle to hand. They traveled through a scattered herd of black cows most all the way out to the Rolling Hills Ranch, and all were part of the Hunt herd. Falcon was figuring out what a ranch was, but it made no sense to him. A man needed one horse. If he was ambitious, he might have a packhorse, too, but Falcon had little enough to pack. Enough cows to give a man meat and milk . . . and all the rest was for show.

A ranch seemed to be some strange possession meant to gather up more money than a man could spend in a lifetime. And that was before arriving at the fancy house, big enough for a family of ten . . . downstairs. Who cut the wood to heat this thing?

There was a large barn no one should need if he had a reasonable number of horses and cows. And other smaller buildings he heard called a bunkhouse and a foreman's house. A ramrod's house . . . what in tarnation was a *ramrod*? It sounded like something a man used to whack pesky intruders over the head.

And that's where he got told to sleep.

Being told where to ride. Being told he didn't need his own horse. Now being told where to sleep.

It made him feel like a child. More than that, it told him he wasn't good enough for their fancy house. Like an unwanted guest. And likely that described him pretty well. Might even be fair.

Didn't mean he liked it.

He walked into his assigned house and dropped off his bedroll. He took a smaller fur bag out of his satchel, slinging it over his head and across his torso, and headed straight for the hills. He considered asking about a horse, but Wyatt had taken off, and the only people here were as much guests as him.

Didn't matter. He liked stretching his legs. And those mountains called to him. As he hiked, he headed for the high ground. He wanted to just keep going. Never come back. If he had it to do over, he'd've brought his satchel and bedroll along. Now he had 'em to fetch sometime, elsewise he might never have gone back.

He found a likely trail on an uphill slope, leading into thick woods. They called to him like he was a horned owl looking for the treetops. When those trees closed over his head, he felt like he could breathe for the first time since he left the Blue Ridge Mountains.

Oh, it was mighty different. In the mountains back home, everything bloomed. There were flowers everywhere in the spring and summer. For a time, as he walked along, he was homesick enough he couldn't enjoy this land. He'd come from a cabin set back in a near forest of mountain laurels. His home was on a ridge, and along it strung azaleas and rhododendrons. The trees bloomed as big and beautiful as the bushes. And tucked beneath the bushes were wildflowers in every color and size.

Here in these mountains, it was all leafed-out oaks and maples and cottonwoods. He recognized them. And the pine trees with their clean smell. But there were other trees he didn't know. Clumps of trees, tall and skinny, with leaves on them that danced in the wind, almost like the whole tree quaked.

He wondered about the animals. He'd heard tell of grizzly bears and elk with huge racks of antlers. And deer, mule deer much bigger than the deer back home.

There were big cats. He had mountain lions back home, but he'd heard these were bigger. Meaner.

He knew people liked to brag up their own land, so he only believed about half of what he'd heard. But he kept his eyes wide open just the same, lest a grizzly taller than a man came roaring at him from the forest.

There were differences aplenty, but he let loose of missing home to take on the exploring. As he did, the new hills and trees eased a lot of his temper. It would be easy to just walk on forever. Find new lands. Find an empty wilderness, build a cabin, and never come back. Never have to face the angry people back at the Rolling Hills Ranch.

Not sure what he'd do, he settled in to

walk. He was a long-legged galoot with tire-less strength. He could set a fast pace and keep it up for hours. He had his rifle over his shoulder and a pistol on his hip, he wasn't careless enough to leave them be-hind. He could live forever out here. He'd hunt up a few rabbits or catch some fish if he found a stream, roast a meal, sleep, then just go on and on, up into the hills.

He could hunt his clothes, bring down a couple of deer, and build a shelter from downed trees and stones. He could live up here for good.

As he walked, he thought of how Kevin had asked, "Pa, is that you?"

It dug at him. It'd always just been him and his ma. Her folks were long gone. Pa had taken off. And they were a long way from neighbors. Ma had never talked much about Pa 'ceptin' he was dead. Though she had told him he looked like his father.

But then, she'd died before Falcon was full grown. He'd thought little enough of looking like his pa after that. But even before she died, she hadn't talked of him much. The two of them were busy diggin' a living out of that hardscrabble mountain dirt. A garden was hard to bring along. They always managed it, but it took both of them working long days to raise and put up

37

enough food for the winter. There wasn't much time for spinning yarns about a man who'd deserted them.

If a third of this land was his — and who could know where the boundaries lay? — then maybe he could have a stretch up here.

He didn't see any cows. Would they pasture cattle on a mountainside? They raised cows in the mountains of Tennessee. Not huge herds, but a milk cow or two could live on this rugged land. He wanted to be farther from all of them than this, but it just might work to be up here.

But he had no need of a stretch of land from his pa. The land was his by law, but he had little enough interest in it.

Again, he heard Kevin say, "Pa, is that you?"

It'd struck him. Kevin had for one minute believed he was seeing his father again.

Falcon knew what it was to long for him. To miss a man he could barely remember. To love someone he had just found out was a betrayer and a cheat, a man worthy of hate.

That moment, that tone in Kevin's voice, was what would keep Falcon here. He found he liked the idea of having a family. Even one as mixed-up as this one.

He'd walk awhile. Maybe even for a few

days. But he'd go back after that and sleep in the ramrod's house. Get to know Kevin and Wyatt. See if there was anything to this family besides anger and betrayal.

But not yet. For now, he walked on and let the mountains and woods call him home.

FIVE

Wyatt was afraid of her.

The cowpokes were afraid of her.

The cows were afraid of her.

The horses were afraid of her.

Truth be told, she was a little bit afraid of herself.

When Cheyenne saw Wyatt come back, she saw in his eyes that he'd brought those land-stealing, sons-of-a-sidewinder to her ranch.

Already working with the strength and speed of two, she threw herself into branding like a mad woman.

Her land, her heritage, her whole world had been stolen.

She'd prayed about it. She really had. Prayed and prayed and prayed to accept what she could not change.

And still she was roping and throwing calves with a ruthless speed. Not hurting the calves, just fast and without ever allow-ing herself one second between. She wanted no time to think.

Rope them, throw them, brand them. Rope another one.

The branding was going double speed as everyone tried to keep up with her.

And stay out of her way.

"Hey, Wyatt, Cheyenne, Winona's here." Their foreman, Rubin Walsh, shouted at her. When she turned, he was looking somewhere else, like he was afraid to accidentally catch her eye.

Cheyenne turned to see her friend Winona Hawkins come riding up. Wyatt didn't speak to Cheyenne but strode out toward Win and whoever that brown-headed man was who came along.

She knew who he was though, or had it narrowed down. Either Falcon or Kevin Hunt.

The two men who'd stolen her ranch.

Or rather their father had stolen it.

Stolen it legally, but there was no justice in what had happened. Her land. Her ma and pa's land. The ranch had been built and run by Nate and Katherine Brewster and was always meant for her, while her grandpa's ranch was for Wyatt.

And somehow the twisted laws of the land gave it all to Clovis Hunt. Grandpa's, Ma's, all of it. And he turned around and left it to sons she didn't know existed. One-third to Wyatt, and one-third each to Falcon and Kevin.

None for her.

The Sidewinder. The name she and Win called Clovis Hunt until they'd almost forgotten he had another name.

She clenched her teeth tight to keep from screaming that word at the newcomer. Her fingers itched to just start shooting. But the one who needed shooting was under the sod. And Cheyenne found an unadmirable part of herself that wished him to the devil. Oh, she had no doubt his twisted soul had been cast into eternal flames, but to wish for it was a powerful sin, and she fought it — with little success.

Well, she'd refused to go to town to fetch them. She'd been gone from the house when the surprise brothers had come home. But she'd be hornswoggled if she'd cower here in the dust while one of the varmints came riding out to the branding. He probably wanted to claim one-third of the cows and drive them off to market right now. She walked out beside Wyatt to face the son of a thief. Of course, Wyatt was the son of a thief, too. And she had no desire to shoot him.

The men kept on with the branding while Cheyenne and Wyatt took a break to have a palaver with their company. Maybe he wanted cookies and tea. Clovis had been fond of such.

Cheyenne walked at Wyatt's side. She had her rope in hand, coiled and tapping against her thigh.

Win faced her, giving her a look that helped Cheyenne remember that no one knew how she felt as well as Win. Win's loyalty was unshakable. That she brought this man out here was probably something she couldn't avoid.

The newcomer looked her straight in the eye and offered her the land back. It reminded her that she'd been acting like a rabid badger for a while now.

Cheyenne felt her heart lift. It still wasn't right, but this was a generous offer. She looked a little harder at Kevin Hunt. Maybe she could see past her anger with him.

Kevin paused as if something was making it hard for him to speak. It was probably hard to give away thousands of acres of grazing land. "If we could, we'd just go, and leave you to this stupid ranch."

We? Cheyenne didn't know what that meant, did he think the other brother, Falcon, would make the same offer? Or did he have a wife in tow? Or his mother?

Cheyenne whacked the side of her leg with her lasso. "Listen, you son-of-a-sidewinder, you stole my land, and I'm supposed to be grateful that you give some of it back to me? Keep your stupid charity."

"Now, look here —"

Cheyenne whirled around and stormed back to the branding.

SIX

Falcon had been wandering for a time when the shooting started.

He thought of those men who'd come gunning for him back in Independence and headed straight for the new trouble. Not the way most folks would've acted toward shooting, but Falcon never could resist a fight. When most folks might've set out running for their lives, Falcon ran toward the action, not wanting to miss a thing.

He got close about the time it stopped, and he slipped around, looking for signs. He found two horses with the RHR brand. That meant the trouble involved his family. He wasn't overly fond of nor interested in his family, but in times of feuding back home, a boy grew up knowing you had to side with kin.

He dealt with the horses while he listened and hunted.

He found Kevin kneeling beside Win, that

feisty woman who'd come to the train to meet him.

He grinned when he thought of her sass, and then he saw her back was bleeding.

His grin shrank away. The only thing he hated more than a back-shooter was a man who'd hurt a woman.

Kevin noticed he had company when Falcon knelt beside him. The two of them braced themselves for trouble as footsteps approached.

But instead of Falcon getting a chance to teach a back-shooter that he was a no-account polecat, the man coming down the trail stopped, turned, and ran. Getting away.

"You see to her." Falcon spoke in a voice no one could hear if they were more than two feet away. "I'll go after whoever shot her."

He meant it with a rage that surprised him. "Get back on that trail where you left the horses." Falcon pointed with his gun to the trail just ahead. "Keep going forward. I tied your mounts down the trail a ways. That trail will lead you to the ranch house. It's not far."

Falcon moved with one goal in mind. To find out who was low-down enough to shoot a woman in the back.

He was fast and silent as he put all his

46

long-legged speed into catching up to the gunman. The back-shooter was running flat out and had a head start, but if a man lived who could lose Falcon Hunt in the woods, Falcon had not yet met him.

He closed in on the man ahead, who was making enough noise to raise the long dead and deeply buried.

This one was fast. Falcon was impressed, though maybe he shouldn't have been. He was dealing with a dry-gulching coward. It figured when he ran, he'd do it right.

Falcon kept going. A steady runner, he had no need to step carefully because his prey was far enough ahead — and the coward ran like he was stoked with fear, so he was hearing pursuit whether there was any or not.

Suddenly the trees thinned, and Falcon ran out into a clearing. A fast-moving stream with steep banks came twisting out of the woods just a few yards to his left. The man he was after was several yards ahead of him in the wide clearing divided in half by the stream.

Falcon ran on, and then in disgust, he fired a warning shot and hollered, "Stop right there, or the next one goes through your spine."

The man stopped so suddenly he fell

forward, then spun around, flat on his belly. No gun drawn. No fight. Only fear. Nothing but a yellow coward. A yellow coward Falcon had seen before.

In Independence, Missouri.

The Tree Climber. Where was the other one? The skilled one.

Bright red pain exploded in his head. He tumbled into the water. He hit hard enough it could've been solid stone. Then he was under the icy surge, being swept along.

Another bullet fired. The second man was unloading his six-shooter.

Fighting for consciousness, shocked into it by the cold water, Falcon slammed against the bank closest to the firing. Then Tree Climber was on his feet, laughing, his gun pointed.

"This water goes straight over a cliff," Tree Climber shouted. "Let the waterfall get him."

Falcon got dragged under. The stream was surprisingly deep for a waterway so narrow. He heard more laughter. This time both men.

He surfaced well past them and behind a stand of trees at the far side of the clearing.

His head roared with pain. Or maybe the water roared.

And then he went flying out into space

and hurtled into a free fall.

Cliff.

He'd heard that. A cliff and a waterfall. Falcon soared like a diving eagle.

He struck the water and was swept into a pond or a lake, but it had a current blasting through it. Then he was out the other end, and instead of flying, he was hammered. Stones and drowning water. Agony in his head that kept trying to send him into darkness.

He struck a jagged rock, then another, too many to count.

Until the darkness won.

49

Seven

Here came that son-of-a-sidewinder again. This time Cheyenne was going to ignore him and keep branding.

"Wyatt, Cheyenne, Win's been shot!"

His words hit Cheyenne like a lightning bolt. She dropped everything without seeing what was in her hands. It might've been a calf.

"She's not bad hurt. She's been doctored. But she needs someone with her."

Cheyenne ran for her horse, slapped a bridle on it, and swung up bareback. "Where is she?"

"At the ranch —"

She spurred her horse and was riding for home between one heartbeat and the next.

Bent low over her horse's neck, she heard hooves pounding behind her and glanced back to see Wyatt was astride, taking out after her. Kevin barely a pace behind.

She faced ahead and left them in the dust.

"She's not bad hurt."

Those words echoed in her head, helping her fight the terror.

"She's not bad hurt."

It was impossible not to think that somehow, in a land that had gotten purely peaceful in recent years, this shooting didn't have something to do with these surprise brothers.

When she reached the ranch, a blond, gangly kid came running out like he'd seen a gunshot wound.

"She's all right." The boy waved his hands at her and broke off the mad dash. "You go on in. I'll put your horse up."

That was mighty neighborly of him. Maybe he was making himself useful because he knew he was as wanted as a swarm of locusts.

"I tend my own horse." She just could not stop snarling at everyone. She made a dash for the barn and stripped the bridle off her mare, and turned her into the corral. Then ran for the house. The kid stayed at her side, yammering about a scratch and a few stitches.

It helped her to enter the house in less of a panic.

As she went in, she heard Wyatt and Kevin coming into the yard.

51

Cheyenne surveyed Win. "You're sitting up?"

"Yep, and near ready for supper." Win sounded unsteady, and she was milk white. She sat straddling a chair so her arms were crossed on the back of it. But she wasn't, in fact, hurt badly. Cheyenne could see that.

"I've got a shirtwaist on that buttons down the back so you can check it." Win reached up and grabbed Cheyenne's hand, and their eyes met. An anchor. Cheyenne realized something that threw her like a branded calf.

Win was the strong one of the two of them.

It'd never been like that before. Win had always preferred the RHR to her home. She stayed in Bear Claw Pass teaching school when it was in session, but the rest of the time, ever since she'd returned from finishing school, she'd been out here. She didn't even go home for holidays. Her pa came over here instead.

Her pa seemed like an easygoing man to Cheyenne. Lazy but harmless. A tiny part of her admitted he was a man who looked like he needed someone to run his life.

Cheyenne and Oliver Hawkins had spoken a few times, and he'd let it be known he admired her.

Since this . . . this disaster of having her land stolen, she'd talked to him a number of times.

Whatever Win's reasons for being over here all the time, Cheyenne had viewed her oldest friend as needing support. And Cheyenne had been that support.

But looking into Win's eyes, Cheyenne felt like she was looking at solid ground in the middle of a raging flood. Win had been that solid ground since the will. And Cheyenne had let Win shelter her as best as Win was able.

It struck hard for Cheyenne to see herself as weak, but there was truth in it. She couldn't get her feet under her. She'd fight to do it, then before she knew it, off she went, raging along with the floodwaters again. Win had helped her, at least kept her head above water.

"Molly did a great job tending me." Win gestured toward a young blond woman. "This is Kevin's sister. And his brother, Andy."

Molly stood at the stove, wearing a tidy calico dress, blue splattered with white flowers. A young woman so feminine and pretty she made Cheyenne feel like an uncivilized savage.

Andy stood beside Molly where they both

cooked. Something about them seemed strange, like they were all three, Win, Molly, and Andy, trying to appear unnaturally calm when there was a gunshot woman in their midst.

"Kevin's ma remarried when she heard the Sidewinder was dead," Win said. "And that means their parents weren't legally married, and it caused no end of trouble for them back in Kansas."

Cheyenne studied them. Molly and Andy. Just perfect. Kevin hadn't just come here to steal her land, he'd brought his whole family with him to aid in the invasion.

Cheyenne nodded because the only words she wanted to speak were ugly enough they were better left unsaid. She peeked at the wound but didn't remove the bandage. It was too tidy, and anyway no one tried to stop her. If they had, just to be fighting against someone all the livelong day, she'd've probably insisted on unwrapping the bandage and checking for herself.

"Molly's had some practice doctoring. She sewed me up and bandaged my back. She's very skilled."

"You know doctoring?"

Molly had turned away and was getting a meal. Doctoring, cooking, what was there this little beauty couldn't do? None of this

54

was her fault, and Cheyenne felt plenty of shame at her anger. That didn't make her any more cheerful.

Wyatt came charging in and wanted to know Win's version of what had happened.

"I'm fine, Wyatt."

"Where were you? Where exactly did —"

As they bickered, Molly set a meal on, and after a lot of fussing, they all sat down at the table. Kevin began a prayer, but suddenly Wyatt broke in, "Where's Falcon?"

Cheyenne had been trying to forget the third brother.

Kevin quickly explained how Falcon found him and Win in the woods and had gone after the man shooting at them. Kevin and Wyatt looked hard at each other, then shoved back from the table, grabbed what food they could tote along, and rushed for the door.

"Be careful," Cheyenne warned grimly. "If Falcon's as good as you say he is, and they got him, then we're all in terrible danger."

After Wyatt and Kevin left, the rest of them ate, but the meal liked to have choked Cheyenne.

As Molly finished her stew, she said they weren't going to take Kevin's full third of the land, like they were giving her a nice generous gift. Kevin had said it earlier, but it made Cheyenne's jaw clench tighter and tighter and tighter. She held herself in control, fought for it.

Win got Molly and Andy talking about their lives back in Kansas, which sounded miserable enough Cheyenne could see why they didn't pass up a chance to steal her land.

"You two need to sleep in here tonight," Win said. "Wyatt will be in here, but we should get Kevin in here, too. There is safety in numbers."

Cheyenne had been holding up through all the talk until Win invited these fools into the house. She slammed her fists hard on the table.

Win jumped and gasped in pain from the sudden movement.

"I'll not take charity from such as you all." Cheyenne shoved her chair back hard, knowing she was acting the fool, but the hurt inside churned until she couldn't keep it in. She wanted to cry, but that was a weakness she couldn't let them see. So instead she erupted.

"I told your brother, and I'll tell you — that land is mine. You've stolen it from me. To give me a good chunk of it back as if it's a kindness? Well, that makes me want to pull a gun and start firing."

56

Molly moved to put herself between Cheyenne and Andy. Cheyenne fought the urge to roll her eyes. As if Molly could stop her if Cheyenne was really of a mind to do violence.

With a mean kind of laugh, Cheyenne made her decision. "I'm not going to shoot you. Hanging would be the result, and that would probably just make things easier for everyone."

Cheyenne ignored the sinking feeling that she might actually be right about that. "I've had an offer of marriage. It'll get me out of here, and I'm taking it."

She stormed toward the stairs, going to her room to pack, though she wasn't going to tell this lot her plans.

"Cheyenne, stop!" Win shouted.

Cheyenne looked back. Only staying because her friend asked her to.

"What offer? Who proposed?"

"I'm surprised you don't know. I thought he'd've told you."

"Told me? Who do I ever talk to? One of the cowhands here? Some friend of Wyatt's?"

Cheyenne hadn't meant to announce it. Hadn't even decided to do it until she couldn't stand to be in this house anymore.

"Your pa proposed to me, Win. After he

heard I'd lost everything."

"Pa?" Win looked truly shocked. "He's too old for you."

Cheyenne brushed aside her friend's objection before glancing at Molly and Andy. "I won't share a home with thieves. I'm leaving first thing in the morning. Tomorrow I'll accept your pa's proposal."

"Calling him 'your pa' instead of by his name seems like a real bad sign." Cheyenne didn't miss the sarcasm in Molly's soft voice.

She left the room at a near run and didn't stop until she slammed her bedroom door. No one came after her, and that was lucky . . . for them. She'd said she was leaving in the morning, but she began stuffing things in a satchel. Planning, thinking, running away. And high time.

Cheyenne spurred her horse. Fighting tears. Furious tears.

And she didn't let them fall.

She'd sworn long ago to never again let Clovis Hunt make her cry.

Oh, she might've gotten carried away a few times, but if she had the control she usually had, there were no tears. And there wouldn't be any today.

She should have just ridden straight over

to the HR and accepted Hawkins's proposal.

But nightfall was coming. She couldn't do that now. Even she, a woman who wore men's britches and worked right alongside the cowhands, couldn't do something that outrageous.

She didn't exactly want to go agree to marry him tomorrow, either, but sure as certain she couldn't do it now.

Because Win's ranch was west of the RHR, Cheyenne rode east. If she had followed the road past the Hawkins Ranch, it would take her to Bear Claw Pass. Another place she didn't want to be.

Her horse thundered along. The sky overhead was still light, but the sun neared the edge of the mountain peaks to the west. She took the only real direction that made sense.

North. Into the wild. She knew a fallen oak that she could use to get across the fast-moving river there.

Her heart chose the direction before her mind caught up.

If she could just be alone for a while. Think. Get away from all these blasted, newly discovered relatives.

Get away from being poked in the face every minute of every day by the betrayal of the man who should have been her father.

Not by blood. She had only vague memories of her birth father, though she'd heard so many glowing stories that she felt like she remembered a lot about him. And they had a picture. But he'd never been a real part of her life.

The man who came along next though, Clovis, he stepped into what should have been a father's place.

Cheyenne's only vivid memories of a father were him, and she'd despised him. And he'd done the favor of hating her right back, it seemed, though he'd treated her no worse than Ma or Wyatt. She'd never thought his behavior toward her had any special cruelty. He was just a sidewinder of a man, and she'd made a bitter acceptance of the fact that he wasn't to be escaped.

And then he'd died.

It should have been a happy day to finally get that man out of their lives for good. Instead, he'd found a way to strike a blow of spite from the grave.

And she couldn't stop the searing pain. The only way to stop the tears was to grab hold of a terrible fury.

Wending her way along a familiar trail, she pulled her horse to a stop. Wyatt would be upset about this. He'd come after her. And he knew her well. He'd come this way eventually.

Because she expected that, she'd brought along a pencil and paper. She took the time to leave him a note where he'd be sure to find it, telling him to leave her alone. She used a knife she'd brought from the house with this purpose in mind — not wanting to give up her own knife — and stabbed the note into a tree.

She rode on, higher . . . slower, deeper into the wild. The mountains rose up in this direction. She had a lot of places she could go, and she wouldn't choose one. Instead, she'd just wander awhile. A day or two . . . or ten . . . or a hundred. And while she wandered, she'd think. She'd thrown Kevin's offer of land back in his face. But that was pride and foolishness. Her temper was so crazed that things came out of her mouth she shouldn't say.

So she'd keep riding until she got herself back under control. She probably should have done this right after they read the will. She might be calmer by now.

An owl hooted in the woods, and the trail closed around her like a cloak. The threat of tears eased. She'd always loved the wilderness. If she lost her home to strangers, then so be it. She'd find another home.

She thought it, but her heart wasn't ready

to accept it yet.

Meandering along, she saw how narrow the trail was getting. Lodgepole pine branches were a ceiling overhead. As she went higher, the branches were low enough that she had to push them aside or duck to avoid them.

Finally, she had to dismount and walk.

Wyatt felt terrible about the situation. Since they were children, they'd talked of the day the land would be theirs. Grandpa had been one to speak of handing down his land. He'd loved what he'd built here and wanted his daughter and his two grandchildren to share that love.

And they had. The four of them, seeing as how Clovis was rarely around, had been a good team.

And they'd talked of adding more land, the good and bad of that. Was the ranch big enough? How much could one family handle? Was there a moral limit to how much they should have? There were plenty of others who wanted to ranch.

Grandpa had been a man of God. He'd insisted they all ride into town for the church meeting on Sundays when the weather allowed. They'd gone in many a Wednesday night for a singing when it wasn't calving time or branding time or roundup time or wintertime.

She let the darkness ease into her bones. She prayed. Sincerely asked God to forgive her for how badly the pain had twisted her.

Thought of the book of Job and all he'd lost and how he'd never cursed God.

Well, for heaven's sake, she wasn't going to curse God. This was none of His fault. Nothing about Clovis Hunt had a thing to do with God.

But her anger.

That was a sin.

And that was why she needed to be alone.

It was branding time, and it didn't suit her to ride off like this, but she had to be alone until she could go back and accept what life had given her. Or decide if she'd keep going, strike out on her own, find her own home somewhere else.

Or get married.

Oliver didn't run his ranch beyond hiring cowpokes, but she could. The idea, when she'd had a ranch stolen from her, had a strong appeal.

EIGHT

Could a body be on fire and freeze to death at the same time? Falcon was proving it could, right here and now.

He woke up drowning in icy water, every joint burning with fiery pain.

Only not quite drowning. Not enough to go ahead and do it, and end the fire and the ice.

His head cleared enough that he could breathe before he'd be doused again. At last, he was able to look around and realized his body was hanging in water to his neck. Clawing around, he found a branch hooked into his coat. The water was a blasting stream, and this branch was the only thing keeping him from hurtling along it.

His fingers and feet were dead from the cold. Twisting to figure out where he was, he saw he'd been slammed up against a whole tree that included this branch.

A tree that would let him crawl out of the

water if he could just break free without plunging on downstream.

He reached overhead and slung an arm around the trunk of the tree. He lifted his whole body up, fighting water that seemed angry about his escape.

With a grunt of pain, he managed to throw a leg over the trunk, drag himself far enough out that his weight was on the tree and not depending only on his battered, freezing arms.

He hung there, upside down, his arms and legs wrapped around that trunk, as useless and heavy as a sack of drowned possum hides, gasping for breath, trying to find another burst of strength. With a huge effort, he yanked his coat free of the branch, then dragged himself up and over the trunk and belly-flopped on top of it.

He lay there, choking some water out of his chest, and slowly getting the worst of the brutal cold out of his fingers, till he could rub them together and feel them.

As the worst of the pain from the drowning and cold eased, he could focus on the fiery part of his misery. His head was ablaze.

He reached up and back until he touched a raw spot. A long tender stripe along the base of his skull.

Where had that come from? He looked

around, studied the water racing below him. Had he scratched his head somehow?

Been clobbered by a rock?

Most likely something of the sort.

He lifted his head, aware of something bothering him more than the cut on his head. More than drowning. More than the terrible chill and the terrible pain.

He couldn't touch on it for some reason, but it was there, and it'd come to him. For now, one step at a time, he'd get himself out of this mess and track down the why of it later.

Edging along the trunk, he reached the muddy bank and kept right on crawling until he was on dry land.

As he stood, he looked around and saw woods and mountains. That hollered *home* and *safety* for some reason. And he felt sure it was important for him to find safety. He just wasn't sure why.

He staggered toward the dense woods, realizing that his vision was blurry and sometimes he saw two of a thing. He gained the trees and leaned against the first one he got close to. He walked along the edge of them, leaning when he could, staggering when he couldn't, listening for anyone coming.

Before he could be caught in the open, he found a game trail so thin he had to think it was made by rabbits. He turned into the woods, following it, heaving a sigh of relief to be out of view.

Then he plowed into a low-hanging branch and knocked himself over backward.

Lying there, breathing hard, he had a flash of reason that told him why he was in such an all-fired hurry to find a safe haven.

He didn't remember anything that had brought him to this moment.

Why was he in that stream? Why did he feel hunted?

And then as he chased those thoughts around, a real big one hit him hard.

He realized he didn't know his own name.

His thoughts echoed. His head was empty and in agonizing pain. Who was he? How did a man go on if he had no idea who he was?

Looking up through the dappled leaves, he wondered if he knew a thing about how to go on. Touching his holster, he knew his gun was gone. In fact, just knowing he'd had one — or for that matter, what a gun was — was a lot of remembering.

But he couldn't remember his own name. Putting two hands flat on his face, he knew nothing of his own looks. He felt the scratch of a few whiskers on his cheeks but no beard.

He looked at his hands and felt no recognition. The impact of realizing it almost knocked him sideways, and it might've if he weren't already lying flat on his back. He stayed right where he was to think.

The tender head.

He had no idea what it meant, but he felt danger. Even that was all instinct with no reason to it.

Time helped steady his pounding heart.

With no idea whether to hide or hunt someone up to help him figure out what was going on, it settled into his brain . . . or maybe his gut, that he needed to lay low until his thoughts cleared.

And he needed food. His belly was mighty empty, and food was strength. Did he go back to that stream? Maybe walk upstream figuring he'd been swept down. Find a shallow spot, see if there were backwaters where the fish weren't being swept along at a dangerous pace.

And he needed to get warm. Dry clothes. For that he needed a fire.

All of that would give him time to heal his sore noggin.

There was too much to do, so he decided he'd just do what came next. Food first. How did a man find food? He saw himself spearing a fish. Fumbling in his pockets, he found a knife. He'd sharpen a stick. Catch a fish, build a fire.

But should he build a fire?

He realized he knew how. But should he oughta do it?

He'd be mindful, and if no one was about, he'd build a fire, the thought of being warm and dry was too much to resist.

But first, the sharp stick and the fish.

He rolled onto his side and saw a tree full of berries. Of a sudden, his worries for food were set aside. That gave his rickety brain time to worry about everything else.

NINE

After a couple of days, Cheyenne got tired of wandering and decided to climb.

Since she had no place to be and no time that made hurrying needed, she reined her horse back toward the RHR and rode for home. She waited until long after sunset. After the cowhands had come in from their long day of branding.

She felt a twinge of guilt for not helping them. Then the notion of working her fingers to the bone on a ranch that was in no way hers got her all lathered up again, and she shoved the guilt away. But that easy anger convinced her she wasn't ready to stay at home yet.

She waited until after Wyatt, Win, and all those fools invading her house went to bed.

Feeling a smug assurance that no one would notice her if she was careful — and she was — she rode her horse right to the barn, stripped the leather off, and turned the mare loose with the other critters in the corral.

She snuck into the house, smack-dab into the kitchen, and collected plenty of food and a slicker because it looked like rain, and walked out. It was a long distance — especially on foot — but what difference did distance make when she wanted to be alone?

Three days now, she'd been camping and wandering and thinking. Her head was swooping left and right, mad and resigned and calm and furious, all churned up going from one feeling to another. The point of getting away was to get control of herself, and she hadn't managed it yet.

And then, by the full moon's glow, she saw signs that someone had passed through on foot.

She could track well enough to be sure it was no one she knew. Another invader. Could it be the man who'd shot Win?

All her mental fussing went flooding away. Someone was skulking around her land. And she didn't care what the law said, the land *was* hers.

Not only did she have an invader to catch and throw off the RHR, she had something to do besides wrestle with her own half-crazed thoughts, and that was such a relief she jumped into finding out who it was.

The signs were hard to read. In fact, it got harder with every step. She could see that whoever it was had started out careless but then quickly switched to concealing his tracks.

And concealed by a man who knew what he was about.

Once in a while, she was lucky to catch a half-wiped footprint or a broken branch. She lost him repeatedly . . . and it was a him. She could tell by the size and weight of the occasional track that it was almost certainly a man. The tracks were odd though. Moccasins, she thought, but not those made by her Cheyenne people.

Was this man from another tribe? Without being able to say why, she was sure this was no Indian.

She'd lose him for a stretch and start circling, casting out a wider area until finally she found him again.

It was a grimly satisfying use of skills she didn't employ often, and she was glad she hadn't lost the knack, but at the same time, she knew she wasn't near as good as the man she trailed.

Her skills were enough to keep her on the trail and judge the trail to be fresh. He was ahead of her but not far. She never caught sight of him, let alone caught up to him.

She considered herself a fine tracker, as good as anyone around, save the people from the Cheyenne tribe. They were her pa's family, and Grandpa had gotten on well with them, her ma even more so. Cheyenne had spent time with them and learned a lot from them.

But not enough to find this man.

The search kept her busy, giving her a focus for the intense feelings inside her, especially since, in all fairness, she probably had no business being furious with Kevin Hunt anyway.

So she searched and the days passed and her confusion built along with admiration for the man she tracked. And she thought maybe, just maybe, after she found this invader and threw him off her land, or dragged him in to face the law, she might be ready to go home without chewing everyone's head off.

TEN

Falcon felt like a savage. An animal. He decided he liked feeling that way. In fact, that might describe him pretty well.

He'd learned to trust his hands. Funny business a man's hands knowing something his head didn't. Like how to rig a snare.

He'd unraveled thread from his shirt and set one, not thinking, not planning, just letting his hands take charge. When he tried to think, plan something out, he'd get confused, and then his head throbbed.

But if he just trusted his hands, he built a good snare, though he hadn't caught anything in it yet.

The first night, he'd quickly tired of hiking alongside that stream looking for fishing ground, so he roasted acorns and pine nuts and plucked ripe berries.

Come morning of the second day, he woke up feeling stronger but still with no working head. Letting his hands guide him, he speared a fish and roasted it. Then, feeling steady, he speared three more and feasted.

His belly full, he took a notion to lean out over the stream and stare at himself. He saw a dark-haired man who had a few days' worth of beard on his face. Hair sticking up in all directions.

He had strange eyes, brown but with a funny golden glint to them.

His clothes were battered after his time in the water, though how did he know? Maybe he'd only barely been dunked in the water and he always dressed in rags.

Besides the clothes on his back, the only other thing he had was a small fur bag that had stayed strapped around him during his trip in the stream. But it only held a few supplies. No clues to who he was.

It was no use staring at himself, but it gave him some comfort to know his own face. It was a hot day, and he wandered away from the stream into the woods. The shade felt good. He found a clear spot that he stacked with dead leaves and tucked himself into. And he slept.

On the third day, the throbbing in his head eased off, except when he tried to dig out some memories. He still couldn't remember a thing before he woke up hooked on a branch, being pounded on by the rushing stream trying to tear him loose from that snag. He ate more fish and nuts. Then he slept.

Hunt, eat, sleep, walk.

It surprised him that he could curl up and sleep several times a day. That couldn't be how he normally went on. The head injury and near drowning must still be wearing on him and sleep gave him time to heal.

The fourth day he snared a bird. Then, when he got out his knife to get the bird ready for roasting, he studied that knife and had a bright idea.

The next time he went hunting, he used his knife strapped onto a pointed stick as a spear and got a rabbit.

After five days, he woke up with only a quiet ache in his head. He had leftover rabbit so hunting breakfast didn't sap his strength. With steady hands and less wobble in his knees, he finally took to thinking of his troubles.

There wasn't so much as a flicker of memory of who he was, where he was, or how he'd come to be here.

It didn't seem to be coming back to him through rest and time. He thought of that stream. He had to've been swept down it, it stood to reason.

So he'd walk back up it and see where

he'd come from.

He had been hiking along for most of the morning when he felt someone following him.

Cheyenne couldn't get a look at him.

She'd been trailing him for two days when she realized he knew she was out here. A chill went down her spine. Like a slap across the face, she was hit with a knowing that he was now trailing her.

She'd seen enough signs to know he was there, but she'd never seen him. Once she knew he was aware of her, she decided to cut and run for home. It was one thing to scout around, track down an intruder. It suited her because she'd had plenty enough of intruders on her ranch.

But to be the hunted. To know you had a predator after you.

The woods, always a place she felt at home, now felt deadly. There were overlooks and hideouts everywhere. She knew them all, and she sensed that this man knew them, too.

She was too far from the RHR to get back in one day, and she had to rest eventually, or she'd make stupid mistakes and get herself caught. Finally, in the relative safety of darkness, she curled up to sleep against a stone wall, covered by a thicket. As she faded off, she decided putting up with the newcomers on her ranch might not be so bad after all.

Falcon looked in her little shelter and smiled. She slept like an innocent baby. Womenfolk who set out to wander the earth alone oughta sleep lighter.

From where he crouched behind a bush, so close he could have touched her, he studied the woman and wondered what she was doing out here.

She wore trousers, an improper thing to do, but he didn't mind overly. She had on a shirt that looked like something a man would wear. But then Falcon didn't remember much so how could he know for sure about what men and women wore?

Her head was resting on a bedroll. She was covered with a stretch of cloth that looked like it'd shed water. Her rifle was near to hand. He saw the bulge under the cloth that said she wore a six-gun. Her hair was dark and long, braided and hanging down her front while she lay on her side.

He thought she was about the prettiest woman he'd ever seen. And of course, with his mixed-up head, she amounted to the only woman he could remember seeing so that wasn't that much of a contest. Still, she was mighty pretty.

He'd turned aside from following that stream to play with her. He'd made a game of leaving enough signs to keep her hunting but not enough to ever find him. He'd spent most of his time behind her, watching her.

Watching her sleep, he was struck by the notion that they might be the only two people in the world. He sure as certain hadn't seen anyone else. He reckoned there were others, but a man couldn't help but wonder. It niggled at something deep in his head. Something about a garden and two people alone.

The flicker of memory sent a shaft of pain through his noggin. He was feeling mostly better, but the cut on the back of his head still ached, and he was prone to stabs of pain as sharp as his knife.

Dodging any efforts for his brain to remember, he considered that he should stay with her. Wake her and talk to her. To walk away from the only other person he could find was foolish.

Or was it foolish to be playing games out in the wilderness when he should be following his own back trail?

The stars went out overhead, and the moon vanished under a cloud. A soft mist started falling. He was tempted, oh, mighty tempted, to crawl into that thicket and share her shelter, share her warmth.

A'course she'd probably shoot him. Though he had no trouble hiding from her, she was mighty good and seemed tough enough to draw that gun and protect herself.

And that got him moving. Leave the poor confused woman alone. He took one more look at her. At that long braid. It was a hard thing to slip back from her. Then again, if he wanted to look at her some more, he could hunt her up anytime he wanted to.

When he was back far enough that she couldn't see him if she happened to wake up, he stood and, heading toward where he'd woken up that first day, started tromping upstream. As the sun rose, it only turned the black to gray. Fog rolled in so thick it was a wonder a man could breathe the air.

Taking it slow, not wanting to fall into the stream in the fog, he heard the storm coming louder, meaner. He knew he shouldn't be out in the open when lightning struck. But neither should he be by the tallest tree around.

That left him with it being wise to find shelter. The thunder boomed and the lightning cracked, closer with each blast of light and noise. The rain turned from mist to slanting bullets of water. Then a lightning bolt hit an oak standing tall alongside that stream.

He saw a downed tree that looked to have a gap under it and dove for cover.

And by the time he was done diving, landing, and collecting himself, he saw that he wasn't alone.

A man and woman sat together at the other end of the tree trunk.

They were both looking at him like he was a ghost come to sit down beside them.

Then the man said, "Falcon?"

That question made no sense. He'd heard of a falcon. A bird. What did this man mean? But the voice. To hear another voice after so long. It kept him from jumping right back out of the shelter.

"Falcon, we thought you were dead." The man made a move toward him, and Falcon's knife was in his hand before he gave it thought.

The man moved back. "What's the matter?"

He thought to ask a whole lot of questions. "Can I . . ." then he thought better of it. To admit his head didn't work right would put him in a weak position.

"Can you what?" The man waited.

Only silence.

The man all of a sudden burst into words. "We thought you were dead. You went over a waterfall, possibly shot."

Waterfall, that could be right. Shot? The cut on his head?

The man said something about a hat, and a flash of something went through Falcon's mind. A hat. He remembered a hat. Maybe. Thinking of the hat brought a vision to his head. A memory. And with the memory came pain.

The man started into yammering, and Falcon tried to listen, tried to glean from this flood of words what was going on. At least the man didn't start shooting. In fact, he seemed genuinely concerned.

It was a long chance, but Falcon didn't see as he had much choice. "Who are you?"

The man shut his mouth. The woman hadn't said a word yet.

They stared at him with eyes so wide he knew he'd thrown them. And then he really looked at their eyes. Especially the man's. He'd just seen eyes like that, looking in a stream.

"He's your brother." The woman finally talked.

"My brother?"

"Yes, your brother, Kevin Hunt. And I'm his wife, Winona Hunt." She seemed to collect all her nerve before she spoke again. "And you're Falcon Hunt. You've come from Tennessee to Wyoming to claim an inheritance from your father."

Falcon. The man, Kevin, had said that — Falcon.

He was named for a bird? It didn't unlock any memories, not counting the hat, of all the stupid things to remember. But a falcon was a noble bird. And Tennessee? Wyoming? Father?

It was all new to him. He shook his head. A surge of relief at knowing his name twisted together with a deeper fear that it didn't help. He could be told his name, but that wasn't the same as remembering it.

"I've been wandering for days."

"You disappeared a week ago, Falcon." Kevin kept staring at Falcon with those eyes that matched his. "You must have been out here alone all this time."

"First thing I remember is waking up on the banks of a stream and didn't know nothing. Not a dad-blasted thing."

"Not even your name?" Kevin asked.

Shaking his head, Falcon stared down at his hands, thinking on how he'd relied on them, as if they were his mind. "I didn't know where I was . . . I mean, sure, in the mountains, but they didn't look like anywhere I'd ever been, but then, I couldn't remember being anywhere ever. I knew I should've had a gun. Why would I remember I'd normally have a gun, when I didn't remember my own name?"

He touched that wound on his head. A gunshot wound? "I knew how to unravel the threads from my shirt and rig a snare to catch birds. I could start a fire using my knife and a flint I found in my pocket."

"All that but not who you are." Kevin sounded bewildered.

"I didn't exactly *remember* how to do those things, I just knew how." He looked at Kevin, then Winona, then he looked down at his hands. "It was like the knowledge just came out of my fingertips without me thinkin' much about it."

"I've heard of someone losing their memory." Winona got his attention. "A sickness or a blow to the head can cause it. *Amnesia* — that's the word I learned."

"Amnesia?" Falcon tripped over the strange word. He'd never heard it before, except how could he know for sure? Maybe he knew it and had forgotten.

And his brother? That didn't sound right at all. How could a man forget he had a brother?

All of a sudden he had a hundred ques-

84

tions. His brother could tell him everything.

A bullet blasted louder than thunder and wood exploded against the tree trunk.

Falcon launched himself out of that shelter and vanished into the fog.

Gunfire! And not one or two shots. A whole hail of bullets.

The only shooting around here lately was Win getting a bullet wound on her back.

Cheyenne launched herself out of her little shelter. She tugged the hood of her slicker low over her face and ran. She dodged behind a tree, listening, judging where those shots were coming from . . . and where they were aimed, and ran some more. Straight for a firing gun.

Not smart. But Win had been shot. What if that man who'd shot her was out here shooting at someone else she loved?

The gunfire kept up hard and steady as the rain — but not aimed in her direction. She moved quickly, keeping silent, though the rain and wind, the thunder and lightning, the gunfire for heaven's sake, had to cover most any sound she made. No one was going to hear her coming.

And she was coming . . . fast.

Falcon might not know his name, but he

knew how to fight.

Matter'a fact, from the excitement, even eagerness, he could tell he was a man who liked to fight.

Once he was away from that shelter, he listened for Kevin and Winona to get away and heard them running the opposite way. Heard 'em. Which meant these would-be killers could hear 'em, too.

He held his knife ready. Two guns blazed, and they aimed in the direction Kevin had gone. Drawing back, melting into the woods, Falcon considered how best to save his kin. The gunfire ended, and he made out the shadowy forms of two men following after Kevin.

Once they were past, Falcon fell in behind them and lost them in the fog. It was like walking in a sea of milk. Just as wet, just as white. He followed by sound.

He couldn't hear Kevin anymore. His brother either got mighty quiet or stopped moving. Either was a big improvement.

And he only heard one of the shooters. It tickled in the back part of Falcon's head that he should know something about these men. Kevin had done some talking about an attack. About thinking Falcon had been shot.

By these two men? If he could remember

anything, maybe he'd know more about who he was.

He heard the sharp crack of a gun cocking straight ahead, took another step to make sure it wasn't Kevin, and hurled his knife.

He saw Kevin jump on the man and go to whalin' on him. The man was down and out though. A sick twist in Falcon's stomach told him his knife had gone true, and the man was dead.

A sharp jab of metal poked him in the back.

Another metallic click. This one Falcon could feel as well as hear.

"Don't move."

Kevin's head came around.

"Stand still, or I'll kill all of you."

Falcon had no knife. Nothing but his bare hands. He'd pick his time and take that gun away from this varmint.

"Get your hands up."

He raised his hands high.

Falcon saw Kevin's hands raise, too.

"Stand beside your brother."

"Why are you doing this?" Winona sounded near panic. Falcon liked to see a woman keep her head, but this was a big ol' mess, so he didn't hold it against her.

"Did my father hire you to kill Kevin and

87

Falcon? Does he want you to kill m-me?"

That's when Falcon knew Winona was planning something. A distraction at the least, 'cuz no one pure afraid would ask such a clear question. He waited for his chance, ignoring the back-and-forth talk.

The man pointed his gun at Falcon. "We tried to kill you in Independence, Missouri."

Kevin looked at Falcon. "Someone tried to kill you, too?"

A stupid question, and Falcon had no plans to admit his head wasn't working right.

"Never figured it to have much to do with this."

"You're a hard man to kill, Falcon Hunt. You not only got past us, you stole our horses, guns, money, and supplies and headed on west. You're a thief."

Falcon stared at the man threatening to kill them — mighty bold of him to complain about another man being a thief — and said, "Sounds like justice to me."

Cheyenne followed the sound of voices.

The fog was heavy enough she couldn't see a thing beyond where she took her next step. Even with that, she moved as fast as she could.

"Stand still, or I'll kill all of you. Get your

hands up."

Who was speaking? He sounded familiar, but she wasn't quite sure why. She wasn't about to start blasting until she knew what was going on.

Another step.

She could finally see past the man to Kevin Hunt. And two other people, one behind Kevin whom she couldn't see and the other . . . was a slap to the face.

Clovis Hunt. The man she wanted to kill until it gnawed on her guts was alive and well, and someone was getting ready to kill him for her.

No, not possible. He wasn't old enough. This had to be the other brother. Falcon Hunt. But he couldn't look so much like Clovis, could he?

If she stayed quiet, stayed back, whoever this was might just finish off something she was ashamed of wanting.

"Stand beside your brother."

She knew that voice. Bern Tuttle from the Hawkins Ranch.

She should stop whatever Tuttle was up to.

Sidling around, wanting a better look, she heard a new voice.

"Why are you doing this?" Win.

Win was here.

Cheyenne finally got far enough to the side she could see Win hiding behind Kevin's back. How in the wide world did Win get out here? And so early in the morning, this far from the ranch, she had to've been out here overnight. Win would never do something so improper. Had she been kidnapped?

"Did my father hire you to kill Kevin and Falcon? Does he want you to kill m-me?" Win's voice broke. Cheyenne had seen Win cry before. She was more prone to it than Cheyenne, but knowing her friend well, it was clear Win was faking her fears and tears. Why else would she say something so awful about her own pa? Which meant she was getting ready to do something desperate and was trying to distract Tuttle.

Tuttle stood there, sneering and talking of a plan to kill Oliver Hawkins and force Win to marry him so he could take over the ranch.

A cold, ugly part of herself hadn't minded overly if the new Hunt brothers died. Oh, she'd've never done it, never stood by for them being shot. But she was so twisted up inside that she'd thought it. But she couldn't think it anymore. She had to save Win.

Not one speck of hesitation there.

While they talked, she got in position.

"And then what about Baker?" Win asked. "How was he going to profit from any of this?"

Baker? Cheyenne only knew one Baker. Ross Baker was the ramrod at the RHR. Ross Baker who'd claimed his pa was dying and asked to be allowed to ride for Texas to say goodbye. He'd come up with that right after they'd read Clovis's will, but Cheyenne hadn't connected one incident to the other.

And yep, that was Ross Baker lying there dead. He hadn't ridden to Texas. He'd been plotting against her family with Bern Tuttle right along with him. Hoping Win would keep Tuttle talking, Cheyenne shifted again.

"His part was to marry up with Miss Cheyenne."

Oh, now Cheyenne was going to enjoy shooting him. But not kill him. She wanted to have a hard, little talk with him.

She raised her rifle, drew a bead, and shot the gun out of his hand.

At the blast of gunfire, Kevin dove at the gunman and slammed a fist into his face. The man went over backward, crying out. Cheyenne rushed in to get between Win and the rest of this madness.

"Cheyenne!" Winona came running to her.

Cheyenne stared at the Clovis Hunt look-alike. "Who are you?"

Win slammed into her and caught her in a hug. Cheyenne barely heard the "Falcon Hunt" muffled into her shoulder.

In the middle of the hug, she looked at Tuttle, groggy, barely unconscious, bleeding from his hand, or maybe his wrist. She'd shot him. For all the years she'd carried a rifle and a six-gun, she'd never pulled the trigger on a man before.

She'd shot a few rattlesnakes and a cougar that'd been thinning her herd. Some rabid skunks and raccoons and such. But to pull the trigger on a man . . . Sickened, her stomach lurched, and for a minute, she fought to keep from casting up her belly.

Holding on to Win helped, and Cheyenne hugged her back hard.

Cheyenne took another long look at the man she'd shot. He looked purely unconscious, and the bullet wound to his wrist didn't look serious. Cheyenne could pay attention to other things for a minute.

"Who's she?" a gravelly voice whispered.

"More family," said Kevin. "She's a sister . . . sort of."

"I am in no way your sister," Cheyenne said sternly.

So this was Falcon Hunt. One of the worthless brothers who'd come a-runnin' to steal her land. But this one wasn't pure worthless. He was better in the woods than anyone she'd ever met, save her tribal relatives. "Falcon, huh? I've been following you for days."

"Yep, I saw you back there tracking me and didn't want to talk. Once I was close enough to tap you on the shoulder and say, 'Leave me alone,' but I let you sleep."

That bothered her, added another twist to her stomach to think someone had been that close, watching her while she slept. She probably hadn't oughta wander in the woods anymore. It wasn't safe. Then, because she didn't like admitting he was better than her, she looked around at the mess they'd made out here and saw that Tuttle had lost all color in his face. She rushed to his side and saw a heavy pool of blood under his hand, soaked under his body.

Quickly, she grabbed her kerchief and wrapped it around his wrist, but it was no use. "He's dead."

She looked up as Kevin and Win walked to Tuttle's other side. Despite her horror, she noticed with confusion that Win and Kevin were holding hands.

Win looked from Tuttle's wrist to his ashen face and flinched. "It's an artery." She slipped an arm around Kevin, leaning into him for support.

Cheyenne had just shot his hand. How could he be dead? She swallowed hard and didn't know what else to do other than back away.

Needing to think on something else, Cheyenne stood, her eyes shifting between Kevin and Win. "What is going on with you two?"

Win smiled at Kevin. "We're married."

"What?" Cheyenne shoved the hood all the way off her head.

The rain had stopped, and that was a shame. She could use a solid dousing to clear her muddled thoughts.

"Yep, well and truly married. Vows spoken before God and man." Kevin put his arm around Win.

Cheyenne considered knocking the arm off. Especially when Kevin smiled. But Win snuggled closer like a brainless sheep, and Cheyenne figured attacking Kevin wasn't going to go over well with her friend.

"You're married. Falcon has been wandering in the woods for days. Armed gunmen hunting everyone." Cheyenne flung her arms wide. "I can't leave any of you alone for a minute or trouble comes flooding."

"This one's dead, too." Falcon knelt by Ross Baker. He tossed the ramrod onto his stomach and retrieved the knife, wiping off

94

the blood before sticking it in his sheath.

Cheyenne couldn't help but admire the man's style.

Win said, "We were going to be kicked out of the ramrod's house with Baker coming home. I guess we don't have to worry about that anymore."

With a sigh, Cheyenne started leading the way home. They'd have to come back for the bodies later.

They hiked for hours. She was the only one in good shape. And the only one who knew where they were going.

She had a lot of questions, and the group talked as they went until she mostly knew everything. Win being married, that just didn't make a lick of sense. But what about Cheyenne's life did?

And Falcon Hunt. That's who she'd been tracking. Despite hating these two men fiercely, she had to admit a deep respect for Falcon.

When they reached the main trail home, they met Wyatt riding out. He'd dragged those two other invaders along with him, Molly and Andy.

Wyatt swung off his horse, and out of the four people in their ragtag bunch, Wyatt ran straight for her and hauled her up into his arms.

Her little brother, taller and stronger than she was, and he had been for a long time. She still had to do most of the thinking for the two of them, but this hug felt as good as anything she'd felt in a long time.

Then the bunch of them took to chattering. When Cheyenne heard enough of their stories to realize Falcon might've been shot — and everyone seemed too scared of the wild-looking man to check — she examined him and found what looked like a bullet crease at the base of his skull, but she was no doctor.

He was such a mess that she left the crease alone, figuring to scrub him up when they got home, otherwise the wound might open and all his filth would get in.

Win rode double with her on Wyatt's horse, and they left the three brothers to walk. As the horse plodded along, she and Win talked some until Win started in about her pa and Cheyenne's announcement that she was going to accept his proposal.

Cheyenne didn't want to hear it, and it didn't take much to scoot Win off the horse. Cheyenne would have spurred on the horse, but she decided not to leave them all behind in case she needed to save the day again.

The afternoon was hectic. When they finally reached the ranch, Falcon needed to clean up and be bandaged. It appeared Kevin had also been scratched by a bullet. Win needed her stitches removed.

There was the sheriff to fetch and the outlaws to haul to town and Cheyenne was the only one who was sure where they were, so that was a long ride out again.

By the time Cheyenne sat down to a late supper, she was worn clean out.

The rest of the family came to sit at the table. Cheyenne looked at Falcon and almost smiled. He'd had a bath, shave, and haircut. He had on clean clothes. He looked purely civilized. And somehow by him looking like less of a savage, she saw the wounded man underneath and wanted to help him.

Would he stay? Would he get his memory back?

"You have family now." Cheyenne met Falcon's gaze with her black eyes. "Stay here and we'll be able to help you through whatever confusion lies ahead."

After a long hesitation, that shouldn't have mattered to Cheyenne as much as it did, Falcon said, "I'll stay until I'm . . . healed, or whatever it is that needs to change for me to remember."

He looked back at them with those strange hazel eyes the brothers all shared. "I can

97

remember a Bible verse about honoring your father and your mother." He frowned in thought. "It's one of the Ten Commandments. The fifth commandment says, 'Honor thy father and thy mother: that thy days may be long upon the land which the Lord thy God giveth thee.' And I remember another verse that says something like, this commandment is the only one with a promise."

"Land." Cheyenne clenched her fists on the table and thought of all that she'd lost. She fought down the anger.

"It's really about the Promised Land, Cheyenne," Win said softly. "That's the land that God had promised the Israelites."

"And I think it's about heaven," Molly added.

So if Cheyenne lost her land in this life, she'd have heaven in the next, and no one could take that away from her.

"And Cheyenne" — Wyatt reached across the table toward her — "honoring your father and mother is an easy thing for you. Your ma and pa were fine folks. And you will continue to live on this land no matter what my pa did to you."

It was only when he rested his big hand on one of hers that she realized her fist was clenched and tried to relax. She wanted to believe him. He was right about her ma and pa. They were fine folks she loved dearly.

Kevin added, "It's us that has trouble. Falcon, Wyatt, and me. We're the ones left with the mystery of how God expects us to honor our coyote of a father. A man who, in his last act, stole a ranch from you, Cheyenne, and a nice chunk of it from you, Wyatt."

"Mine was no great pillar of decency, either," Molly muttered. "I think honoring him is going to have to be one of those sins I just have to ask forgiveness for."

Cheyenne set aside her own anger long enough to wonder what Molly's pa had done.

"We may never be able to abide by this commandment," Kevin said. "And I'm not even sure it'd be right to do so. But —" He held out his hand to Win, who smiled and took it. Then Win held out her hand to Molly, who clasped her hand.

Molly moved a little slower, but then Falcon was a little scary. Finally, she offered her hand to Falcon, who reluctantly grabbed hold. Falcon didn't reach for Cheyenne, but Kevin took Wyatt's hand, Wyatt took Andy's, and Andy reached hesitantly for Cheyenne. Which Cheyenne took to mean she was a little scary, too. She took Andy's hand, then looked at Falcon. Not sure she wanted to touch him, but it seemed right to create a circle.

A circle that created a family.

Cheyenne tightened her grip and looked at Falcon. Not a man to disrespect. Not a man who'd lie and cheat and steal like Clovis. Kevin and his family were decent people, too. These people she could honor.

"I'm proud to know all of you," Kevin said so solemnly it was like the prayer before the meal. "I can say with an easy heart that I will honor family."

Every one of them, with one voice said, "I will honor family."

"Can we quit talking and eat?" Andy broke in.

Laughter bubbled around the table, ending the sober moment. As everyone reached for bowls of food, Cheyenne said, "Do you think Tuttle and Baker came up with the idea to take over the ranches on their own?"

That stopped them in their tracks.

"You don't think so?" Wyatt asked, appearing to force himself to lift a bowl of mashed potatoes.

"It sounded like they went back east to try and kill Falcon."

"Back east of where?" Falcon asked.

Cheyenne arched a brow at him. She had

100

no idea what to do about his addled head. "But how did they know where he'd be coming from? Did we even talk about him? I was mighty mad about the whole thing. I'm sure word got out about the will, but it seems to me they knew details that very few people would have known. How'd they find out so fast and head straight east to stop him?"

"And get back here fast enough to attack Kevin and his family?" Win served herself a slice of ham, then passed the heavy platter.

"You said I got off the train from Omaha. Where's that from Independence?" Falcon took a slice of bread and began eating it until more food came. "Those two men said they'd attacked me, but if I took the train out, would they have had time to beat me back here?"

"They had to have gotten here before you in time to attack Kevin."

"They said I took all their horses and guns. I might've been a few days selling them."

Andy laughed. "You stole all their stuff?"

"So they said, and took their money, too. How'd they get back here so fast? The train costs money, don't it?"

"It would have worked," Win said, "if they'd walked to Independence and gotten

101

some money. Bought new horses and ridden hard for Omaha."

"So did they rob a bank in Independence?" Falcon buttered his bread. "Because I doubt I left them horse-buyin' money."

There was quiet while they ate, thinking.

"If they had accomplices, they could have wired them for money. That works fast," Win said.

"Wired money?" Cheyenne hadn't heard of that. She looked around the table, and no one else seemed to understand, so Win explained about money going between banks with permission given over telegraph lines.

Wyatt scrubbed his face. "If that happened, what you're saying is, there might be more of them."

"If there are, then our troubles might not be over." Falcon, for all that he'd cleaned up good, sounded like the voice of doom.

And this from the man whose memory had started only a week ago.

"I had planned to start building a cabin somewhere right away." Kevin turned to give Win a worried look. "But we don't dare to unless we're sure it's safe."

"I wonder just what my pa had to do with all of that mess." Win tapped her fork on the china plate. "Sheriff Corly is going to ride out and talk to him. And it'll probably come out that we are married."

"We should go tell him," Kevin said.

"Not necessary. I'd as soon let him come here. I'm sure he'll ride over tomorrow."

Cheyenne was watching the two, thinking of Win and her problems with her pa. Something passed between Kevin and Win that was very private. She wondered what. Win had never kept secrets from her before. Married life was going to ruin their friendship.

"I'm going to sleep in the bunkhouse," Andy said. "I asked Rubin if I could, and he said four men quit today because branding is over, so there's plenty of room." Then he added to Falcon, "Rubin said you're welcome, too. We should clear out of the ramrod's house and leave it to Kevin and Win."

Falcon nodded, chewing.

"We've got four bedrooms upstairs," Wyatt offered. "You can sleep in here."

"Nope." Andy had a gleam in his eyes that wasn't about the good food. Cheyenne suspected he liked being a cowboy so well that moving into the bunkhouse suited him just fine.

The clink of their forks and knives as they scooped up food had a friendly tone. Molly had done a wonderful job. The meal was delicious, better honestly than the food Win made. She was an uninspired cook. Must not teach cooking in finishing school.

Molly got up and fetched a pan of apple dumplings. She brought sweetened cream to the table and started passing dessert. Cheyenne took a bite, and her admiration for Molly's cooking grew. Maybe Molly could teach Win a few things.

Maybe she could teach Cheyenne a few things.

As they ate, Cheyenne thought of all those nights when it had just been Wyatt and her in here eating. Those had been quiet meals, and her cooking was nothing to get excited about.

It looked like there was no getting shut of this crowd, so Cheyenne grimly decided she'd accept them. She feared it would get old fast.

Eleven

"Win can take the cooking and housekeeping back over, and I could apply for her job as schoolmarm," Molly said as she cleaned up after breakfast.

Falcon didn't know nuthin' about ranching and didn't care to learn, so he'd come in and eaten breakfast in the big house.

Kevin and Win hadn't shown up. Molly said she'd been told Win would cook for them in the ramrod's house and not to plan for them.

Wyatt had gone out to look over the branded cattle, Andy with him.

Cheyenne was grumpier than usual this morning, and that was saying something. She'd stayed at the house.

She reminded him of someone. Falcon wasn't sure who, but he found he liked Cheyenne, despite her quick ways with a scowl. He felt like maybe he'd known tough women before and they suited him.

Falcon really didn't know what anyone was talking about most of the time. "You're a schoolteacher?"

Molly nodded.

"Win too?"

"She was. She's been teaching in Bear Claw Pass ever since she came back from finishing school in St. Louis. And I was a teacher back in Wheatfield, Kansas, before I moved here. Her pa went in and told them she was quitting without her permission. Then she got married, so she can't work anymore."

"Her pa did that?" Cheyenne lifted plates off the table and took them to the sink.

"I wonder if a teacher could teach me to — to — remember? Or help me remember things I'm supposed to already know?"

Molly settled a plate into a basin of hot water and turned slowly to look at Falcon. "Teach you . . . your past?"

Falcon shrugged. "I know it ain't reasonable, exactly, but what about this is? I know my name. Now. I know this is Wyoming and the nearest town is Bear Claw Pass. I know most everything I've been told, and I remember all of it. So if I can't remember things, maybe I can start over and be taught things again, and it'll be like I remember."

Cheyenne began wiping dry the plates

106

Molly washed. "We could just spend the morning talking. I could tell you all I know about this situation."

"We had to study Tennessee in school, so I could tell you what I know about it." Molly scrubbed a cast-iron skillet and handed it to Cheyenne. "Tennessee is where you came from. The Blue Ridge Mountains."

"And we've got papers here saying a very few things about the unknown brothers," Cheyenne said. "Just where you lived so the lawyer could send a letter to you telling you to come and steal my land."

Grumpy. Falcon ignored it. "So I'm from the mountains?"

"Yep." Molly wiped out the basin and hung it on a nail over the sink. "But the mountains way back east."

"Must be why, when first I come around in that river, I headed for the mountains as soon as I could get land under me. They seemed safe. It's like I was called to them, like a bird heading for its nest."

"Can you read?" Molly asked, untying her apron.

Falcon knew what reading was. Memory was a strange thing. "Nope. Well, I'm not sure."

Cheyenne came and put a piece of paper

in front of him with a pencil. "Write *Falcon*."

He stared at the paper for a long moment, then picked up the pencil and wrote his name.

"I reckon that means I can. Not sure about anything else though."

"Let's go in my grandpa's study," Cheyenne said. "We left the will in there and copies of the letters that were going to you and Kevin. You can at least know that much about yourself. I can tell you about the ranch and Wyoming. Molly can tell you about Tennessee."

"Maybe," Molly said, "we'll say something that'll shake loose a memory."

Falcon hated to get his hopes up. Hopelessness seemed called for at this time.

"Is that your ma?" Falcon stopped in the doorway of the front room and looked at the huge painting on a wall above the fireplace.

"Yes, it is. That's Katherine LeRemy Brewster Hunt."

Falcon heard sadness in Cheyenne's voice and wished he had words that would make her feel better. But that seemed foolish. How could anyone feel anything but sadness over losing her ma? Falcon wondered about his own ma. Someone here had said she was dead, but he must've told them that. He couldn't remember it.

The picture was hard to look away from, so he paid mind to it and not Cheyenne's sad, beautiful face. Katherine Hunt had on a blue dress. Her brown hair was down in curls around her shoulders. She was standing in front of this very fireplace that the picture now hung over. Her arms came together in front, holding something Falcon didn't recognize. A fancy thing, a fanned-out blue thing that matched Katherine's dress. She had about the prettiest smile on her face Falcon had ever seen. Her skin was tanned, and her eyes snapped blue.

Falcon might not remember much about himself, but he knew this was a fine room. Pretty blankets were thrown over the backs of a settee and two chairs, and fine lacy circles draped over the chair and settee arms. He saw a small basket with something half-finished in it. It had to be Cheyenne's work, or Win's maybe? Cheyenne didn't seem like the fine lacy type.

Looking back at the picture, he said, "She looks like you." He knew Cheyenne had never smiled that way since he'd met her, but he wished she would. "You've got dark eyes, but other than that, you're of a kind with your ma. Both beautiful women."

109

Cheyenne turned away from the picture. "And you look like Clovis Hunt. I can't tell you much about yourself. But I could tell you a lot about him." She didn't make that sound like he wanted to hear it.

She stepped through an open door and went behind a massive desk of solid oak big enough to nap on and opened a side drawer. She pulled out a packet of papers. "Here's the will, and it contains instructions about contacting you and Kevin, including information about where you lived."

"Then you know more about me than I know about myself." He picked up the papers and unfolded them and stared awhile. Then he said, "I reckon I can't read much besides my name."

Molly hadn't followed them into the study, but now she came in with a sheet of paper. "This is the map of the ranch. Kevin got it at the land office, and I had it in my room. You said you might build a cabin."

"I did?"

"Yep," Molly said. "You could use the map to decide where you want to build it. Maybe Cheyenne could tell you about highlands."

Cheyenne took the packet of papers from Falcon and tucked them back in the drawer. "You didn't need to get that in town. We've got a map here."

Molly tipped her head and gave a tiny shrug. "I don't think Kevin wanted to ask you for it. But he planned to ride your boundaries and find a likely spot, far enough away we wouldn't bother you none."

Cheyenne's eyes glinted in such a way that Falcon knew the newcomers were always going to bother Cheyenne.

She went to a large wooden table standing in front of a bookshelf and pulled out a deep drawer. From inside she brought out a tube of paper. She brought it to the desk and unrolled it. Falcon saw it was a map. Very detailed and impressive compared to the quickly hand-drawn map Molly had.

Cheyenne picked up a book, a paperweight, and a stand that held an inkwell. She used them to weight down three corners of the map. She kept the fourth corner from rolling with her hand.

She began talking.

Falcon was impressed by how well she knew this land. Knew where the old boundaries were between the land her pa had owned and the Rolling Hills Ranch. Talked about how they'd joined them after her pa died.

"I was really young. I have only shadowy memories of my own pa. Ma and I moved over here after Pa died, bucked off a horse he was breaking. Grandpa was living in the foreman's house then. He insisted we needed a fine house for the three of us, and built this. It was finished about the time Clovis Hunt came along."

"And you're saying Clovis was still married to my ma and Kevin's ma when he married your ma?" Falcon rubbed one hand over his face as if he wanted to scrub that information away.

"Pa, is that you?"

Falcon jerked his head up. He looked around the room, but they were the only people in here.

Who was that? It was a man's voice, and Falcon thought the question had been put to him.

"Pa, is that you?"

For a horrifying moment, Falcon thought he might have children somewhere. A wife. Where were they? Who called him Pa?

Falcon tried to focus on that strange voice he'd just heard. It had to be a memory, but thinking on it made his head throb. The women were poring over the map, not looking at him at all.

They didn't notice him checking the room for someone.

Should he tell them? The headache grew, and to escape the pain, he forced his mind back to what was going on around him.

The lack of a memory made him feel like a strange kinda critter. He had no idea what was wrong with him, and he had a flash of, well, it wasn't right to say he was ashamed exactly. But he felt so odd. Like he had a terrible weakness, and that made him a man who'd be picked out of a herd like a three-legged elk.

"Mark on my map where some highlands are for Falcon. And do you know where fertile farmland is for us?" Molly slid her modest little map onto the corner of the big, colorful map Cheyenne had.

"You drew your map wrong." Cheyenne pointed to a curve on Molly's map. "Our land goes out way farther than this. You drew your boundary so it follows the east side of Mount Gilbert, but it goes around the west side of it."

Cheyenne took the pen off the desk, dipped it in an inkwell, and redrew Molly's map to add a whole big stretch to match hers.

"No, Cheyenne. Kevin said he talked to the land agent the whole time he was drawing. He could've been off a little, but not that much. That stretch you just added to my map is part of the Hawkins Ranch. Win was with him and look at those tiny letters."

Molly tapped on the line that Cheyenne had added. "They wrote *HR* for Hawkins Ranch."

Cheyenne's always somber face twisted into anger. Falcon was getting used to seeing her that way.

"Then the land office is wrong, and Win is wrong."

Molly and Cheyenne looked at each other.

Cheyenne said, "Win doesn't know her ranch's boundaries as well as I know mine."

"Are you sure your grandpa and your pa really bought their land?" Falcon moved to stand beside the two women and looked closer at the map. "There couldn't've been a land office out here when they settled. Maybe he only claimed the land, but when Hawkins came along, the land office showed open range, and he bought it."

Cheyenne's head snapped up, and she glared at Falcon. "This land is ours." She slapped her hand on the map, and Falcon got the notion that she might want to slap him.

Weren't his fault about the maps.

Her eyes narrowed, and he saw she was thinkin' something as if she could see inside his head.

He surely wished someone could.

"Let's go to town," Falcon suggested.

"We should wait for Wyatt."

Falcon smiled right in that cranky face. "You reckon he knows this land better'n you?"

Molly flinched at the challenge in his retort. Falcon saw it as she stood behind Cheyenne, and it was a mighty big flinch. But he didn't let it move him from the stare locked between him and Cheyenne.

"No one alive knows this land better than me."

"Considering that there might still be some varmints chasing after us, I'll ride with you, if I can borrow a horse?" Falcon asked.

"This ranch owns about a hundred horses. And you own a third of them." Cheyenne looked like she wanted to scream.

Just like always.

But without knowing a thing about what was normal, he decided he liked a feisty woman. By that measure, he liked Cheyenne Brewster more every minute.

"I think I'll stay home and make a meal." Molly drew his attention.

He'd forgotten she was in here.

She shook her head in a way that made no never mind to him, then turned and walked out.

Falcon said, "It's a funny thing not to have any memories."

Cheyenne's scowl relaxed some. "I'll just bet it is."

"I've no notion of what I like and what I don't like." Then, bravest thing he ever did, or so he suspected, he chucked Cheyenne under the chin. "But I am finding myself liking you real well."

Instead of biting his head off, she arched her brows, and her eyes went wide. She seemed frozen and didn't say anything back.

Probably for the best. "Let's go to town."

Shaking her head, then nodding, finally she found her voice. "I'm bringing the maps."

TWELVE

After Falcon took his hand away, Cheyenne still felt that chapped, callused finger on her chin. She even rubbed the spot he'd touched a few times while she saddled her horse.

"You remember how to do this?"

Falcon was slapping a saddle on with no sign of confusion.

"It makes no sense." Falcon paused from tightening the cinch to rub the back of his head.

The wound had to be a bullet crease. Tuttle had talked about Falcon being hard to kill. He'd mentioned attacking him and being bested by him in Independence. And here Falcon stood while Tuttle and Baker were dead and, no doubt, being buried today.

Cheyenne wondered what Oliver Hawkins had thought about his foreman being shot. About the man being involved with an attempt to kill Kevin and Falcon. About his plans to kidnap Win and keep her hidden away until she had no choice but to marry him.

It hadn't missed Cheyenne's notice that Win had yet to go see her father. Tell him about her wedding. The sheriff was going to his place first thing this morning, so Oliver would be over here as fast as he could move after Sheriff Corly left his place.

As they rode, Cheyenne thought of Win's pa. She should've stayed home. She'd declared a week ago she was going to marry him. Now was a chance to see him — if she guessed right about him coming over, upset at Win's marriage. Instead, Cheyenne was riding off.

Well, she looked to be getting her land back, though only in a verbal agreement, not legally. She could live with that, but it still burned bad. She had to find time to seriously consider Hawkins's proposal.

She knew he was no great rancher. But she saw the good side of marrying a man she could be in charge of. And he didn't run off like Clovis. Even as she thought of it, her stomach sank. She realized she had no real interest in the *marriage* part of saying, "I do," with Oliver. But as a partner in a ranch where she got to be in charge, that part of it could work. And maybe if she was the right kind of wife, he might take to running off, too. She could hope.

As they left the ranch yard at a fast walk, Cheyenne rubbed her chin again over the spot Falcon had touched. She couldn't stop herself.

That made her say something she might've been better off keeping quiet about. "We've hired a lawyer to track down just when your ma died. If she was still living when Clovis married my ma, then Ma's marriage wasn't legal and Clovis had no ownership of the RHR. That'll cancel the will and any claim you and Kevin have on the place."

Falcon turned to look at her. Really study her. What was he thinking? Maybe *he* didn't even know what he was thinking.

"I can't help you. I-I think I'd tell you so I could get shut of the land my pa stole. The land's been kinda hung on me permanent, ain't it? Didn't you say it's in the will that I can't sell it?"

"It's very carefully worded so you have to keep it. It can't be put up for sale for ten years."

Falcon scratched his head and turned to watch the trail.

"If I ever get to rememberin' things, I'll know how old I was when Ma died." With a disgusted snort he said, "Heck, I don't even know how old I am now. Older'n Kevin, I reckon. Beyond that, I can't remember. But my memory will come back after a time, surely. When it does, I can figure out if she died before Clovis married your ma. But for now, I can't even remember having a ma."

Cheyenne managed a harsh laugh. "Pretty good chance you had one. We can count on that. You should have stayed around and gotten to know us before you got your brains knocked out."

"I don't remember a'course, but I expect I didn't feel all that welcome. I'm just guessin' that, on account of how y'all have acted since I found you."

"Let's pick up the pace." Cheyenne kicked her horse into a ground-eating gallop, and Falcon stayed with her.

They reached Bear Claw Pass, and Cheyenne rode straight to the land office. Hitching their horses, Cheyenne charged through the door, in no mood to wait another second to figure out why the map she had at home didn't match the one in town.

She'd brought hers along, carrying it carefully. It was a prized family possession. But she didn't see how she could challenge the land office's map without proof.

Gordon Spellman was behind a counter,

sitting at a desk writing when Cheyenne slammed the door open. He jumped at the loud noise, then smiled when he saw her. He was a gray-haired man with a tidy white moustache and golden-framed glasses. Cheyenne had known him for years. He and his wife went to church with her on Sundays. Whatever was going on here, she believed that Gordon's honesty was beyond reproach.

"Cheyenne, what brings you to town?" He frowned a bit. "Winona Hawkins was in here only a few days ago with some stranger, looking at a map of your property. Is there a problem?"

He wore a white shirt that buttoned down the front. His sleeves had black armbands, which Cheyenne knew many men wore because the general store didn't get in ready-made shirts in sizes that were overly particular. So the armbands shortened up long sleeves.

"There's a mighty big problem, Gordon." Cheyenne slapped her map on the counter and began unrolling it. "We have our own map out at the house, and it doesn't match yours."

Gordon watched the map unroll, studying it briefly before looking over at the map he had in his office.

"This right here." Cheyenne drew her finger on her family's map, then over to the land office's map. "There's an inward curve on your map while there's an outward curve on mine."

She tapped the map hard on the area she said was hers.

"It's Mount Gilbert." Cheyenne looked from Spellman to Falcon and back. "This here is Falcon Hunt, brother to Wyatt. He's come to claim his inherited land. It's real important we get the ranch's boundaries right if we're going to have new ownership." Cheyenne leaned down close to compare the two maps.

Gordon looked at Falcon, then returned to studying the map. "I'll admit to you, Cheyenne, that your ownership of the land is old. It was settled before I moved here. It's not a map I pull out and study."

"And see here, in fine handwriting, it says this is the boundary with the Hawkins Ranch. Now, I know Mount Gilbert is ours. I know it. Some of the land, well, there might be a question about details. But Gilbert here" — she tapped again — "Grandpa had a love for that land. He used to say it wasn't good for grazing, it was good for gazing."

"Are you sure he owned it though, Cheyenne? This was all open range when your grandpa Jacque settled. Does he actually have a deed that shows what land he owns?"

Cheyenne paused. "There are deeds somewhere. I know Grandpa was like a lot of others on the frontier. First, he just stopped, put up a cabin, and reckoned the land around him was his. When there was finally a way to own land, after he'd been here for years, he started buying it up. First the water holes, then the best grazing. But I know he pushed himself hard to own his land tight and legal. And Ma did the same for the land my pa had settled on."

"Your pa, Clovis Hunt?" The man glanced at Falcon. It was plain to see he'd known what Clovis Hunt looked like because he was seeing a young version of the man right before him. He for sure didn't question for one second whether Falcon was truly Clovis's son.

"No, my real pa. Nate Brewster. He might've died before the land was even surveyed and for sale, but Ma was mindful of owning her land. Grandpa and Ma worked hard to get their land under their legal ownership."

Gordon went back to studying the maps. "And you say this is a mountain good only for gazing? Why would your grandpa spend

123

money to own what is, in practice, a wasteland?"

Gordon leaned closer to study his version of the map. "You've got the Hawkins Ranch as owners of this disputed mountain area, but that's not right." He touched a spot on the map. "This section isn't owned by Oliver Hawkins, either. He doesn't put his money toward wasteland no matter the view." Gordon sniffed. "Hawkins has little interest in the wonder of the land around us. He only wants property he can profit from."

"But Win came in to check on the maps with Wyatt's other brother, Kevin. Why would she write on that line that it was the boundary between her father's ranch and mine?" Cheyenne knew better than to call the ranch "mine." It for a fact was not hers. But it best described the property so she said it.

"I was here when she visited with Kevin. I watched Kevin draw a map, and he asked me some questions about it as he worked. I remember Win saying your land bordered hers. I suppose she just made a quick note of that? As far as I know, Winona has never shown any interest in her father's property lines. Unless perhaps she also has a map at home."

Cheyenne considered that. Win never went home if she could help it. It was doubtful she spent any time studying maps there. Cheyenne nodded and looked at that strange oblong circle cut out of her property. "Does that land have an owner, then?"

Gordon turned to open a drawer and thumbed through the files. He came to the spot he was searching for and pulled out a sheet of paper.

Bringing it back to the counter, he said, "I've got a deed here listed to Percival Ralston."

"He's from the Hawkins Ranch. He's been there for years." Cheyenne frowned. "He was the foreman there for a time, then he had his leg badly broken riding a bronc. I think he does bookwork for Oliver now. I really don't know what he does, I only know he's got a bad limp and doesn't work cattle anymore. Ralston owns this stretch?"

Gordon nodded.

"What's the date on the sale?"

Gordon looked in his files. The drawer slid farther open, and the papers crinkled as he thumbed through them. At last, he pulled out a sheet of paper and read for a bit. "He's owned it for nearly ten years, it seems. That was before I came to the area. Actually, the date he bought it was only weeks before I started this job."

Gordon frowned at the date. "Odd, I know the land office was empty for a time before I got here because the former agent died at his desk. It looks to me like Ralston bought it when there wouldn't have been anyone to sell it to him."

With a shake of his head, Gordon said, "Maybe someone appointed a temporary agent. The agent might have moved on when he heard I was to arrive, but he wasn't here when I got to Bear Claw Pass. At any rate, Ralston must have come in hunting a home and found a gap in the rugged land between the two ranches. Maybe he was struck by it the same as your grandpa. Looking to spend his old age on that mountain gazing at the view."

"Grandpa owns that land and did so long before ten years ago. I'll go home and hunt through our deeds. You may have to refund Ralston's money."

Gordon peered at the paper. "That will be no hardship. There's a thousand acres on that hill, but he was charged only two pennies an acre."

"That's twenty dollars. He bought all that land for twenty dollars?" Falcon landed a hand on his hat as if the surprise of it would knock it away.

"It's listed as wasteland. It has little to no value. I admit that's an exceptionally low price, but a mountain with no grazing land, well, it wouldn't be worth much." Gordon read the papers with a frown. "The name of the land agent on the deed isn't right though. It's the name of the man who died. And I *know* the purchase date was *after* his death. Maybe they dated it wrong. But it's irregular."

Gordon looked at Cheyenne, then at Falcon. "I'm going to check into this more closely. I can compare the previous land agent's signature and look into other land sales from around that time. I'll see if any other sales were made between when I know my predecessor died and I arrived. And I'll check the older documents and see what your grandfather bought using those older deeds."

As he tapped the counter, his eyes lit up. "Yes, if your grandpa bought this land, there should be an old deed saying so. You bring me in a copy of the original deeds, and we'll check them against each other. If this is your grandfather's land, then there is some skullduggery at hand."

"I can come in with the deed tomorrow. Or wait longer if you need time."

"Tomorrow would be fine."

"I might bring Wyatt with me. We both heard Grandpa talk about that land. We both believed he owned it. He certainly spoke of it as if he did."

"Wyatt's voice added to yours is a good idea. We'll get to the bottom of this, I promise you."

Cheyenne reached out her hand. Gordon hesitated; shaking a woman's hand wasn't the usual thing, but he took her hand anyway.

"See you tomorrow."

Cheyenne nodded and pulled her gloves on as she walked outside with Falcon behind her.

They reached the horses before she said, "Let's ride out to that mountain. I haven't been there for years. It was more Grandpa's way to gaze at pretty scenery than mine. But I'd like to see if Percy Ralston has put himself up a cabin on my land."

"Let's find the deed first." Falcon swung up on his horse. "No sense charging in to land when we don't have the law on our side."

"That's my family's land, Falcon."

"I believe you. Now let's prove it."

Cheyenne gave Falcon a steely-eyed look, then reined her horse around and rode out of town for home.

■ ■ ■ ■

Molly heard the door open and turned to see her new sister-in-law come in.

"I've been shirking here in the kitchen," Win said. "I'll make the next meal. We've been leaning hard on you for a while now."

The dark curls, bright blue eyes, and pink cheeks. A woman so colorful and with such a sunny smile. Molly could see why Kevin was drawn to her.

Molly didn't spend a lot of time looking in a mirror, but she knew she was a washed-out, colorless woman. Blue eyes, but so pale they didn't matter much. Flyaway blond hair that always straggled loose from the tight little bun she wore. And the only time she had any color in her cheeks was if she stayed out in the sun too long. Then she looked red as an overripe beet and was, no doubt, about as appealing.

Stifling the envy she felt at the pretty woman who'd turned her brother's head, Molly prayed to be delivered from her unkind feelings of resentment. "I've got it started already. Rubin brought in a beef roast last night. I put it on early so it'd be done by noon. I've peeled the potatoes, and I've got carrots ready to bake, and room in the oven for them in just a few minutes when I take out the pound cake I've got baking."

Uncharitably, she wondered what the woman could be thinking to come in here an hour before the noon meal and expect it wouldn't already be cooking. Unkind feelings again.

She was unnecessarily hostile to Win. Again she prayed for God to guide her. "But I *would* appreciate it if you took over."

She had other work.

"Tell me what's left. I'm sorry I didn't come over sooner, but I had to clean up after breakfast with Kevin. Then just now, Andy came in and asked Kevin if he wanted to go look at the branding. Learn a little about handling cattle. So Kevin left, and I finally got over here."

"Kevin and branding." Molly shook her head. "I wonder if he'll take to it. Do you want to be a rancher's wife? Instead of a farmer's wife?"

Those pink cheeks turned a bit brighter. "I want to be Kevin's wife. Whatever he works at, I'll be working at his side."

Win's eyes turned thoughtful, as she studied Molly. "I-I don't talk about it much, though I told Kevin, but my father wasn't a-a decent sort of man. I know you had trouble with your own pa."

Molly knew Kevin had told Win about the way Molly's parents had died. But even Kevin didn't know the whole story, and Molly was determined that no one ever did.

"O-our parents died when I was quite young. But after . . . well, after . . . Kevin was there to help." Molly's chest hurt just from talking about such a terrible thing.

Mentally squaring her shoulders, she shook off the old times. "I was old enough to manage the house and care for Andy, until I felt more like his ma than his big sister. I reckon that's why it comes natural to cook for you all and keep the house tidy."

"Is there anything you'd like to do, just for pleasure? Take a break?"

"Not really. I guess I could wander into the study and find a book." She never sat around idle during the day.

Win's eyes lit up. She smiled. "Get yourself a cup of coffee. I'll get the pound cake out of the oven, and there" — her eyes went to the bowl of icing on the counter — "you've got a glaze made for it. I'll frost it, and you can drink coffee and eat cake while I work."

Win laughed. "Won't that make you feel like a lady of leisure? And we can talk while I get the potatoes stewing and the carrots on to bake."

Her laughter was contagious enough that Molly managed a true smile.

Before she sat, she said, "Let me check the cake. It should be done by now. Then yes, I'll sit down. I'll let you take over while I rest my weary bones."

Win smiled back, then got a coffee cup down while Molly checked the cake and found it done. She drew it out of the hot oven, set it on the folded kitchen towels she'd gotten ready to handle the hot pan, then slipped the carrots in. She moved the already peeled and quartered potatoes forward to begin their boiling.

Now that everything was done, sure, she could sit and rest. But it had been nice of Win to offer, and the cake did need to be glazed while it was still hot.

Win set the brimming coffee cup on the table and made a wide sweep of her hand. "My lady, your coffee is served."

Molly sat and picked up her coffee. If she wasn't so frightened and sad about losing Kevin, her partner and best friend forever, she might come to like Win.

But she wasn't going to rush into anything.

Cheyenne slammed the door open and

stalked across the kitchen without looking left or right.

Falcon, a pace behind her, said, "Molly, dinner sure smells good. Hi, Win. There's a mix-up between the land office and Cheyenne's memory of the ranch boundaries. We're huntin' the deed. Gonna straighten this out."

With a flinch, Cheyenne wondered how it'd happened that the roughhewn, barely civilized Tennessee mountain man with the addled brain had better manners than she did.

By the time she was done flinching, she was through the room and forgot Win and Molly in her rush for Grandpa's study.

Cheyenne went straight for a row of drawers built into the wall of shelves behind Grandpa's old wooden desk chair, always squared behind the massive oak desk Cheyenne's pa had made for Grandpa as a Christmas present years before this house had been built.

Cheyenne knew her ma and Grandpa had worked hard to make the study worthy of that pretty desk, and she always thought of the love of her family when she looked at it.

She dropped to her knees by the first drawer and went straight to the *D* section. It was all real tidy. And she remembered right where those deeds were.

They weren't there.

Scowling, she looked up to see Falcon standing there with his hands in his back pockets.

"Aren't you going to help me?"

"Can't read."

"Oh. Well, you won't be much help, then."

"I reckon teachers like Molly and Win might help."

"I suppose. And this is now one-third Win's ranch." Cheyenne said it like she was taking bites out of the words. "She oughta come in here and help, except . . ."

"Except what?"

"The deeds aren't here."

"Stolen? By Pa?"

Well, that hadn't occurred to her. She realized she was still wearing her hat. She reached up and tore it off her head. "Why would he do that?"

"Um . . . maybe something about the map being changed . . . it might . . . if he was around . . . If that sale went through when there wasn't a land agent, then it's someone up to no good. And that sounds like Pa."

Sinking back from where she knelt to sit on her heels, she whacked her hat on the open drawer, then slammed it shut with a loud thud.

"Or maybe it ain't under *Deed.* It might be under *Land* or *Ranch* or *Boundary* or . . ." he trailed off.

Whacking Falcon with her hat, which did no harm as he was standing and she was sunk down on the floor, she said, "I get it. I haven't looked at those deeds for years. And maybe I haven't ever looked at them. Maybe Ma and Grandpa had them out, and I was just standing around here listening. So I'd better go through the files more carefully."

She whacked Falcon's ankles again, then tossed her hat on the desktop. She went back to the first drawer and slid it open. This ranch was an old one, and the files piled up. Still, a ranch didn't run much on paper. It was mostly done with hard labor, sharp thinking, and a strong back. But the files had been years accumulating, and the job was a big one.

Before she started, she looked up and sideways at Falcon, still standing there. "You should learn to read. It's real handy."

Falcon shrugged.

"We've got two teachers here at the house, and near as I can tell, not counting cooking and cleaning, mending and gardening, milking the cows and gathering eggs, neither of them have much to do."

"I think you have to count all of that. They

have a lot to do."

"If they aren't roping and riding, I don't count it."

Falcon gave her a smile so small it mainly flashed in his eyes. "It counts. But come winter, if I'm still here, there might be some long evenings trapped inside. I might ask for help."

"Go now and ask them. I'm going to be a while."

Falcon looked over his shoulder at the open door, then he whispered, "I don't want to talk to them."

"Why not? They're your sisters."

His expression of horror made her laugh, and she sure hadn't done much of that in a while.

"They are *not* my sisters, and neither are you. Wyatt and Kevin are just barely my brothers. I like the idea of having a family, but I'd've preferred a less troublesome one. One where I get shot and drowned less often."

Cheyenne would have preferred a less troublesome family, too, so she could only agree. She decided to leave him to do whatever he wanted and turned back to her drawer.

"I'm going to go through all the papers here, and I need to look in a chest that had

136

been in Grandpa's room and another that was in Ma's. This is going to take all day."

"Get the teacher ladies in here to help."

"I will. We can spend the time after we eat going through everything."

"You're fussing about a deed to land that isn't even yours all right and legal, but, Cheyenne?"

She ignored the churn of anger that lived day and night in her gut. "What?"

"Whatever the law says, that land *is* yours. I won't stand in your way. Pa used a bad law to cheat you, but I won't be part of it."

"That's real decent of you, Falcon." Her stomach churned just a bit less. "I need to remember that Clovis did this to me. Neither you nor Kevin did it. I've been mad at all of you, and there's no fairness in that. Not a lot of common sense, either. I'm going to try and behave better."

She closed the distance between them. "Thank you."

He nodded his head with a light in his eyes that could be humor.

"Once I'm through with this, we're going out to Mount Gilbert and see that stretch of land and find out how Ralston came to own it."

Win came to the office door right then and said, "Dinner is ready. Come join Molly and me. I don't think Kevin or Wyatt will be back."

The meal was delicious, but Cheyenne barely tasted it in her haste to go straight back to sorting papers. The more she searched, the more she found in places she'd never considered. Molly and Win threw in with her, and Falcon went around and found eggs and milked cows to pass the hours.

For all their searching, they didn't find any deeds.

When they sat down to talk with Wyatt and Kevin while they ate, Cheyenne told her story of the missing deeds. She'd accepted that they were gone. "I've got to give up."

As Wyatt sliced his roast beef, Falcon said, "Tomorrow, Cheyenne and me're gonna go look at the land."

"I'll go back out to the cattle," Wyatt said. "Doubt you need a crowd to ride over there and see what's what."

Cheyenne wanted to get to the bottom of this, and she wasn't going to wait one day longer than necessary. "We'll ride out at sunrise."

THIRTEEN

If Ralston had built a cabin on Mount Gilbert, Falcon didn't give it much chance of surviving the coming wrath of Cheyenne Brewster.

They were making tracks, and Falcon kept up, but it was taking all he had. He was a fair hand at riding and wondered how much of it he'd done back in Tennessee.

A cabin came into his head. Faded in, then vanished. An old, tumbledown cabin that looked like it was nigh onto hangin' off the edge of a mountain.

His head, along the back where he'd taken that bullet swipe, gave a sickening throb that cut deep and stretched around to the front of his head.

And he thought of the cabin again, then it was gone.

What did that mean? Was that his cabin?

He forced himself past the pain to go over that vision of a cabin.

"Pa, is that you?"

He wanted to punch himself in the head to make it work. But his head was already considerably tender, so he didn't do it.

"We need to walk the horses awhile." Cheyenne slowed her mount, and Falcon did the same. Nice and easy. Forcing himself to put the fight to remember aside and pay attention to here and now. He realized they'd done a lot of riding, and somehow, he knew how to do that.

"I'm mighty good at handlin' a horse." Falcon looked at Cheyenne, a hand herself.

They walked along, toward a big old mountain. It was a cool morning, but it'd warm up soon enough, so Falcon just enjoyed the ride. Before he'd had near enough of it, Cheyenne interrupted his painless thoughts.

"The horses are rested." She was sounding cranky again.

Honest, Falcon was used to that tone and didn't mind it overly. "Then let's pick up the pace."

They were a long time reaching that section of the map. There was plenty of rough ground to ride through, but Cheyenne knew this one mountain rose up by itself, right on the boundary of the RHR and the Hawkins Ranch.

Slowing to a walk again, she said, "If Percy Ralston made some kind of land grab, he was slick about it. I've never heard him speak of land of his own. Not that I've spoken much to him in my life. But he lives and works on the Hawkins Ranch. A man who owns his own land would live there, wouldn't he?"

"Unless he likes his job and intends to keep it until he's ready to settle into a rockin' chair. He could be providing for his old age," Falcon suggested.

The mountain grew in front of them. It was a mountain that could be ridden up on a winding trail that went for a long ways, curving all the way around, snaking back and forth on the steeper stretches.

But that's about all it amounted to. A nice trail to ride for a day's outing. Grandpa had liked such things, but Cheyenne, well, she'd kept busy at the ranch.

"I'm not sure what we're looking for," Cheyenne said as they wound up the mountain. "All of this is ours. I'm sure I have the deeds to prove it, but where to search now? And if the Sidewinder stole them, where would he have taken them?"

Cheyenne skirted along a trail that went

crossways of the mountain for a stretch. She saw signs that it'd been ridden from time to time, but that didn't prove much.

"Hold up," Falcon called.

She reined in her mount and twisted in the saddle to watch Falcon study the ground along a stack of boulders. Not huge ones, but good-sized. In fact, she realized they were all too much the same size.

Swinging down, Falcon landed with the grace of a big cat. She couldn't help but admire the way he moved.

She'd never even met him before he'd lost his memory. Wyatt had barely spoken to him, either — he may not have spoken to him at all. Kevin and Win, as well as Molly and Andy, had exchanged a few words with him, but very few.

How could anyone judge his character?

"We tried to kill you in Independence, Missouri," Tuttle had said before Cheyenne shot the gun out of his hand. *"You're a hard man to kill, Falcon Hunt. You not only got past us, you stole our horses, guns, money, and supplies and headed on west. You're a thief."*

Falcon, with no memory, had said it sounded like justice. At the time, that had amused her.

Cheyenne alit as she watched Falcon study the stack of rocks, each about the size

142

of his head.

Then he looked up the hill with sudden alert attention.

Cheyenne remembered how good he was with a trail and was sure he'd seen something.

She ground-hitched her well-trained horse and came to his side.

A whine drew her head up. "Look at that."

Falcon was already looking, his hand on his pistol. A dog. A black, long-haired dog with a white streak angling down its face, giving it one black eye and one white.

"It's hurt. Any wounded animal can be dangerous." Falcon lifted his hand from his weapon and spent a few seconds moving rocks aside, then took his first step on a trail that had been very carefully covered.

Cheyenne thought of Percy Ralston. Pretty badly stove-up, and he had been for years, with one leg that barely worked, leaving him with a limp that made hard work impossible. And yet she could see that about ten boulders, maybe twenty — some might be fifty pounds — blocked this trail. Hard work lifting them aside. She'd just about swear the chore was impossible for a man with Percy's struggles.

Had he been faking his injuries all these years? Of course, she'd rarely seen him. If he'd been around her, she might've noticed a phony limp.

The dog's ears folded back. It bared its teeth but stayed lying on its belly. A low growl rumbled. The dog's shoulder was soaked in blood.

"Let me go first."

Falcon was closest, so it figured he was going first, but she still said, "Why? Do you have a way with animals?"

Falcon looked over his shoulder at her, glaring. "I don't know."

He turned to face the dog again. Cheyenne kept forgetting he had forgotten everything. Which was a strange thing to realize. Forgetting he'd forgotten.

But he was able to do most everything. Handle whatever came along. She had a hard time thinking of him as less than fully healthy.

Falcon moved forward slowly. He lowered himself into a crouch and spoke quietly to the dog in a voice that almost crooned. The dog was about twenty feet up the trail.

Cheyenne couldn't make out what had made the wound. A wolf attack maybe?

Falcon reached another row of boulders. Rather than take time lifting them aside, as Cheyenne saw had been done many times before, he stepped over the rocks, then went on talking, inching forward. The growling stopped, and the dog went back to whining.

Falcon, making no sudden moves, reached into the fur pack he always had along and pulled a strip of jerky out. He extended his hand to offer the meat to the dog with a crooning voice.

The whining stopped. The dog leaned forward, drawn to Falcon and that gentle voice. Falcon closed in on it.

When the meat almost touched the dog's muzzle, it lurched forward to a small extent, accented by a deeper whine of pain, then snatched the meat away and dropped to its belly, chewing and swallowing fast, as if it was starved. And Cheyenne suspected it was.

It was too badly hurt to use that leg without terrible pain. She'd seen that with the dog's unsteady movements.

Falcon eased forward again, producing another stick of jerky. He broke this one into four pieces. In the gentle talk, Falcon said, "I'm afraid it'll choke."

Cheyenne realized he was talking to her. Maybe he'd been talking to her the whole time, and she'd assumed it was all for the dog.

When he was close enough to touch the dog, he didn't. He set one of the small chunks of jerky on the ground so the dog could reach it without moving. The jerky went straight down its throat.

"What's your name?" Falcon set another piece of meat down and inched forward again, keeping low.

Cheyenne saw those fangs bare, the ears lie flat on the dog's head.

Another chunk of meat, gobbled down, then a fourth.

When the dog was swallowing the meat whole, Falcon reached out and rested one of his big, callused, competent hands gently on the dog's head.

The dog whined, flattened itself even lower on the ground, then Falcon had his knife out with an almost silent swish of steel against leather.

Was he thinking the dog needed to be put out of its misery? Cheyenne had to fight the reflex to launch herself at Falcon and stop him. Before she could do it, Falcon's hand slid toward the bleeding spot. His knife came forward, and with a single swipe, he cut something his hand was resting on.

Cheyenne saw a wire. Barbed wire. She hated the stuff. Her eyes followed the line of wire, and she saw more, rusted and twisted up with the rocks and dirt, barely visible.

146

The dog leapt to its feet. Only three of them. It stumbled backward. It had obviously been trapped, held down by that wire. It let out two loud barks that sounded like "thank you." Then it turned tail and ran, limping up the trail.

"Did you see that?" Falcon rose to his feet and turned as Cheyenne did the same. She'd kept as low as he had.

"See what?"

"That dog is a nursing mother. I was angled enough to see when she jumped up. And she looks like she's been pinned down here a long time, kept away from her pups." Falcon turned and strode uphill. Calling over his shoulder, he said, "Let's see where she's going."

Cheyenne hurried to keep up, following what she could now see was a clear trail.

The lines of small boulders crossing the trail had covered up that it was even a passable stretch. With the boulders gone, they could've ridden their horses up — if the barbed wire didn't get them.

They walked it, and it took them right to the top of the mountain. When Falcon crested the mountainside, he gasped quietly. Cheyenne was two paces behind him and caught up when he froze in place.

She looked down at something she'd never

147

seen nor suspected was here.

A mountain valley.

It looked to spread out for a few hundred acres. But that wasn't why Falcon had gasped. At least she didn't think so. It was the herd of cattle. Some black, some Hereford. But mostly black cows with white faces. Hundreds of them, grazing on lush grass.

"Where did they come from?" she asked.

"They have to be Ralston's cattle, if he owns this land."

A sharp bark drew Cheyenne's attention to the dog. She limped with near frantic speed painfully across the side of this beautiful grassy bowl. She tumbled once, and Cheyenne took two steps, afraid the dog was going to fall to the bottom of the bowl, but the mama caught herself and dragged herself into a fissure in the rocks. Cheyenne wouldn't have noticed it, nor recognized it as a cave, if she hadn't seen the dog vanish into it.

She realized she could hear a faint mewling sound from inside the cave. Within seconds of the dog entering, the mewling stopped.

"Puppies finding a meal." Cheyenne's throat felt a little thick to think of that mama dog hurting herself in her fight to escape that barbed wire. Knowing her babies were hungry.

"How long do you think she was there?"

Falcon shook his head slowly. "Judging by that cut on her shoulder and that there was dried blood under the newer, deeper cut, I'd say she's been trapped away from her babies for days."

"I hope they all survived."

"We'll give them time to get their bellies full."

"Ralston's dog?"

Falcon shrugged. "More'n likely. For now, let's talk about these cows." Falcon turned to the herd. "What are the chances a hired man at the Hawkins Ranch owns this slice of property between the two ranches, has a herd of cows — some of 'em with a powerful look of your herd — and ain't never mentioned it to nobody?"

"I suppose it's possible Hawkins knows."

"And Hawkins ain't never talked about it? Seems the kinda thing that'd be known. Mostly folks know who owns land around them, don't they?"

"They for sure do. But how would I ever wonder who owns this land when I know I own it?"

"Did your grandpa know about this valley?"

Cheyenne looked at the land. "I don't think so. He'd've run cattle on it. And this is a big old mountain. Grandpa could have wandered awhile and never seen it."

"I wonder how Ralston found it."

"Happenstance, maybe. He saw a deer or elk go bounding up a trail no man would normally notice."

"Then he worked mighty hard hauling rocks to hide the trail."

A man who could barely walk, Cheyenne thought. "As for this land and herd coming to Ralston in some honorable way, the chances are somewhere between slim and none. Hawkins has Herefords, the red ones with the white faces. We have Angus, the all-black ones. And if you crossbreed the two kinds of cattle, you get cows that look just like these."

"I wonder if he rustled your cattle at first, along with Hawkins's. Then, once his herd got big enough to grow on its own, he quit adding from other herds. You said he's been out here a long time, and Spellman said Ralston already owned this mountain when he came to the land office. Ralston could've been doing this for years. Letting his herd grow. Maybe even slipping a few head out to sell."

"From what I can see, they're mostly all

branded with that stick with two loops: a *P* facing back, an *R* facing front, sharing a center stick. PR — Percival Ralston. I'll bet it's a registered brand. But not on the few Herefords and Angus." Cheyenne gave a snort of disgust and pointed to a majestic black bull standing apart from the cattle and above the cave where the dog had gone. He stood sideways to them, his head swung around to keep an eye on the newcomers. He had an *RHR* branded on his hip and a second brand beside it. "Especially not on that one."

Cheyenne's voice took on a snap. "I recognize those two brands. One's ours. The other is the brand of the man we bought the bull from. The bull had a real official name, Texas Midnight. He was a yearling calf when we brought him home, bred to be a prize bull. We lost him his first winter, years ago. He cost a lot of money, and he just up and vanished. We figured he fell afoul of that stream or maybe wolves, but wolves would've left a sign, and believe me, we hunted. Searched for that young bull, or at least his carcass, for a full growing season before we gave up and accepted he was gone."

"Looks like you didn't hunt hard enough."

"No, we didn't, and that's a fact. If we

had, we'd've caught on to the rustling. It was after Grandpa died. Right after, because Grandpa bought Texas Midnight midsummer. Then Grandpa died that fall, and for a while, we weren't doing a good job of tending the cattle out of grief."

Cheyenne felt a spark of rage. "He used our grief to steal from us."

"I'd say we've got some cattle to herd home," Falcon said dryly. "One at least, but I say we take the whole herd."

Cheyenne looked at him with a furrowed brow. "Isn't that how you handled the men who attacked you in Independence?"

"That's what that varmint Tuttle said."

"And you said it sounded like justice." Cheyenne slapped him on the arm. "I like the way you think. I expect the two of us would make a hash of driving them, especially because you probably don't know what you're doing. We'll go home and fetch Wyatt and a few other hands and come back. I want it done before we talk to Ralston. If we're making a mistake, Ralston's gonna have to come over and explain how he came to have his name on a deed for land that's mine." Cheyenne had the thought flicker through her head again that the land wasn't hers but the Hunt brothers'. But it was. In her heart it was. "And how he came to own a herd that looks like it's mostly mine mixed with Hawkins's, and why he neglects his dog."

"Might be best to talk to him first, rustling being a hanging offense and all."

"Horse thievin' is a hanging offense, too, and you did that."

"I can honestly say that I have no memory of doing any such thing."

"Fair enough. We'll leave them, though that bull is mine, and I can prove it."

"We'll prove it all — and soon. I'm mighty eager to hear how he explains all that." Falcon stared awhile longer.

Cheyenne didn't mind standing there gazing at her now fully grown, majestic bull. "Let's go check on the dog."

FOURTEEN

They went back for their horses and led them into the valley. The cattle seemed tame and uninterested in them. The bull only looking at them once in a while.

They hitched their horses and left 'em grazing, then walked to the little cave.

Mama was flat on her side with three skinny pups goin' mad, eating like they'd been missing their mama for too long.

Mama didn't like the company.

Falcon smiled at the poor critter. She'd had a hard few days.

He dropped to his knees to fit inside the small cave opening, and it wasn't much bigger than just to fit a dog and her pups.

Falcon slid over to let Cheyenne in. When she got all the way in, she was a sight too close, but he couldn't bring himself to object.

They sat shoulder to shoulder. Cheyenne crossed her legs at the ankles, and pulled her knees up nearly to her chin, then wrapped her arms around them.

Falcon copied her and rested his back against the cave wall, watching those babies fill their bellies.

Time passed. Crowded in like this, Falcon felt all the aches he'd been shuttin' out of his thoughts. But they were healing. He'd be his own self soon.

Whoever that was.

The mama quit keeping an eagle eye on them and let her head drop to the ground as if it weighed a hundred pounds. Falcon leaned forward and rested a hand on the mama's weary head. Her eyes blinked open. She watched but didn't bite or run away. The puppies might not've let her loose. He caressed her and studied that nasty cut on her shoulder.

"She probably oughta have someone put some thread in that cut. Don't know if she'd allow it."

Cheyenne nodded, then rubbed the old girl on the forehead. The dog's eyes closed again. She seemed to be getting used to her new cave mates.

The puppies fell asleep, one at a time. The mama had settled in and was snoring quietly. Worn out nearly beyond surviving by her terrible situation. Falcon saw no meanness in the dog. She might go for a throat to save a puppy, but he chanced it and slid a hand under the closest pup. They were all black with white markings, like their mama. This one had a straight blaze down the center of its face and four white paws.

It didn't stir when he lifted it, nor did the mama. It worried him some. Just how exhausted were they? How close had they come to dying?

He pulled the puppy against his chest and cradled it there, then, thinking of Cheyenne, he handed it to her. She smiled at him. Her black eyes full of bright pleasure.

Once the baby was comfortable against her chest, nearly tucked under her chin, Falcon got another one. This one pure black except for one ear and the tip of its tail.

After a long spell, Cheyenne said quietly, "They usually have more puppies." Cheyenne still sat shoulder to shoulder with him. Her only other choice was to get out, and she didn't look like she had any plans for that.

"Let's just sit here and be quiet until the babies wake up. They all need sleep and more to eat, I reckon. Mama included."

A long time had passed when the one puppy still lying against its mama stirred and started suckling again. Figuring if that puppy had slept enough for hunger to again take charge, then these had, too, Falcon set his little white-eared pup down, and it flopped around and found food. Cheyenne added hers, and the mama woke up and licked her babies.

"How old do they look to you?" Falcon felt like he should be able to guess such a thing, maybe if his head was working right.

"No idea. A month at least. Their eyes open at about two weeks. So maybe a month. They're still really young." Cheyenne shrugged.

"Funny thing." He watched the dog when he spoke. She must be getting used to them because she just attended to her babies now without a growl or a fang showin'. "I kinda like it in here. It feels like I'm in a sheltered spot." He looked at Cheyenne. "You reckon that means I lived in a cave back in Tennessee?"

That got a smile out of her as he'd planned. He pulled out more jerky and fed the dog.

"You lived with the bears and cougars no doubt," Cheyenne said. "You've got the ways of the wild on you, Falcon. I'm thinking you lived in the mountains there. You like the mountains here too much. Took right off for the hills when you got here, almost as natural to you as a bear hunting a cave."

Nodding, Falcon pulled his canteen off his shoulder. "Cup your hands. We'll give her a drink of water."

The dog, wary but buried under puppies and too worn down and thirsty to resist, lapped water out of Cheyenne's hands.

They let her empty the little serving of water, then Falcon poured more. He said, "I need to doctor that shoulder, but I'm not sure how, and I don't have anything with me to use if I did know. If she's been huntin' her own meals, she probably won't survive out here hurt like this. Must've managed it before, but now she can't outrun much. We can wait on the cows, but we have to take her and the pups home with us."

Cheyenne looked away from where she watched the mama lap up water fast enough it wasn't all dripping away through Cheyenne's fingers. "We're turning dog thief?"

"This dog and her pups would've all been dead in a couple more days. We don't even know for sure she belongs to someone. She might be a dog running wild."

"So we can have her?"

"Your land. Your cows. I say that makes her your dog. We'll talk it over with the sheriff about the cows. I s'pect he'll want to have a talk with Ralston. After that, if the sheriff says it's legal, we'll take them to the RHR, too. If Ralston comes after those cows — and with his brand on a lot of them, there's a chance he could, though I don't know how he's gonna explain your bull in here — then we'll brace him with how he took over land that doesn't belong to him. And if he can prove he came by it all honest, we'll let him have everything back that doesn't have an RHR brand on it. For right now, I'd say he's got some explaining to do and what better way to make him do it than to . . ." He looked at her. At those black eyes and that dark hair twisted into one long braid hanging over her shoulder so it dropped nearly to her waist.

"Than to steal his cattle?"

"Yep."

She wore somewhat less manly clothes today than he'd seen her in before. A brown riding skirt, not the britches she wore in the mountains. She had on a shirt the color of a biscuit. Blouse not shirt. Blouse was what it was called. Buttoned up the front with pretty tucks and wooden buttons.

He poured more water.

"Pa, is that you?"

The voice. Who had said that? It was gone before he could focus on it.

Like a flash of lightning he thought, *Harvey.*

C-could Harvey have been who said, "Pa, is that you?" Could he have a son named Harvey?

The pain came fierce. He bent his head forward to force himself to bear it, hoping more memories would come.

Then he knew Harvey was a . . . was a *mule.* That came clear.

"Falcon, what's wrong?"

A hard tug on his arm brought his head up. He didn't know it was down. He capped the canteen, set it aside, and rubbed on the back of his neck. The crease was scabbed over, hardly even tender anymore.

"I-I think I — maybe I had a mule named Harvey." Of a sudden, the front of his head throbbed so hard his torso fell forward again. He'd've fallen over, laid out on the cave floor, if there'd been room. He braced his forearms on his knees, rested his head there, and forced himself to reason it out. He tried to picture Harvey.

"An old rawboned mule."

Cheyenne clutched his arms. "Named Harvey?"

"Harvey, yes. I'm sure that's from before. Out of my memory. Harvey was mine."

Forcing himself to think made his head

160

throb until it pounded, like someone hammering on it. He pushed on. The things buried in his brain seemed to be trying to get out, but they were using a hammer and chisel to make their way.

"You're remembering?"

"I think so, yes." A mule named Harvey. But then who had asked him, "Pa, is that you?"

He couldn't get any image of children who'd asked that question of him. The question was asked by . . . by an adult man. That seemed right. The voice was clearer now, and he was sure it wasn't a child speaking. Could it have been him? If it was, who had he asked? Clovis? From what he'd been told, he hadn't seen his pa for years.

Keeping his head bowed, he found a prayer inside him. He could remember there was a God, but not what his own believin' had been like. He couldn't get that out of hiding in his noggin, either. And the pain was carving his head up. But he pushed on. It was there. Right there to hand, if he could only —

A hand touched his chin and lifted. He raised his head.

Their eyes met. He saw only kindness. Kindness and something else. Her hand moved until it slid up to rest her palm on his cheek. "Stop now. You're in pain. I can see it in your eyes, in the expression on your face."

"It's givin' me a powerful headache." He covered her hand with his. It felt so nice, that strong, callused woman's hand. "But I need to keep at it. It all feels close, and if I can just —"

She brought her other hand up until she held his face. "Stop. Don't hurt yourself like this."

"I have to, don't I? I have to keep —"

She moved one hand to rest her fingers on his lips.

That drove his headache away and all thoughts of digging around for memories.

He said quietly, "I have to remember, Cheyenne."

"You will. The pain has to mean you're not done healing. With time, you'll remember. But, for now, stop fighting through the pain. You have courage, and I like courage in a man, but I hate seeing you hurt."

The soft suckling of the hungry pups faded. He forgot about the cool shade of the crowded little space, almost too little to be called a cave. All he could feel was her callused fingertips, and he smelled the warm scent of a woman. She looked at him, and he saw goodness in her eyes. Considering

162

how cranky she'd mostly been, it was a fine moment.

"You've had a few memories. Give yourself time, and you'll have more."

"You don't know that."

"It stands to reason."

He smiled. "So you touch me, lean close to me, all to distract me from my pain? An act of kindness? Or are you really starting to like me?"

Something dangerous flashed in Cheyenne's eyes. A look that, if Falcon had any common sense, would make him hightail it before she started swinging a fist.

Then her eyes flashed with something else, and she whispered, "I'm starting to like you real fine, Falcon."

He forgot every sensible thought in his mostly senseless head.

FIFTEEN

Falcon Hunt had handed her a puppy.

That was no reason to think such warm thoughts of him, but it was a sweet thing to do. A quiet, gentle, happy moment in her life, which had been loud and harsh and sad for too long.

And then his pain. Such a gentle act with the puppy. A man she'd trailed in the woods long enough to know how strong and smart and woods-savvy he was. And so wounded.

Those rugged, callused hands handing her that soft puppy. Its belly so full of milk she could almost feel it sloshing as the little critter slept. Her hands touched his as he gave the baby over. An expression on his face. Not a smile. Falcon wasn't a big smiler, nor a big frowner. He didn't laugh or yell. Not overly anyway.

He was a man in control of himself. It was a relief after the treatment she'd received in that will at the hands of Clovis, whose only type of control was to lie well enough you had no idea what went on in his fermented mind.

Now Falcon, who'd come here to invade her land, had saved that mama dog. And whatever his outward appearance, that injured, fiercely protective, half-wild dog saw inside to someone she trusted.

Cheyenne found herself trusting him, too.

She'd told him if he could remember when his ma died, if it was late enough that Clovis's marriage to Cheyenne's ma was illegal, the will wouldn't stand. That meant Falcon would lose everything.

And still he'd faced pain, trying to remember.

She'd always hoped to marry someday, but her measure of a man was her grandpa. He was the kind of man she wanted to share her life with. And on the other end was Clovis. Her ma was a strong, wise woman in so many ways, but she'd let herself be fooled by Clovis. And a big part of that, Cheyenne knew, was because she'd married too quickly. Cheyenne believed Ma would have seen the truth, the rot at Clovis's core, if she'd just gone more slowly.

Cheyenne was going to give any man she was interested in plenty of time to reveal his true self.

And here she was, thinking warmly of a man she hardly knew at all. Moreover, a man who didn't know himself. For a moment, she'd thought he would kiss her.

She'd never imagined wanting such a thing, but she had. Inside, she was churned up, heated up, melting. It was the oddest feeling, and she wanted more of it.

Especially because it was only now that she realized how cold she'd been. How frozen inside. Yes, she'd known of how hard and angry she'd been since the reading of the Sidewinder's will. But she now knew even before that she'd kept much of herself lassoed and hog-tied, never to run free.

Never had she imagined wanting to be touched and held by a man.

She thought of her hasty plan to marry Oliver Hawkins. She'd known him a long time. He might not send her pulse racing, but she knew him and wouldn't be fooled by him. But now that she'd thought of kissing Falcon, she realized how impossible it would be to let Hawkins kiss her.

Here she sat with Falcon's face still held gently in her hands. His eyes on her. He was so still, so silent.

She should pull back, but she didn't want to. Didn't want to let go of him. His eyes drifted closed, then, from deep in his chest, the words so quiet they reminded her of the dog's growling, he said, "Thank you."

The mama dog yipped, looking at the entrance to the cave, and Cheyenne turned to look out, reaching for her gun, afraid Ralston had come to check his cattle and saw the boulders moved.

The bull, Texas Midnight, poked his nose into their cave. Cheyenne's nose almost brushed his. He bellowed hot breath right in her face and bunted the roof of the cave opening.

Cheyenne scooted back, which wasn't hardly possible in the cramped space. The dog barked with more fury, wasted on the bull and upsetting for her and the pups.

"Do you think he can get in here?" Falcon whispered, and his warm breath from behind her was all the way different from the bull's.

"Nope, and I think, for a while, we can't get out."

She looked over her shoulder and grinned at him. Then she said, "You try and calm down that mama dog. I want to hold a puppy again."

"Don't answer this if it's going to make your head hurt."

Falcon turned to look at Cheyenne, who

carried his bag, filled with puppies. He had the mama dog draped across his lap. Once the bull had tired of staring at them and wandered off, they'd loaded up the dogs, giving the mama plenty of time to sniff her babies to make sure they were all right, then they'd carried them down to the horses and headed for home.

"I'm going to come back for my bull whether the sheriff lets me have those cows or not, and to get rid of that barbed wire."

"It looks like he kept the top of the trail wired up. But it's all fallen down."

"I suppose by the time it fell, the cows were used to the canyon and didn't try and get out. But he should have wound up the wire and gotten rid of it."

"We'll find plenty of places where this Ralston will turn out to be a careless fool," Falcon guessed.

"He got away with this thievin' for a long time," Cheyenne observed.

They wound down the side of the mountain.

"Give mama another sniff of her babies. She's fighting my hold," Falcon said for the umpteenth time.

Finally, he just took the bag, puppies and all.

"No." Cheyenne made a swipe for the bag,

but the mama growled and her ears went back.

Cheyenne scowled. "Why do you get to carry all the dogs?"

Falcon laughed. A nice change from the pain. "What did you start to ask? About me not answering if it made my head hurt?"

"Oh, that's right. I want to talk about Harvey."

Falcon, paying close attention, didn't feel a single pang. "Just you asking about it didn't give me pain. Let's see." When they finally reached the bottom of the mountain, and Falcon could pay less attention to his horse and the dogs had settled in to sleeping, he could think on Harvey.

"Just tell me what you see. Don't search for more."

"A mule."

"What does his bridle look like? Does he have a saddle? Are you riding him or leading him?"

They were mighty good questions, and it set him to thinking, not of what he couldn't remember but on the details of what he could.

After he'd told her all he knew about Harvey, he said, "And I saw a cabin. A little, ramshackle thing. It's built into the side of a hill, or probably a mountain."

169

"In the paper work we got, your address was a town called Chickahoochi Cove."

"That rings something in me, but I can't really remember it. It's just a name that somehow seems right."

"That's probably your cabin you're remembering."

They rode along, a friendly sort of ride. Falcon talked of his cabin until his head started aching.

"Enough now," Cheyenne said. "We've used up the day, and we'll be lucky if they haven't thrown our supper out to the chickens."

"I hope they've saved enough to feed the dog."

Cheyenne looked at the dogs, then her eyes raised to meet his. It was there between them. Falcon could feel her hands resting on his face. How it upset her to see him hurting. How close they'd been in that tight little cave.

"I'm starting to like you real fine, Falcon."

It helped get the pain away from him.

"Let's pick up the pace if the dogs can handle it," she said. "I want to talk to Wyatt about those cows."

Sixteen

"You found Texas Midnight?" Wyatt had barely washed up and sunk to his chair.

Molly and Win were putting a meal on the table. They'd turned the noon beef into shepherd's pie, with meat and vegetables in a thick gravy and mashed potatoes over the top.

No one had ever cooked like this at the RHR. Ma was no hand at it. She was good enough to keep them fed, but she was working long hours with Grandpa. She'd never had time to fuss over preparing a meal.

Cheyenne had followed in her footsteps.

And Win, who'd cooked here off and on for years, was a whole lot better than Cheyenne, but she'd never made food like this.

Cheyenne told Wyatt all that had gone on. He looked under the table and saw the mama dog nursing her babies right there in the kitchen.

"And how many cows again?" he asked.

"I don't blame you for finding it all hard to believe," Cheyenne said. "Where do you think those deeds are, Wyatt? Where'd we put them? Or have they been stolen by your sidewinder of a pa?"

"What makes you think he took them?" Kevin stopped eating.

"The only reason I thought of Pa," Falcon said, "is he was the only low-down coyote around. There's no proof he did it."

No one seemed interested in fighting to clear his name.

"There are some old papers of your pa's, Cheyenne, your real pa, Nate Brewster, in a . . . in a chest somewhere. I think," Wyatt said. "He didn't exactly own land, but he might have some records and maybe Grandpa put their deeds together."

"You can help me hunt," Cheyenne said. "Then we'll go in tomorrow and talk to the sheriff."

"I can't go." Wyatt jabbed a thumb at Kevin. "And he can't go. He's been some help with the cattle. Not much, but enough I want him out there. He can at least watch after his little brother. Keep him from spooking the whole herd all the way to Denver."

"I'm glad to try," Kevin said.

172

"Falcon and I will talk to the land agent tomorrow, and to the sheriff again," Cheyenne said. "It's time to stop asking questions and start getting some answers."

At that, Molly set a custard on the table and a bowl of peaches she'd found jarred in the root cellar, but she'd done something fancy to the peaches and the custard smelled like a slice of heaven. She added coffee, and it distracted them all from their planning, which was just turning into a repeat of Wyatt asking the same questions from different directions over and over.

Falcon found himself enjoying the way the family ate and talked and sometimes squabbled. He tossed a few hunks of tender roast beef to the dog, then glanced under the table to see a chunk of beef coming from the other side. He looked up and saw Cheyenne blush at being caught.

Family, it was an interesting business. He found it suited him.

Cheyenne shoved the trunk back under the big sofa in the front room. She'd forgotten it was tucked under there. This house hadn't been dug into like this in all the years she'd lived here.

"Nothing. I'm done," she said in exasperation. "We're going to have to hope Gordon Spellman found what we need."

She stood and crossed her arms, thinking of any other place she could search. The whole family had been at it for over an hour. Wyatt had even gone and looked in the barn, where they had a few things stored. Even though Grandpa would've never left them out there.

She and Falcon were alone in the front room. Kevin and Win had gone to bed. Molly had the kitchen clean and bread baked for morning. She'd looked in every corner of the kitchen and her room, and as Cheyenne had known, there was nothing.

Wyatt had come in from the barn and gone to sleep. Falcon had the bunkhouse to look forward to. The dog was already tucked in there with Andy.

"Let's get some rest." Falcon came up to her and rested one hand on her arm. "We'll start again tomorrow. We'll get it figured out."

Nodding, it all caught up with her. The shock of the Sidewinder's will that had thrown her whole life into upheaval. Long days branding. A week in the wilderness, and now the worries about the ranch deeds.

She was exhausted. But maybe, even though there was a lot to figure out, they were on the way. She let her shoulders sag with fatigue, and it brought her too close to Falcon. He wrapped his arms around her.

"Rest against me for a bit."

She couldn't resist letting him bear her weight for just a moment. She thought of the puppy. With her head resting on Falcon's strong chest, she let a faint smile curve her lips.

The moment between them stretched, then it became something more than a moment. She raised her head at the same time he did, and their lips almost touched by accident.

"Patsy," he whispered.

She jumped away from him. "What?"

A bucket of ice water couldn't have cleared Cheyenne's head any faster.

Falcon stumbled back. His eyes wide. She saw the knowledge in them. He knew what he'd said.

He didn't say it again, but he didn't try to pretend those words hadn't come from his mouth.

"You." She jabbed a finger at his chest. If it had been a bullet, she'd've shot him in the heart. Which sounded real good right now. "You . . . are *married.*"

Falcon's jaw clenched so tight she thought she heard his teeth creak.

He didn't deny it. "I-I just . . . I don't think so."

He put space between them, when they'd been so close. He rammed his fingers deep into his hair.

She saw the pain. It came when he was trying to remember. How could she feel compassion for him and want to clobber him at the same time?

"Patsy. Who is that?" he asked.

"You're the one who said her name."

Falcon didn't respond.

At last she was able to say, "I believe you when you say you don't know. But if you left a wife back down the trail . . ."

The anger of it, the hurt. The wanting. She turned to get out of here, get away from him.

"Cheyenne, wait!"

She turned as she reached the door. Only after she'd obeyed him, did she realize she was doing it. She fought down the urge to go kick him. Truth was, she wanted to kick herself for trusting him.

For obeying that cracked-whip voice.

But here she was, stopped in place by his command and staring at him. An odd urge to cry swept through her at his rugged good looks. His gentle confusion. His pain. Even guilt. She saw all of that. Maybe he did have a wife, and even without remembering her, he felt guilty on a very deep level.

And maybe his memory had hidden her, and the way he'd held Cheyenne close hadn't been meant as any disrespect. But he'd come out here without her, hadn't he? He'd never said a word about a wife. Kevin had brought his family along. If Falcon had a wife and he hadn't brought her, then he had abandoned her. Just like the Sidewinder.

She fought back tears. They didn't fall, and no sob escaped, but she was crying inside in a way that reached to her heart.

She hated that she wanted to do such a foolish thing as cry. She hated that he'd made her yearn and care and want.

"I'm sorry."

A sorry excuse for a man.

"I'm sorry I spoke another woman's name. But who is she?"

"A woman you left behind, I'd say."

His jaw clenched tighter, nodding as if he had to force his head to move up and down. "You're right to be furious. I can't . . . that is, *we* can't be . . . well, we can't be . . . close to each other. Not until I remember." He came closer to her right after he said they couldn't be close. And she didn't run.

He was absolutely right. Cheyenne's

heart, previously neatly frozen and safe, was now aching.

"I do know one thing, Cheyenne. If I'm a polecat like my pa, then losing my memory might be for the best."

"Why? So you can abandon a wife, maybe children, with a clear conscience?"

"No, because if I'm a low-down side-winder of a man, then today I can become someone new. The thought of abandoning a family is sickening. I can't believe I have it in me to do such a thing. Talking of it makes me ashamed to the bottoms of my feet. If that's who I was, then that's not who I will be anymore."

He came toe-to-toe with her. He reached up that rough, gentle hand and caressed her cheek with two knuckles. "From this moment on, I am going to be a decent, godly man. No matter how beautiful the woman is. And no matter how my head is full of you when it comes to thoughts of a woman."

He meant it. She could see it plain as day. But then he had no idea of the kind of man he was. Nothing he said now would hold when his memory returned.

"From this day forward, I intend to be a better man than my pa, and that means nothing passes betwixt the two of us until I know for certain I'm free."

It was a noble promise. She wished him luck keeping it. Then she left the room on the silent vow that free or not, men couldn't be trusted. And that was what she needed to remember.

SEVENTEEN

Wyatt stepped out of the back door of the
house.

From her mount in back of the herd,
Cheyenne saw his mouth drop open. He
shoved one hand into his hair and knocked
the Stetson clean off his head.

And then his eyes landed on the bull. He
went from shock to pleasure. Then anger.

Shouting, Wyatt ran for the nearest corral
gate. "Rubin, get out here! Andy, Kevin,
you too!" There were horses in the corral,
but it was a good-sized yard. They could
live together for a bit if they had to.

Andy came out of the bunkhouse. He ran
in exactly the right direction to keep the
cattle from turning away from the corral
gate. The kid was learning.

Cheyenne would have probably been able
to haze them in the right direction, but the
boy was helping. And she'd taken five RHR
hands along to drive the cattle back. Falcon,

too, but she wasn't speaking to him.

Rubin charged out of the barn, more cowhands on his heels. They all took off to block cattle from picking the wrong direction.

Kevin stepped out of the ramrod's house in his socks. He saw the cattle, vanished back in the cabin, and was out again in seconds with boots on. Win came to the door to watch in wide-eyed confusion.

She wasn't much of a ranch woman, but she knew her pa ran Herefords and the RHR ran Angus, and there were a few Herefords here with the HR brand.

The cattle were gentle critters. Cheyenne had expected them to be wild as deer. Instead, they were fat from a life of easy food, plenty of water, and enough contact with men that they didn't get overly upset at the sight of a horse and rider. They were broke to the trail by the time they got them up and out of that meadow.

It had been easy for her and her cowhands to guide them home, despite Falcon being next to useless. He seemed to figure out the way of it enough that he could ride along behind while everyone else hazed the herd. They'd made their way to the RHR with little fuss.

Now those mostly black-and-white cattle

walked calm as you please into the corral.

Rubin ordered the men to get the horses out of that corral, away from the cows. Horses, especially cow ponies like these, would sometimes make a game out of herding cattle they shared a space with, which, in a pen like this, amounted to bothering them.

Best to separate them as soon as possible.

Wyatt had the gate closed, and Cheyenne was on the ground.

Falcon swung down, and reached for the mama dog, who'd come hobbling out of the house. Molly had kept her inside until the cattle were penned up. But now Molly stood at the kitchen door, and the dog was loose, coming straight for Falcon. The mama was already looking stronger. She needed to put on some weight, but she'd survive.

Andy came up to them and picked up one of the puppies. "Can I have one of these for my own?" His question was about the only normal thing anyone had to say about this mess.

Better than talk of cattle rustlers and land grabs. Betrayal that had gone on, maybe for years. It had to be for years.

"You can have all four of them as far as I care." Cheyenne dragged in a chestful of air to calm herself, before saying, "Let's go inside."

"The sheriff told you to take the cattle?" Wyatt watched the cattle crowd up to a watering tank that stood in the yard.

"Yep, he listened to my story, went with us to the land office, rode out to that valley and checked it out, then said he was going to bring in Ralston."

"So the land agent found evidence Ralston's deed was forged?"

"Yep. Spellman's got proof of our claim and is transferring the deed to that. There's a whole lot to tell about his checking old records, old signatures, dates from the time Ralston recorded his purchase. There weren't any other purchases besides Ralston's because there wasn't a land agent. The date alone shows it to be a fraud. He must've broken into the land office and put a forged deed in and stole the original one."

Cheyenne wanted to talk to Rubin, too, but he was busy riding a horse into the corral to lasso the horses in there. The other men were with him, and though she hated being suspicious, she wasn't sure whom she could trust. The last trouble they'd had was with their own ramrod partnering up with the foreman from the Hawkins Ranch. And Percy Ralston was another HR hand.

Was he the only outlaw left? Or were some of Cheyenne's own cowhands in on this?

"I still can't believe you found our bull," Wyatt said. "He's a beauty."

Cheyenne turned and marched to the house. Wyatt fell in beside her. In fact, he passed her, eager to get her to where she wanted to be so she'd talk.

Falcon considered not going in with them. He could take his dog and her pups, and go to the bunkhouse, which seemed to be his house for now.

Andy came up beside him. Still holding one puppy, he crouched by the litter, then sat right down on the grass and coaxed a second puppy onto his lap.

Which meant Falcon was out here playing with puppies and a kid.

Which seemed like a fine idea. He hunkered down beside Andy and petted the mama dog, who'd lain down again, exhausted, poor girl. "Let's take the pups to the bunkhouse."

Andy smiled as he cuddled the little critter to his chest and giggled when it licked his face. "Okay."

Andy looked away from the pup, dodging its tongue but not very hard.

"Falcon," Cheyenne shouted from the

184

back door, scowling at him, "get in here."

She went back inside, not waiting to see if he'd obey her.

Jealous of the kid, Falcon said, "Can you see to them for a while? I think they'll let her stay in the bunkhouse. She may turn out to be a good cattle dog."

"I'll feed and water her and find some kind of nest for her and the puppies."

"She's half-wild so don't upset her overly. If you touch that shoulder, she might bite. I sure would."

Andy grinned. "There's a good-sized bone left from yesterday. I'll probably leave the shoulder alone if it don't start in bleeding again."

The kid probably had more sense than Falcon did. He wondered if the boy had ever had a dog. Then Falcon wondered that about himself.

He meandered to the house. Goin' slow, at least partly because he didn't like Cheyenne's bossy ways.

He thought of that almost kiss. Maybe he liked her bossy ways a little.

Who was Patsy?

He pictured that cabin again.

It caused a deep throb in his noggin so he quit thinking and went inside.

The whole family was sitting at the table

squabbling, 'ceptin' Molly. She was by the stove like usual.

Mostly the noise came from Cheyenne and Wyatt.

"I wonder what you two were like before this whole mess with Clovis's will. 'Cuz I ain't never heard neither of you do much but complain."

That shut 'em up.

The pair turned to glare at him.

Wyatt said, "I've climbed that mountain a few times. I've never seen a trail on the side you and Cheyenne were on."

Falcon explained how the rocks were stacked to disguise the trail. "I almost went past it myself," he continued. "If that dog hadn't whined, I might've." But he wouldn't have. He'd seen those rocks had been moved. It had been well hidden, but he'd seen it all right.

"I can't believe Percival Ralston stole our bull. And that was years ago. He's been at this for a long time."

"And faking how hurt he is, Wyatt," Cheyenne insisted.

"I know him just well enough," Win said, "to know he couldn't lift a bunch of heavy stones. At least not if he's really as injured as he acts."

"Well, he's a skilled liar, clear enough,"

said Falcon.

"My father probably didn't even notice he had cows missing," said Win. "Especially because Percy Ralston does most of his bookwork. He's —"

They were all jabberin', one on top of the other.

Molly was the only one not talking, not angry. She was busy getting a baked chicken out of the oven. It was late for dinner, but she must've planned to wait on him and Cheyenne. The woman was a fine cook and had a good head on her shoulders.

Falcon's head, on the other hand, was a wreck. All this talk was too much. He shut it out, and suddenly his thoughts were flooded with flashing, stunted memories.

The same things.

Patsy. Harvey. A cabin. *"Pa, is that you?"*

The pain was too much to let him talk to these folks. He should put his thinkin' aside and help figure out what to do with the cattle he'd just stolen . . . or maybe taken back. But he had to get through this wall in his head, memory was just behind it. And hurt or not, he had to pound his way through it to remember who he was.

He backed slowly out of the kitchen. He wanted to go out the back door and find Andy and help him care for that nice little family of dogs. But he didn't think he could swing a door open and not be noticed, even with them all stewin' over this rustling mess. Besides, much as he wanted to spend time caring for a dog, he needed to remember.

Instead of trying to sneak outside, he left the kitchen for the hallway and kept backing up until he reached that room they'd been in before with the big picture of Cheyenne's ma on the wall.

He stood in there, the kitchen noise faint from here. His ears were grateful for the quiet, though his head still hurt.

He stared at that picture. It was Katherine, he knew, but it was so close to Cheyenne. Katherine's coloring was a shade lighter. She had blue eyes instead of black like Cheyenne's. But the pretty face, the size and shape of her, was pure Cheyenne. A beautiful pair of women.

His pa had been married to this woman.

"Pa, is that you?"

A sickening throb sent him stumbling backward. His hands clasped his head. He came up against the wall, and his knees weren't steady enough to hold him. The pain sent him sinking to the floor. He'd found a corner. His back was to a wall of bookcases that met right here in the corner with him.

There was a soft rug on the floor that made it as easy to sit on as any chair.

He sat there with the picture of Katherine LaRemy Brewster Hunt staring down at him. As if she knew he wanted to kiss Cheyenne.

As if she knew he . . . what? He'd like to dredge up all sorts of guilt to lash himself with, but he didn't even know what kind of man he was.

Was there a woman somewhere he'd left behind? Patsy? Abandoned like his own ma?

A face swam into his vision. Patsy. A big girl. Blond with a good smile. Patsy. His . . . his . . . it was right there. A stabbing pain went through his head, so sharp it turned his stomach, and he thought he might empty his belly right there on the floor.

He clutched his head, sank his fingers deep into his hair and pulled, hoping pain on the outside would help him bear the pain on the inside.

Who was she to him? The memory came with what felt like a kick in the head, but he had to know. He couldn't be anything to Cheyenne if he had a wife.

Patsy. His wife.

The cabin he'd shared with her.

The cabin he'd ridden away from to head from Tennessee to Wyoming.

He waited, wanting more to come through that door, or for him to step through it into his memories.

But that one glimpse.

Cheyenne had been a betrayal. She had to have been, if Patsy was his wife.

Pushing himself, he knew, if he could just hang on a little longer, bear the pain, he'd remember everything.

EIGHTEEN

He wasn't sure how long he'd been hunkered down there when a movement to his right brought his head up. His eyes were almost blurred through the pain.

"Are you bad off?" Kevin rushed to his side and dropped to one knee.

Falcon's wavering memories slammed shut. He wanted to swing a fist into Kevin's face and tell him to go away.

Then he thought of what Kevin had just said — and the voice he'd said it in.

"Did you, uh, o-once s-say . . ." His memory wavered. "Did you ever say 'Pa, is that you?' I mean, say it to me . . . ever?"

Kevin's cheeks turned a ruddy color. One corner of his mouth turned up in an embarrassed smile. For some reason, the expression helped Falcon push aside the pain in his head.

"Yep, when you stepped off the train." Kevin gave Falcon a worried look, checking him over. Then he rose to his feet. "For just that one second, with you turned mostly away from me, you looked so much like my pa, uh, our pa, a man I hadn't seen for twenty years, that I let those words loose. I knew even as they left my mouth you were too young."

"And you knew Pa was dead, the will and such?"

Kevin gave a little one-shouldered shrug. "Considering I'd known pa was dead for most of those twenty years, and I'd just found out he was dead again, seeing you and not being all that sure he was dead was an easy thing to have flicker through my mind."

"Makes sense."

"Is your head still sore? Is it worse? You've been moving and acting like you're feeling fine. Except for losing your memory —"

"Yeah," Falcon interrupted, "except for that."

Kevin smirked. "Anyhow, I thought you were pretty well off. But you look like you're hurting bad."

Falcon didn't like talking about how weak he felt when he was hunting inside his head. A man needed to hide if he was weak. The weak were prey. Supper. Animals and people were both dangerous. "Aren't you supposed to be in the kitchen arguing?"

"I reckon. But I can't add much to it, and they're yelling just fine without my help." Kevin reached a hand down to Falcon, who, after thinkin' it over a bit, took the hand and let Kevin haul him to his feet.

It was a good strong yank. Falcon was eye to eye with his brother. Their eyes matched. They both had a little dip in the center of their chins. Beyond that, they didn't look much alike. Falcon was an inch or so taller than Kevin. Probably broader. They both had brown hair, but Falcon's was darker, straighter.

"When you went missing —" Kevin swallowed hard — "when we thought you were dead, it made me sad to think a brother I never knew was a brother I never *would* know."

Kevin clapped him on the shoulder, and it was a gentle slap. He was acting like Falcon was fragile. Prey. Though Kevin didn't seem to be hunting.

Falcon met his gaze. "A brother. And you have a little sister and brother. I-I don't think I had anyone else. Except, I think . . . a wife."

"A wife?" Kevin's brows arched.

"I had a flash of memory. Patsy. I can see her face and a cabin. We were married, I think. Were or are married."

"You don't remember anything else?"

"I remember I had a mule named Harvey, and I remembered a man's voice — you, I guess — sayin', 'Pa, is that you?'"

"Yes, you came out here on the train and arrived the same morning I came riding in with my family. And you heard what Tuttle said about Independence. So you had a run-in with him back there."

"And then I went missing later that day I got off the train?"

"Yep."

"Did I say anything else?"

Kevin thought a second. "When I said, 'Pa, is that you?' you said, 'Ain't no one's pa, mister.'"

Falcon straightened. "I said that?"

"Yep."

"So I didn't abandon my children?"

That struck Kevin into a dead quiet. It was all there in his eyes how their pa had abandoned them. Falcon didn't want to be that kind of man.

"Have you been worrying that you might've done that?" Kevin asked.

Falcon shrugged, but he was feeling better. The pain lessening in his head and his heart. "I thought of Patsy's name when I was —" He snapped his mouth shut. He

194

must've taken another beating on his head to've almost blurted that out.

"What happened?"

Falcon didn't know what he must look like, but it had to be tellin' Kevin something. And suddenly Falcon was glad he had a brother. Maybe talking to a brother would help him a little.

He looked at the door to the hallway, which led to the kitchen. Plenty of squabbling in there still. Dropping his voice, he said, "I thought of Patsy's name, said it out loud, when I-I —" he cleared his throat 'cuz it was clogging shut — "when I had my arms around . . . Cheyenne."

Kevin staggered back, caught himself, his eyes as round as twenty-dollar gold pieces. "You and *Cheyenne?*" Whispering didn't hide the shock.

Falcon nodded, afraid she'd somehow heard and would come charging into the room, looking to pound on him worse than the rocks in that stream had. He'd already lost his whole past. What else did he have to lose?

His life.

"And called out another woman's name after?"

Honestly, it was more *during,* but Falcon didn't see any reason to mention that. Bad enough he'd thought of another woman, but to have said her name out loud . . . And now Kevin saying it out loud, it all made him feel even worse. Which surprised him because he wouldn't've believed he could feel much worse.

"And you're still alive?"

Falcon *was* alive. He was sitting right there. And still . . . "I'm a little surprised myself."

They heard a commotion in the kitchen.

"If you repeat this," Falcon growled, "you're the next one going headfirst over a waterfall."

Kevin held up one hand, palm flat at shoulder level. "I swear I'll never mention it."

"Not even to your wife?"

Footsteps came from the hall and Kevin turned. Without, Falcon noticed, promising a thing. But Falcon had to clamp his mouth shut 'cuz someone was coming.

NINETEEN

"I want to have one more look for the deeds. I was wondering if Grandpa might've stuck them inside a book. Maybe he had a thought to hiding them." Cheyenne turned to leave the kitchen.

"Or maybe Pa did take them out of the drawer and hide them."

Cheyenne glanced at Wyatt. "Why would he do that?"

Wyatt shrugged. "Like Falcon said, he's just the only low-down coyote who spent time in the house."

She looked around the kitchen. "Where is Falcon?"

"He might've gotten tired of listening to us squabble." Wyatt shrugged and came after her as she headed for the study.

"Does he have a safe somewhere?" Win asked, following. "My pa has one."

"It's time to eat in just a few minutes," Molly protested. "Your grandpa didn't stick valuable papers between the pages of a book."

Cheyenne looked over her shoulder at the hardworking young woman. For some reason, Molly bothered Cheyenne. *Annoyed* might be a better word.

She wasn't sure why, but she had a sneaking suspicion it was because Molly was acting like a woman ought, and Cheyenne did no such thing. If that was so, then Cheyenne oughta be ashamed of herself. And she would be, just as soon as she had any spare time.

Cheyenne knew womanly skills. She could knit like nobody's business, and she enjoyed it. There were blankets and doilies and what-not scattered all over this house. It helped untangle her thoughts. She oughta be knitting right now, but lately all her knitting had gotten tight. The last thing she tried to knit had ended up a hard, little square about a fourth the size it should've been.

Beyond knitting, she didn't prefer work in the house when there was ropin' and ridin' to do. Didn't mean she couldn't cook. She could. Preferred not to, but she could.

Win was better than Cheyenne, and Molly was better than Win. They were eating well these days. Molly being part of this invasion

198

of surprise family was the best part of it. Or the second best.

Meeting Falcon had been the best part. That . . . well, that wounded, gentle, good-looking, puppy-sharing Falcon. That was the best part.

Except he probably had a wife. Which meant she oughta tie him up and drag him behind her horse at a full gallop for a mile or two, over rocks and scrub pines. Then maybe back her horse over him.

Even so, he'd held her close enough to turn a girl's head to mush.

Cheyenne shoved all that mushiness out of her head. She was not letting her thoughts go to him. She turned away from that annoying Molly and charged after that deed.

Cheyenne rushed down the hallway and into the front room, then she stopped so suddenly she almost fell over her feet. Wyatt, who'd been following, slammed into her from behind and knocked her forward a few steps.

Falcon and Kevin stood together, and both of 'em were looking at her so strange.

What had she interrupted?

Only one thing came to mind, but Falcon was a quiet man. He'd've never told Kevin about what happened between them in that cave or in here last night.

"Watch what you're doing." Wyatt bulled past her, heading for the shelves and shelves of books. His shove was enough to get her eyes off the two men and pay attention to what she was about.

The deed.

If these two didn't care enough about a plot to steal a ranch that was one-third theirs to stay in the kitchen, then they didn't deserve to hear what was going on.

She did sneak one long look at Falcon. She thought he looked pale. And there were lines that looked like pain around his eyes and bracketing his mouth. He'd been having those headaches again. Trying to remember. She wanted to ask him what had come to him. And she wanted to clobber him if he'd remembered a wife and six kids. Worse, if he'd remembered three wives and six kids.

But he needed to remember. That's why he'd left the kitchen and come in here. And Kevin had found him and was worried about him. So was she.

Falcon's eyes met hers.

Wyatt pulled a book off a shelf and fluttered through the pages. "Take the next shelf, Cheyenne. Win, the one on past. Kevin, get over here, we're searching each and every book to see if the deeds are stuck in one of them."

Cheyenne noticed Molly hesitating by the door.

"Should I set dinner back in the oven to stay warm?" Molly asked in a resigned voice.

"Sure," Wyatt said without looking up from the book in his hands. "We'll eat whenever we have time. You can just go back to the kitchen."

Cheyenne glanced at Molly, who glared at Wyatt. Cheyenne hoped Molly didn't kick Wyatt's backside. Instead, she turned and left the room.

With one more look at Falcon, Cheyenne forced herself to quit worrying about him. Well, no. She didn't quit worrying about him, but she quit looking at him and took her worry with her while she searched for Grandpa's deeds.

"I'll do a row of books," said Kevin, "but I reckon it's a waste of time."

Wyatt fluttered through another book. "We've been through everything else, and we remembered the books and decided we should be thorough."

Kevin patted Falcon on the shoulder. "You should sit back down. You're not all the way well yet."

Falcon nodded, rubbed his temple, and looked around the room.

Cheyenne saw him glance in the back

corner like he wished he could get as far away from them as possible.

Instead of standing in the corner, he picked a soft chair that sat to one side of the fireplace, which wasn't lit.

When he sat, he looked almost like he was collapsing. She wanted to go to him. Scold him for not stopping with his efforts to find his memories.

But she had books to go through.

She worked quickly, thumbing through book after book. On her second shelf, she pulled out a book, and a leather packet came with it, dropping to the floor.

The top was a flap that was tied down with a leather string twisted around a flat brass button. She untwisted it, flipped it open, and pulled a stack of papers out that looked older than anything she'd found before.

The paper on top was a record of a land purchase. Not the mountain but the land the house was built on.

"Wyatt, everyone, I think I've found something."

Win left her neat stacks of books behind. Kevin came up beside her. Wyatt was next. She divided the thick sheaf of papers between the four of them.

"The top one's a deed for the house. The

second one is about some cattle Grandpa bought dated about the time he settled out here. Let's go through it all."

Unable to control herself, she went and sat on the settee that faced the fireplace. Falcon had slumped low in his chair, and his head rested against the top of his wingback chair. Another chair, matching Falcon's, sat straight across from him. The matching dark green settee sat between them.

Everyone was busy carefully studying the papers she'd found. She'd wondered if Falcon was asleep, but he slowly sat forward, rubbing his right temple, and spoke so quietly she didn't think anyone could hear him but her. "I remembered just a bit more, Cheyenne. Patsy was my wife. I know that for sure." His eyes, such a perfect match for Wyatt's, met hers.

Her stomach twisting with anger, Cheyenne asked, "A wife you left behind, just like the Sidewinder left your own ma?"

The roomful of people, already quiet after Cheyenne handed out papers to sort through, went silent.

"You abandoned a wife to come out here?" Wyatt's hazel eyes flashed with anger.

"I don't know much else," Falcon said. "I don't blame you for being suspicious, but the feeling attached to remembering her . . . it's solid and good. I don't want to believe I left her behind. The land wouldn't have meant much to me. I don't have a hankerin' to be a rancher, 'lessen I did but I've forgotten it. But when I think of home, I feel no guilt for leaving her."

"Any memories of your ma?" Cheyenne really just could not stand to talk about his wife anymore. Not when she could still feel the strength of his arms.

Little cracks were snapping across her heart to think how close she'd been held by a married man, how interested she was in him. She was tempted to go hunt up a puppy and hug it in a quest to feel better.

Shaking his head, Falcon said, "I don't remember details, for certain not about Ma. I just think there wasn't nothin' back there for me anymore. I think that means no ma, no young'uns. No wife. No brothers or sisters. No family left. No one."

Cheyenne nodded. But he could be sure things were over and done between them. Then she caught Kevin looking at her. His eyes immediately snapped back to the papers Cheyenne had handed him.

That had been a mighty strange look. What had these two been doing in here?

With a deep sigh, Cheyenne turned back

to Falcon. "Well, you're neck deep in family now, Falcon. You couldn't be lonely if you wanted to. I think you'd gone off wandering that first day wanting no part of any of us, and after you lost your memory, you spent a week in the wilderness showing no sign of rushing back upstream to find where you'd come from."

Falcon gave her a half smile. "I was planning to do that until I saw I was being followed."

"By me."

"I told you I watched you sleep, didn't I?"

Cheyenne felt her neck heat up. It spread, and she was glad she had a deep tan to hide the blush. "I think you said something about getting close enough you could have touched me."

"A woman I'd never seen before out wandering in the woods, good tracker, woods-savvy."

Their gazes met. A silence stretched.

"I found it." Wyatt whooped and waved a paper in the air.

For the first time in a while, Cheyenne had an appetite. "Bring it to the kitchen table."

Wyatt nodded and headed out, paper in hand. Everyone followed after him. They were fast moving, eager to have a look at that deed, and to get more of Molly's good cookin'.

TWENTY

Another horseback ride.

Without rememberin' another blasted thing about himself, Falcon looked at the wild hills they were riding through and wanted to get away from everyone.

He was bringing up the rear. So he watched his family . . . strange notion to have family. It didn't seem right to him, and yet there they all were. And riding ahead and leading the pack was Cheyenne.

He imagined vanishing into those hills, and taking her with him.

He even thought maybe she'd come along. Then he thought of Patsy and knew she'd've never come, and he'd've never asked her to.

Shoving that aside, he rode along to visit his new sister-in-law's pa. He was havin' some trouble keeping track of who all his family was, and he didn't think that had a thing to do with takin' a knock on the head.

At least, little as he cared about all of this,

the ride they were taking led to somewhere that might be interesting. Falcon had yet to meet Oliver Hawkins, and what he knew sounded like the man was no one to admire.

Trying to ignore the call of those mountains as he rode, he thought about sleeping in a crowd instead of out under the stars. It hadn't suited him. He'd slept in the bunkhouse, shared a set of beds stacked one on top of the other with Andy on the top bunk.

He'd never heard tell of such a thing. Of course maybe he had, but he doubted it. Beds stacked up to crowd lots of men under one roof. Strange arrangement.

Tonight there'd be a stack three high if you counted the dog. Andy had figured out a way for the dog and pups to slip under the bed, making a dark cave for the little family. Every one of the cowpokes seemed to have adopted the dogs.

When Falcon went to the bunkhouse after they ate to stock up on bullets, Andy told him that Rubin had put some salve on the dog's cut. She'd just licked it off. One of the men had fashioned a bandage by wrapping it tight, but not too tight, around her. She'd chewed it off.

In the end, they'd let her be.

Falcon's bed was decent. The cabin wasn't overly warm with the windows open. The cowpokes were friendly, and none too inclined to ask nosy questions.

Falcon liked it in there, but at the same time, he'd considered borrowing an ax, right there in the dark of night, and heading into the woods to build himself a cabin.

And now, because he'd shoved the lunatic inclination to build a cabin aside, he rode with his family to Win's pa's house.

It was strange how Win had to be coaxed and almost bullied afore she'd come along. Turned out she hadn't told her pa she was married, and her pa had never come storming over to complain about it.

They'd all figured the sheriff would tell him the day he went over to talk to Hawkins about Tuttle, and they expected Hawkins to come right over demanding to be told what was going on. But maybe the sheriff figured a woman's pa knew she was married, and it never came up.

Win was the only one of their number who had a pa, and she wanted nothing to do with him.

Of course, none of the Hunt sons wanted anything to do with their pa, either. But with Clovis being dead, there was no real need to consider him and plan to avoid him.

Cheyenne's pa, along with Molly and Andy's, was long dead.

Plenty of ways to die out here, it seemed.

Oliver Hawkins though, he was alive and well, and it was clear as rainwater that Win didn't want to see him.

But she came along, too. Riding overly close to Kevin, which seemed kinda nice. They'd all agreed — well, maybe not Win, but she was foolin' herself and no one else — that her pa was bound to notice she was married. Had to happen one of these days.

She could keep hiding out, or she could go face him now with her Hunt family surrounding her.

So they were all heading over except Molly. That woman seemed to dearly love her kitchen. And Andy had stayed to practice cowboyin'. The foreman, Rubin, said he had work the kid could do.

Falcon rode around a curve in a nicely widened and leveled trail to see the Hawkins ranch house. He gasped. He heard the same from Kevin. The rest, of course, had seen this white-board monster before.

Falcon had thought Cheyenne's house was grand. But it was log and stone, made out of what was to hand in these parts.

This house had to've been shipped in. Every little piece of it.

Three full stories of neat boards. It was surrounded on all sides he could see with a covered porch and white railings. The front doors were wood, with glass panels in them in a rainbow of colors. And the wood was carved in a way that would take Falcon a year of hard work, all fine details, with shining, carved brass doorknobs on a double door, and hinges to match. The windows were all glass, something just lookin' for a chance to break, or so Falcon thought.

His mind flashed to his cabin. Wooden shutters. Leather for hinges. A wooden latch that dropped into place where it might've had fancy brass knobs. His head throbbed, and he turned his attention to the mansion ahead.

This was the house of a wealthy man. Or a fool. In Falcon's opinion, it was probably both.

Cheyenne reined her horse in, swung down, and tied the mare to the hitching post near the barn. Oliver didn't have one close to the house. The rumor was he didn't think a line of tied-up horses looked right standing in front of his place.

Cheyenne would fix that if she married him.

True, a day ago, when she'd been in Falcon's arms, she'd abandoned the whole notion of marrying Oliver. But then she found out Falcon might be married.

She snuck a glance at him.

Knowing he was here to stay, all she could think of was getting away.

And, since she couldn't be with Falcon, she didn't want to be with anyone. That fit with Oliver real well.

And she knew Oliver was willing.

And she knew Oliver would step back nicely and let her run this ranch to suit herself. He'd shown little inclination to take charge, just hired his work done.

She could run this place and do it well.

They all tied their horses and headed for the back door of the house. Cheyenne knew Oliver liked to come to the front door of the RHR ranch house. No one else ever did that. So maybe they should go to his front door, treat him as he treated them.

She hammered with the side of her fist on the back door. Considering the size of this ridiculous house, she didn't expect anyone to hear her. So she'd wait a few seconds, then go barging in and holler until Oliver showed himself.

The door swung open before she could reach for the knob.

A woman stood there, pretty, not very old. Wearing an apron and with her dark hair in a knot at the back of her neck.

The woman's rather sharp blue eyes shifted to Win, then she said, "Hello. I'll get Mr. Hawkins. He's in his study."

Cheyenne nodded. The woman bustled away.

Cheyenne stepped inside even though they hadn't really been asked in. But this was Win's house. Win could come in and bring her husband . . . and his family . . . now her family.

Cheyenne gave Win a long look. "Who is she?"

"Pa's housekeeper and cook. She's been here just a few months. He had another one when I first came back, but she quit. He wrote an ad in a paper back east to get Mrs. Hobart. That's all I've ever called her. She's a widow, Pa said."

"She's your age."

Win followed Cheyenne into a large entry area with pegs for hanging up coats and hats. Cheyenne shed her hat.

Cheyenne noticed her old friend was holding Kevin's hand so tight her knuckles were white. "A few years older, I think, but not too many."

"And what about Percy Ralston? He works in his own office in this house, doesn't he?"

"Yes, and he has his own cabin, it's part

of his pay."

Cheyenne pulled her gloves off and tucked them behind her belt buckle. "I suspect the sheriff hauled him off."

Wyatt muttered. "We probably should've checked with the sheriff before we came here, but it's a long ride out of the way."

Since they'd already talked about doing that, debated it near half to death in Cheyenne's opinion, she wasn't going to start up about it again. They'd already decided seeing Oliver about his land and cattle came first.

Wyatt hung up his hat on an empty peg beside Cheyenne's and dropped his gloves to the floor beneath them.

They all trooped into the kitchen just as Oliver came almost running out. "Winona! Is something wrong?"

He came at her, arms spread wide. Kevin made a sudden move — a surprising move — and blocked Oliver from giving Win a hug. Cheyenne found that shocking.

From the look on his face, Oliver did too.

"What is going on here?" Oliver's eyes noted that his daughter was holding Kevin's hand. "I met you the other day at the RHR when you stopped me from hugging my daughter then."

Some of the color faded from Oliver's

cheeks as he asked, "Winona, is something wrong? Are you hurt again?"

"Pa." Win had to look over Kevin's shoulder to talk to Oliver.

Cheyenne knew Win spent little time with her pa, but why did Kevin think she needed to be protected from him? A new husband's possessiveness? Or was it more?

"I'd like . . . that is, well . . ." She cleared her throat.

"Win and I are married, Oliver." Kevin gave him a smile Cheyenne considered very insincere. "Or should I call you Pa?"

Wyatt started coughing. Cheyenne thought it sounded like he was covering up a laugh.

"You're married?" Oliver squawked like an angry hen. And why not? This was how his only daughter, only child, told her father she'd gotten married?

"Yes, Pa. We eloped. And then there was some trouble, and it's taken me a couple of days to get over and tell you."

About five by Cheyenne's count.

"Yes, the trouble. Tuttle attacked you. Tried to kill you and" — Oliver's eyes shifted to Kevin — "and this man here. Sheriff Corly was out. But that was days ago."

"I was terribly upset, as you can imagine.

215

I'm sorry."

Oliver slipped past Kevin, though Kevin was watching very closely, and patted Win's hand.

Win could play the fragile lady quite well.

"Enough with the wedding talk," Wyatt cut in. "Did you talk to the sheriff this morning?"

"Why no. I haven't been to town."

"He was riding out here," Wyatt said, all business.

"Oh, um, I did saddle up and go for a ride this morning. I must have missed him. Mrs. Hobart didn't mention it."

"We found cattle stolen from our ranch and some from yours." Wyatt told the story rapidly. "Hidden in a valley high up on the mountain that borders our properties. It's land we own, but somehow there was a deed in town with Percival Ralston's name on it."

"What?"

Cheyenne felt some sympathy for Oliver. His eyes were now on Wyatt, but they kept going back to Win as if his eyes were iron and Win and her news were a powerful magnet.

"You say Percy Ralston did this?" Oliver stepped back, then back again until he bumped into his kitchen table. He almost fell over a chair and grabbed it, then sat down hard.

"Yep." Wyatt nodded. "The sheriff knows about it. He was coming out here to arrest Ralston this morning."

"I-I don't know. I haven't talked to Ralston at all today."

"We want to look around his cabin and at your bookwork," Wyatt said. "We want to find more proof that Ralston forged a deed to a chunk of RHR land and see if he's been up to any other trouble. I expect the sheriff hauled him off. Do you know if he searched his cabin?"

Oliver shook his head. Then he snapped his fingers. "Ralston sent one of the cowhands over this morning with a note saying he wasn't feeling well and wouldn't be in." Oliver looked over his shoulder toward the door that led into the rest of the house.

Oliver looked at Win and stopped talking about Ralston. "Win, my baby girl, married. Come and sit down. Kevin, you too. All of you. I want to hear everything. About the wedding and about the rustled cattle."

They heard the slam of a door. Wyatt charged out of the kitchen and through the house, Cheyenne just a pace behind him. They got outside in time to see Mrs. Hobart galloping out of the yard, bent low over her saddle. Heading down the trail that forked to lead to Bear Claw Pass.

Cheyenne and Wyatt turned to look at each other. Oliver was right behind them, then everyone else came out of the house into a clog on the broad front porch.

"Where does Ralston bunk?"

Oliver pointed to a good-sized house made of the same clapboard that the big house was made of, except it was raw boards, not painted the shining white of Oliver's mansion. And those boards looked so new they weren't weathered yet. "That's his place."

"I wonder where Mrs. Hobart went tearing off to?" Win asked. Not sounding all that fragile and ladylike right now.

Her pa didn't seem to notice.

218

TWENTY-ONE

Cheyenne charged toward Ralston's new house. Fearless and tough though she was, Falcon caught up to her. He'd rather not let her run alone into the house of a liar and a thief.

Cheyenne slammed the door open. "Percy Ralston, you get out here."

No one came out.

She went on into the house to search the rooms.

"Mr. Hawkins." A white-haired man with a limp came out of another one of them bunkhouses like the one Falcon was sleeping in. How many men did Hawkins jam into this one?

"What is it, Bud?" Hawkins had followed them into Ralston's place.

"Ralston rode to Bear Claw Pass this morning. He left right after you did and before the sheriff got out here. He said he'd told you in the note he sent."

219

"I didn't see any note until I got back. And he didn't say he was riding to town, he said he was ailing."

"He complains o' them joints worse'n I do." Bud shook his head.

Falcon saw something in Bud's eyes that made him ask, "Don't you think he hurts as much as he claims?"

Bud's mouth made a straight, hard line. "He's mighty faithful to his limping, but I've seen the man move a few steps now and ag'in when he don't think no one's watchin'. It makes me think he's not quite as laid up as he lets on."

Since Falcon knew, considering those boulders, that had to be true, he didn't pursue the comment.

Hawkins did. "What do you mean? He walks with a cane all the time. His one knee won't even bend, and it pains him terribly."

Falcon didn't like something about Oliver Hawkins, maybe his smooth talk. Maybe the way Win acted when he got too close to her, or the way she'd dragged her heels about announcing her marriage. But the man struck him wrong.

If Hawkins was a cheat who'd been cheated by a better cheat, it wouldn't bother Falcon overly, 'ceptin' the man hadn't just cheated Hawkins. When Ralston started in to stealing RHR cattle, he'd done honest, hardworking folks wrong.

That bothered Falcon plenty. He hoped that meant he was an honest man himself.

"Did you see him ride out, old-timer?" Falcon walked up close to cut the herd of clamoring folks.

"Yep, rode the same way his woman just did."

Hawkins shoved Falcon aside. Or he tried to. Falcon didn't move an inch. So Hawkins went around him. "His woman? Mrs. Hobart was *his woman*?"

And what Falcon heard in Hawkins's voice wasn't just surprise, it was shock, even jealousy. It didn't take much figurin' to know Hawkins had considered Mrs. Hobart to be his woman, and not just in the way of cooking and tidying.

Falcon gave the man a disgusted look, then said, "Everyone stop moving around. I need to look at hoofprints, and every step y'all are takin' is scuffing them up. If Hobart went after her man, then I can for sure follow her."

"Bud" — he gestured at the old man — "can you tell me which prints Ralston left?"

"Yep." They walked to the trail left by Hobart. "He's riding a line-back dun. A big gelding." Bud pointed, and Falcon saw the tracks clearly.

"And no reason to take that one except it's strong and fast. The tracks are plain as day. Laid out right in line with the gray mare Mrs. Hobart rode."

Falcon studied them, then asked, "What'd'ya mean no reason for it?"

"Ralston ain't a big man, and if he's going to town like he told me, he don't need a horse that strong. And he's supposed to be lame. Hard enough to mount a normal-sized horse. Why choose a big critter like that unless you're planning to move far and fast?"

"Did you see him mount up?"

"Ralston always ordered someone to slap leather on whatever horse he rode, then he led the horse behind his house to mount up back there. Common enough, too. He rode out for a few hours every couple a days. Said it helped his leg. And behind his house, there's a stump. He said he uses that to mount. But I sneaked a look a few times. Ralston ain't usin' no stump. He just don't want to let anyone see him swingin' up nimble as a squirrel."

Cheyenne came rushing out of Ralston's house. "He's left nothing behind but empty drawers."

"He had two good-sized satchels with

him, now that I think of it. He must have loaded those on while he was behind the house. Then he took off. Didn't have much time to see just what he was about."

Turning on his heel, Falcon rushed for his horse, tied around back of the mansion. "We can catch up to Mrs. Hobart without much trouble and make sure she's on a trail that stays with his. Maybe she's partnered with him in this."

Hard not to wonder if any more of the Hawkins hands were involved, or the RHR hands.

As Falcon swung up onto his horse, Wyatt and Cheyenne were with him. Kevin and Win just behind.

"Win, wait." Hawkins came running after them. "Let them go. Stay here and talk to me."

Cheyenne turned to Kevin, who had a mule-stubborn look on his face as he hoisted Win onto her horse.

"You two should stay. Explain to Oliver what's going on."

Win scowled at Cheyenne as her father reached her side.

Oliver reached up and clasped her hand. "Please stay awhile."

"Oliver." Cheyenne was a lot friendlier to Hawkins than Falcon thought need be. "We think Percy Ralston was stealing cattle from you, and maybe money. Can you let Win and Kevin check the account books and talk to the hands? We need to get to the bottom of this. If we can't catch up to Ralston, we'll at least get Mrs. Hobart and bring her back. We've got a lot of questions for the both of them."

"You think Percy has done all that?" Hawkins asked that question just like a man who didn't have a brain in his head. "And Mrs. Hobart?"

Win's shoulders slumped. She and Kevin exchanged a look Falcon couldn't understand, but it seemed like they were mighty troubled by something.

"We can stay awhile, Pa." Win swung down from the horse, and Kevin slid an arm around her waist.

Falcon was done listenin' to 'em jaw. He rode toward the tracks left by Ralston and Hobart. It was like readin' from a book. He set out at a fast pace, not a bit worried about losing such a clear trail.

"They're heading for town." Wyatt rode up on one side of him, Cheyenne on the other.

"If they keep to the trail they are," Cheyenne said. "But Ralston lied to Hawkins about why he wasn't at work. No reason to

224

trust that he told the truth to Bud. He might've started out for Bear Claw Pass until anyone watching him was out of sight."

And before they were a mile down the trail, Falcon saw the big dun's tracks veer right into the heart of the most rugged stretch of hills Falcon had seen so far.

"Hobart went on toward town, and Ralston turned off. You reckon she thinks she's following him but doesn't know where he went? Or is she making a run for town and the train, just taking off?"

The three of them stopped where the tracks split.

Cheyenne adjusted the flat-brimmed hat she wore on her head to shade her eyes from the sun. "If she's making for the train, then she could get away clean. It doesn't come through that regular, but I think it's due."

"I'll take Hobart," Wyatt said. "You two go after Ralston." He spurred his horse and raced away.

Cheyenne frowned after him. "I should've gone after Hobart."

Falcon reined his horse to follow Ralston's tracks. "Why's that? 'Cuz a woman should chase after a woman? That don't sound like you."

Cheyenne fell in beside him, likely wondering at a man thinking he knew her. "I didn't mean I should."

"It's what you said."

"I *mean* he'd be more likely to want to stay with me and hunt Ralston and send you after Hobart."

"Not leave us alone together?" Falcon didn't figure the tracks would vanish in the next minute so he stared at Cheyenne and her ever-cranky expression.

"He doesn't know there's any reason for that."

"Sure, he does."

Cheyenne gasped and pulled her horse to a stop. Falcon rode on, and she got going again.

"Did you tell him I — you, that is we — did you . . . tell him?"

"That a man had some moments of . . . closeness with his big sister? A man who might be married? Who might be as big a sidewinder as his dead pa? Nope. I didn't say nothin'. But a man like Wyatt wouldn't want to leave his sister alone with a man in the wilderness. It'd go against his notion of what was proper. But he also probably knows, admits that is, I'm better in the woods than he is. That'd be a real grown-up way to think. You're better'n him, too. So he takes the easy trail heading for town. Not hard to follow that one."

"And leaves the highly skilled trackers to head into the wild?" Cheyenne smiled.

He noticed she'd done a little smiling here lately, after a long spell of not one upturned corner of a lip. He hoped she'd admit it was because of the son-of-a-sidewinder.

"I would dearly like to believe my little brother —"

"Who's a full-grown man and a top rancher and tracker. Not as good as us, but still has a fine eye," Falcon interrupted.

"— is growing up. I like thinking it. I'm enjoying the rising respect for him, and it was already mighty high."

"The trail turns off here."

"I know this trail," Cheyenne said. They were headed up. The trees closed overhead, shading them from the strength of the August sun. The scent of pine and rich soil, the breeze ruffling the leaves of oak and cottonwood and aspen, were like a comforting hand sheltering Falcon and Cheyenne. "I love riding in the forest."

"Me too," Falcon said. "I walked through here that week I was wandering."

"That must've been before I caught sight of you."

"I intended to follow the stream that'd carried me along, hoping maybe I'd be able to find out where I came from. But I wasn't

227

real sure that was the right thing. Sure, I could maybe find folks who'd know me. But I might find trouble, too. I was feeling beaten up from that trip down the river. I spent a few days sleeping too much and eating what I could find until I had some strength back."

"This is miles from that stream and miles from where I picked up your trail. You covered a lot of country."

"I'm a long-legged galoot. Even with my head not workin' right and nearly drowned and needing to feed myself with nothing to hand but a knife, I know I came this far."

"And you remember a woodsy trail in a mountain full of woodsy trails?"

"Yep, mighty strange when I can't remember my own name."

"Don't try and remember anything now. We don't have time for the pain you go through, and anyway, it's awful to see. The trees clear out ahead. If Ralston is just flat-out running, if he knows we found his cattle —"

"Your cattle," Falcon interrupted again.

"— found *our* cattle, he'd have to know we were in there, or someone was. We didn't put all the boulders back like we found them. He's making a run for it, but there's a fine lookout on up the trail. If a man were to stop, keep his eyes open for someone doggin' him, he'd have a field of fire and we'd have very little shelter."

"Unless we leave our horses and go into the woods and slide around, sneak up and get ahold of him."

Cheyenne smiled. "Yep, unless that."

Falcon swung down and led his horse a few paces into the woods and found a small area, little bigger than two horses, with enough grass to keep the critters content. Cheyenne was tying her horse up beside Falcon's before he'd finished.

"Let's stay to this side of the trail." Falcon headed out.

Cheyenne clamped a hand on his arm. "Nope, this trail curves close enough to a solid wall of rock up there that we'd have to step out of cover."

"Nice being with a lady who knows her way." Falcon smiled at her, proud to be in her company. "Then let's take the downhill side. It'll be a pleasure sneakin' through the woods with you today, Miss Cheyenne."

The cold look she gave him reminded him of saying Patsy to her. She'd be a partner, but she wasn't in the mood to be friendly, and who could blame her?

They walked across to the downhill side of the trail. The trees here canopied the trail,

229

but it was so rarely traveled that the grass grew solid on it, and some small trees peeked through right on the trail.

Every step was hard work. The trees growing on a steep sidehill were a jungle. There were saplings growing up between ancient oaks, scrub brush everywhere. The ground was uneven, cut by ancient rivulets of water, stones jutting out every few feet. Mostly just animals walked the trail. They'd spent generations finding the easiest way through trackless forests.

"That's poison ivy, be mindful." Falcon pointed to a ponderosa pine, its branches stretched far, weaving in and out of the growth around it. Its trunk was covered with a climbing vine covered with leaves clustered in groups of three.

Easing up to his ear, Cheyenne whispered, "You remember poison ivy, but you don't remember your own name?"

"It's strange, and no denyin' it. But there's nothin' for it but to go on, manage best I can. Hope my noggin starts working again someday."

He pointed to a short tree with long narrow leaves that ran in pretty rows. "And that's poison sumac. It'll turn vivid red in the fall." Shaking his head, Falcon slipped on downhill.

It took time climbing down. Finally, Falcon stopped, crouched low, and pointed. Up the hill a stretch, maybe a dozen yards, barely visible through a thicket of scrub birch trees, a man crouched behind a waist-high boulder, his rifle resting on top of it.

"Percy Ralston," she whispered into Falcon's ear.

Falcon tapped her on the shoulder, then jabbed his finger at her, then at the ground.

A firm nod of her chin, and Falcon slid away.

He moved like a ghost in the woods.

No idea how he'd learned it. He figured it was a need for hunting, but maybe he'd been a sneak and a thief.

It gave him a headache thinking of it. He got down on his belly to stay below the bushes. If he rose up high enough to see Ralston, then it stood to reason that Ralston would be able to see him.

Choosing every inch forward with care took time. He sure hoped Cheyenne didn't get tired of waiting for him.

Smiling at the thought, he could well believe she had the patience of a cougar waiting for prey to walk under the branch. Cheyenne would wait in silence forever.

Another inch forward, then a foot, then five feet. He was close. Ralston crouched right past this clump of stunted trees. Another slow advance and Falcon knew his time was coming now. He had to launch himself. Strike hard and fast as a red-hot rattler. Oh, Falcon had a gun, but he didn't want shooting trouble.

A sickening twist to his stomach reminded him he'd already killed a man in the midst of this. It'd been his knife that did it for Ross Baker.

Another thing he couldn't know about himself. Had he killed before? And was this his next chance?

Made him less partial to Wyoming.

He leaned forward and to the left. He needed one glimpse of Ralston so he'd know where to jump him. Where was the man's gun? Where was he looking?

Leaning out, Falcon couldn't see him. He leaned farther, then farther yet. Finally, he rose up on his knees, an inch at a time, and found no one.

Ralston had taken off.

He pivoted to find the man just as a hard blow knocked him to his back. A fist slammed into his face before he knew what had happened.

Percy Ralston, the disabled cowhand from the Hawkins Ranch, had a punch like he'd hidden an iron horseshoe in his glove.

Falcon caught the next plowing fist in his left hand, then pounded Ralston in the face.

A hard grunt broke free of the man as he grappled with Falcon. Ralston had him down, all his weight on top. He moved with a wiry ease that shocked Falcon at the same time it made him furious.

Another fist to the face, then Ralston wrenched free of the grip Falcon had on his one fist, and in a flash that hand came up with a rock half the size of Falcon's head. The rock came whipping down as a bullet blasted it to pieces.

Cheyenne was on them with a fury. She swung the butt of her rifle into Ralston's head and knocked him off Falcon. Falcon pounced on him with a drawn-back fist, then froze. Ralston was knocked into a sound sleep.

Cheyenne leaned on her rifle and looked down at the man. "He ain't a bit laid up, the low-down scoundrel."

Breathing hard, his face throbbing from too many landed blows, Falcon said, "At least he wasn't before you bashed him in the head."

233

Cheyenne had a few piggin' strings with her. She had Ralston bound hand and foot when they heard gunfire from back down the trail in the direction Wyatt had gone.

"Wyatt!" Cheyenne launched herself to her feet and sprinted down the trail to her horse.

"Either he is shooting Mrs. Hobart, or she's shooting him." Falcon was behind her a half step. They untied their horses and were riding down the rugged, narrow trail as fast as the horses could run.

No talk. The race was against time, not each other, but Cheyenne was in the lead, and Falcon was keeping up, just barely.

A tree branch hit Cheyenne hard enough she almost lost her seat. "Look out!"

Afraid to turn and look back because she needed to be looking ahead to know when to duck next, she heard his horse and hoped Falcon was still atop it and galloped on.

She reached the trail where they'd split off from Wyatt. Falcon came on just a horse length behind her.

He'd made it.

This trail was wider, and they went at a flat-out gallop.

Wyatt's riderless horse came tearing up the trail straight at them.

Cheyenne's stomach roiled.

God, please don't let Wyatt be shot and killed. Please, God. Hold him in your hands. Protect him with a heavenly shield. Please, please, please.

Never had a prayer been torn from her heart and soul as this one was.

They'd been separated for a good stretch of time, and Wyatt had gotten down this trail a piece.

Protect him, God. Please, please, please.

Then she saw him. Flat on his back. His chest a river of blood.

Flinging herself off the horse, she skidded to her knees and touched his neck. "I feel a heartbeat. Weak but steady. He's losing too much blood though."

Falcon was there across from her, stripping the kerchief off his neck and folding it. Cheyenne had one, too, and tore it free. And Wyatt's.

Falcon yanked Wyatt's shirt open and a

neat round bullet hole — high enough to have missed his heart, but not by much — bled freely.

It was as if life itself was flowing out of her brother.

Protect him, God. Please, please, please.

Falcon pressed the kerchief on the wound; gradually but relentlessly, he pressed harder and harder yet. "I've got the blood staunched as much as I can. I'll lift his shoulder, and you can just feel back there under his shirt for a bullet hole."

She pulled his shirt open farther, then slid her hand around to his back, afraid to bump him around at all. She pulled bleeding fingers away from the wound she'd found in back.

"Yep. There's a hole in the back of his shirt, too."

"Good, the bullet went through. I'll hold the kerchiefs, back and front, while you figure out how to tie off a bandage. Once we get the bleeding stopped, I'm going to build a travois. Get him home that way."

Cheyenne dragged piggin' strings out of her pocket. "Tie it off with these. I know how to build a sledge, I think that's what you mean by travois."

"Two poles joined over a horse's shoulders with the other end tied together so we can carry Wyatt?"

"Yep, I'll get to work on it." Her voice was dry as a bone. She had to swallow hard to shut down the tears. Tears were useless.

"Help me tie this off first. It's a two-person job."

She did her best, hating how her hands trembled. Once the bandage was secure, Falcon kept pressure on the wounds, and Cheyenne jumped to her feet and got to work. She found the best branches she could that were close to hand and set to work, using her horse to rig the sledge that would carry Wyatt home.

Please, God, please, please.

She drew the rigging close to Wyatt as Falcon rose from his side.

"I'm ready to move him. I've done all I can here."

"It had to be Hobart." Cheyenne got on one side of her brother. The only person in this world she truly loved and trusted.

"Probably," Falcon said, his voice grim, his face pale with worry. He moved so he stood right across from her. "When we lift, we lift together."

Cheyenne had maneuvered the travois so the wide end of it was by Wyatt's head.

"Move him as little as possible," Falcon instructed. "We'll just lift a few inches and walk him right on up."

Nodding, Cheyenne gripped the side of Wyatt's shirt and pants.

"Can you get him? Is he too heavy?" Falcon's eyes were serious and thoughtful, as if he were thinking of every move, considering all that could go wrong.

"I can do it. I *will* do it."

He wanted Wyatt to survive just as much as Cheyenne did. Maybe not out of a deep love and trust, but because it was good and just that a fine man survive a low-down sneak attack.

"I think the bleeding has stopped, but he's lost a lot." Falcon caught Wyatt's clothes on his side. "Ready?"

Cheyenne nodded.

"Lift."

They made the shift.

Wyatt groaned, and his eyes flickered open. "Whaa happened?"

"Hush, be still," Cheyenne said. "You've been shot. All three of you Hunt brothers have taken a bullet. I hope they don't start on non-Hunts next." She thought of Win, also shot. Well, she was a Hunt now.

"Shot?"

"Did you see who it was?" Cheyenne asked.

"Let it be for now." Falcon cut her off,

and she was glad of it, glad he was taking charge. "I can promise you thinking is a hard business, takes more strength than a man has sometimes. I've sure enough learned that."

Falcon took the shirt off his back, so he stood there with only longhandles on, and twisted the shirt into a rope. He tied the rope around Wyatt, under his arms and to the poles supporting him.

"It'll keep him from sliding off and adding pressure to the wound. Do we head for home or Bear Claw Pass? Is there a doctor there?"

Cheyenne heard the way Falcon said *home,* and it put strength into her. Steadied her when she wanted to cling to Wyatt, tend him somehow right here instead of adding to his pain by taking him on a long rough ride, however carefully they moved.

"Home is closer than Bear Claw Pass, and Molly's a better doctor than the one in town."

"I've been to Dr. Murphy," Wyatt put in groggily. "I'd as soon stay away from him and his shaky hands."

Cheyenne looked at that chest wound. No bullet to dig out, so that'd let Molly avoid operating. Shaking her head, Cheyenne said, "Let's go home."

They moved at an achingly slow pace. Cheyenne riding the horse pulling the travois. Falcon leading his horse and walking beside Wyatt.

They passed near the Hawkins Ranch, and Cheyenne said, "I'm gonna signal Kevin and Win that we're passing."

Falcon looked at her, and she gestured with her gun. No sense surprising the man.

He gave his chin a firm nod.

She fired into the air.

A cowhand came running around a stand of trees, gun drawn. A man ready for trouble. Cheyenne recognized his face but couldn't say his name.

"Tell Win we're heading home, and she should come along." She never let up on the slow steady walking of her horse. "We ran into trouble. Wyatt's been shot."

The man holstered his gun as two more came a-running. "She already headed home, Miss Cheyenne." The man jogged up to look at Wyatt.

"He looks bad, miss."

"I know."

"Maybe you had oughta bring him into the Hawkins place."

Cheyenne considered it. But so much trouble was coming from this direction that she couldn't stand the thought of it. "A woman staying with us has a lot of doctoring skills. I want to get Wyatt to her."

"Did you see anyone riding out from here?" Falcon rarely took his eyes off Wyatt, ready if the bleeding should start up or the ties holding him on the travois should break.

"Besides Mrs. Hobart, you mean?" The other men were gathering around. "And of course Miss Winona and her husband rode away."

Another cowpoke said quietly, glancing behind him, "And that must've made the boss mad because he came out and started hollering and sent us all to bring in a herd that didn't need to be brought in. He wouldn't let up and we figured him to be hurtin' 'cuz his little girl got hitched, so we done what he asked, every one of us."

"He made me saddle his horse before I rode out," the first cowpoke said. "He takes off alone on horseback time to time." Then he said, "I'll saddle up and ride along with you folks. No one should be out without good protection. This is the third shooting we've had around these parts."

He didn't wait to hear what Cheyenne had to say, just pivoted around and took off for the ranch. Two others went with him.

She welcomed the armed guard.

They kept moving, as slow and steady

as . . . as . . . . Cheyenne couldn't help the thought that pounded in her head. As slow and steady as a funeral procession.

But Wyatt wasn't dead, and the things that could be hit right there, heart, lungs, spine, would kill him quick. There seemed to be every chance he'd survive the gunshot wound. But would he survive the fever and what came after?

Sickened with worry, she focused on keeping things slow and steady.

Five men came riding toward her from the Hawkins place. While they were still out of earshot, she said to Falcon, "If there was just one of them, I'd be afraid because I don't know who to trust. But a crew this big is safer. I'm glad for the company."

Falcon nodded, and they moved on. Slow and steady.

TWENTY-THREE

Molly heard thundering hooves. Everything about the sound of that horse coming at full speed shouted desperation to her.

She rushed for the back door and stepped out just as Kevin slammed the door open to the ramrod's house. She noticed he had his gun in hand but wasn't aiming anywhere. Not yet.

The bunkhouse door flung open and five armed men stepped out, one of them Andy.

A single man came racing in on horseback and charged straight for Molly.

"It's Wyatt. He's been shot." The man reined his horse to such a sudden stop, the animal reared up, fighting the tight hold. The man leapt off a second after the horse had four legs on the ground.

Molly put her hand over her belly. It was too much like home. All the trouble. Ma's trouble with Pa. Pa coming home hurt from his night rides. Always something terrible.

Why was there no peace in the world? And Wyatt? Not Wyatt. He was so young and strong, and he'd been so nice to her, well, a few times.

Falcon had been shot and was left with amnesia.

Win and then Kevin had been shot, and two men after him ended up dead. That should have ended it.

Now Wyatt.

But she'd lived through the Civil War in Kansas. Honestly, how did folks live who didn't have to fight for their lives every day?

"Miss Cheyenne said to get ready for him. Clear the kitchen table, boil water, whatever you need to do."

"Talk while I work." Molly clamped down hard on the riot of fear twisting her gut. *Dear Father in heaven, I am no doctor. You know that. I know that, and they all know that, and yet they are expecting me to deal with a gunshot. Guide my hands, Father.*

She forced herself to move, to race against the time of Wyatt's arrival so she could begin helping him right quick. "Tell me what you know. Where's the wound? How is Wyatt? How far are they?"

"The bullet went clear through his shoulder. Miss Cheyenne only sent me running ahead a few minutes ago. They'll be here right away." The man darted out.

She thought of how it was with Ma. Molly had no business sewing up her ma. It all terrified her witless. Her hands were unsteady. Her heart hurt too much. She'd heard somewhere that a person with too much connection shouldn't doctor another, maybe small things like taking a few stitches, or tending a relative when they were feverish. But serious doctoring, she knew she shouldn't. It was said that with someone you knew and loved, you were too apt to fear the worst, and it was too easy to ignore what seemed like small complaints because you were used to listening to them complain.

The two ends of doctoring, caring too much and not taking them seriously.

Just because Wyatt was her half brother's half brother didn't mean she was connected to him. Nor did it matter if she was. She had to do this.

The table had a few things on it. A salt cellar and pepper grinder. A dish of butter and a jar of jelly. She quickly cleared them away. Molly ran to a closet with some folded fabric and set it on the table. She wanted to tear some of it into bandages, but that could wait. Cheyenne would be here this time. She might be able to do some of this work, know where things were.

Molly put three pots on the stove. One large, two small. One small to heat vinegar and herbs to clean the wound. The second was water, to get the first batch hot faster. The third was a big pot of water so they could have all the clean water they needed. There were hot water wells on the stove, too, but Molly wanted to have plenty.

She pulled one long piece of fabric over the table, then went to the small corner of a cupboard where she'd placed all the supplies she'd used when Win was shot. She wanted them close to hand rather than spend time ransacking the house when trouble came again.

As she concocted her vinegar rinse, she thought of Wyatt and prayed over and over again. *Dear Father in heaven, guide my hands. Steady my hands. Steady my mind and heart.*

Wyatt had been so angry that first day at the train station. Not one bit happy to see any of them, yet he'd let them move right in, fed them, treated them decent. And now he'd been shot, and it had to all be tied in with this mess involving Clovis Hunt's will.

She heard more thundering hooves. They wouldn't be bringing him that fast. She rushed to the back door to see another rider coming into the yard. And beyond that, a fair distance, she saw six more riders. She recognized Cheyenne because she favored a beautiful white horse, and that critter was there.

Swallowing hard, she didn't see anyone who looked shot.

Seeming to come an inch at a time, they rode into the yard. They came straight to the back door, and Molly could finally see Wyatt.

Fighting the need to cry, she rushed down just as Falcon firmly took her arm. "We need to lift him, Miss Molly. We'll turn him over to your doctorin' hands as soon as we get him inside."

Cheyenne went to the offside across Wyatt's unmoving body from Falcon. Then Falcon said, "Vincent, get over here."

A strapping young man, who Molly assumed was from the Hawkins Ranch, rushed over.

"Stand there where Cheyenne is."

"Falcon, I'm —"

"He's heavy, Cheyenne." Falcon's voice snapped like a bullwhip. "We don't have time for your feelings to be hurt. Let Vince in there."

Frowning, Cheyenne did as she was told.

Molly knew he *was* heavy, and they *didn't*

have time for Cheyenne to want to help and fail.

Still, to see Falcon back Cheyenne off. It took Molly a minute to notice her jaw was gaped open.

She shoved aside the shock and closed her mouth about the same time Falcon and Vince hauled an unconscious Wyatt into the kitchen.

Not wasting a second, Molly said, "Falcon, cut his shirt away."

Leaving the cutting to Falcon, she rushed to the stove, ladled boiling water into a basin that she had ready, and brought it to Wyatt's side as Falcon finished. She knew he carried a razor-sharp knife all the time, and he seemed well able to use it.

Wyatt was stripped to the waist. Cheyenne stood across from her.

Molly talked to her, recognizing the love and terror in Cheyenne's expression. "Your cowpoke said the bullet went all the way through."

Bathing the blood away, Molly saw the neat round hole. It made her sick that something so damaging could be so small.

Kevin came running in, Win a step behind him. "What happened?"

Falcon began talking, but Molly ignored him to pay attention to what she was doing.

She worked in silent urgency to clean the wound in Wyatt's chest. No bullet, thank the good Lord. Cutting a bullet out of someone was hard, and Molly had no fine tools to make it less brutal.

Cheyenne didn't so much as spare the talking men a glance.

Molly lost track of the time, but it felt like she was hours cleaning the wound. When she was satisfied the wound was as clean as she could make it, she looked Cheyenne in the eye. "Get me the funnel I set beside the stove, and there is a pan of vinegar I added healing herbs to. It's going to sting like blue blazes, but I was taught vinegar has healing properties. I pulled it off to cool a bit after it boiled, but it's still steaming hot, and that's a good thing."

Cheyenne was back with both in seconds.

Molly placed the funnel over the wound, explaining as she set it in place. "I want to try and flush the wound out as well as possible. When someone is shot through a shirt like this, there are threads that go into the wound. I've picked out anything I could find, but it's almost impossible to get it all. A thread or bit of dirt, anything left in the wound can cause an infection."

Without speaking, Cheyenne said, "I'll hold the funnel. You handle the vinegar."

Molly let Cheyenne take it, very careful to keep it centered over the wound and pressed hard against Wyatt's chest.

"I doubt my brew will go in as deeply as I'd wish. It'll flush the wound a bit, then flow all over."

Looking up, she saw Win. It seemed as if she were ready and willing to help.

"Get towels." Molly's hands were full, but she nodded her head in the right direction. "I gathered a stack over there. Use them to collect the vinegar as best you can. No sense making a terrible mess."

Win came with the towels.

Now came the worst of what Molly would do.

Lifting the pan of boiled vinegar, she poured the thinnest stream she could manage through the funnel.

Wyatt, unconscious until now — thank heaven for that — roared. His body surged until he nearly sat up.

"Kevin." Molly's single word brought Falcon and Kevin to the table. They'd finished their talking and been standing ready. "Hold him. I think his collarbone is broken. Everything I do is going to hurt him worse than just a bullet wound would. You have to hold him still."

Falcon, beside Molly, shoved both hands

against Wyatt's chest and held him down on the table. Kevin, beside Cheyenne, threw his weight over Wyatt's legs.

Cheyenne got the funnel back in place. Molly went back to pouring.

A scream, deep and awful to hear, erupted from Wyatt's throat.

Molly glanced up, expecting Cheyenne to have murder in her eyes for Molly after hurting her brother this way. Instead, Cheyenne only focused on holding that funnel, tears raining down without a sob to go with them.

Molly finished flushing the wound. They rolled him over, and she repeated her treatment on the back.

"I'm not as worried about the back. You said the bullet hit him in the front, so it would shove threads along with it. The back, where the bullet exited his body, has a better chance of being clear of trouble."

Still, she flushed the wound carefully, taking as much time as she felt the job needed.

The day was wearing down by the time she'd bandaged him. Molly straightened from the doctoring, and her back kicked up such a fuss, she began to fall.

Falcon caught her and held her until she was steady.

"Thank you."

"Welcome, little sister."

She'd've smiled if she had one ounce of good humor in her anywhere. She did give him a nod.

"We need to keep at least two people with him so he doesn't roll off. I don't want him up in his room yet. And I don't want his left arm to move. We'll have to splint it somehow. This hard surface is a better place for him until he regains consciousness. And besides, I can keep an eye on him better here. Hopefully only for a couple of hours. We can probably boot him off there in time for supper."

Wyatt was lifted above the messy table. A new cloth was put down, and they returned him to lying on it. Cheyenne straightened away from Wyatt, once he was settled again. "How do you know all this, Molly?"

Shaking her head, Molly said, "Learned in a hard school. A doctor should know more, maybe have medicine I don't, but it seems I'm all you have. That's how it was when I was back in Kansas, too. So I learned."

Cheyenne pulled a chair over to the table. Win sat down on the other side of Wyatt. Molly wanted to protest, afraid the two women weren't strong enough if Wyatt got to thrashing. Before she could speak, Kevin sat by Win, and Falcon sat at Cheyenne's side.

Molly gave her back a few minutes to stop jabbing at her, then she began cleaning her ruined kitchen.

A woman's work was never done around here.

"Now tell us who shot him," Win said.

Falcon and Cheyenne exchanged a furious look and started talking.

Twenty-Four

Wyatt had never in his life lain down while the sun was still up.

If his ma could be believed, though in this she might've been exaggerating, he'd given up napping before the age of two, before the age Wyatt could remember, so his memory of naps, or the lack thereof, fit what he knew of himself.

And yet here he was, waking up from a nap while golden sunlight streamed through the windows.

Worse yet, surrounded by people who weren't napping but were instead talking endlessly, or so it seemed to his tired ears.

He needed to get up and slip outside to get to work. To that end, he moved.

The pain came roaring to life along with the memory of what was going on.

"I've been shot?" The words slurred, but they came out well enough.

The whole room fell silent and whirled to

look at him. He thought they should have been looking at him already, considering the bullet he'd taken.

He remembered it all. Not who'd shot him. The bullet came from . . . from . . . behind him. He'd heard something. Thought it might be Cheyenne. He'd turned, and the bullet had struck. He hadn't seen anyone though. He'd been shot by someone under cover.

The cowardly, evil work of a rabid skunk, and whoever'd done it needed to be put down just like they'd do with the skunk.

Except, of course, the skunk would've only done it because he was sick and out of his head. Whoever had hidden themselves and taken that carefully aimed shot had no such excuse beyond evil.

"Wyatt, you're awake!" Cheyenne was at his side in seconds. She rested a firm hand on his upper arm and squeezed, very gently, but he saw her pleasure and worry.

Cheyenne and Win, his childhood tormenters. And he'd tormented them right back. His grown-up friends and family, yes even Win. A sister of the heart and now, married to his brother Kevin, a sister in fact.

Falcon and Kevin looked at him from behind Cheyenne, their eyes a match for their concern and relief.

Then Molly came over and somehow, without saying a word or laying hands on anyone, shoved them all back. She slid an arm behind his head, met his eyes, and said, "Drink some water. You've lost a lot of blood, and you'll need plenty to drink."

Lost a lot of blood sounded serious.

"How bad is it?" He realized he couldn't move his left arm. Not an inch. He glanced down and saw it strapped to his body by someone who was serious about tying him up.

For all that he was surrounded, it was Molly he asked and who answered, the rest of them letting her take charge.

"You've been shot in the chest. The bullet was through and through. It didn't hit anything vital, your heart or lungs. It may have broken your collarbone, only I think the fall off your horse did it because the wound is lower, and the bone seems to be snapped clean, not fragmented like a gunshot. It's going to take time for it to heal. We kept you down in the kitchen —"

"I'm in the kitchen?"

Molly nodded. "You're on the kitchen table."

"Can I get up to my room?"

"In a little bit." She gave him a kindly smile. "We'll need to clear the table before supper, so you'll have to move."

That made him smile back, or at least he thought he did. If his thoughts didn't quite reach his lips, it was because he felt like he'd been run over by a stampeding herd of wild mustangs.

"D-did you doctor me, Molly? Like you did Win?"

"Yes. I'm a schoolteacher by training, but I think I could have a solid career as a doctor, considering the need in this town."

"It's mostly just the need here on the RHR. You can be our doctor. You already are." A stab of pain almost lifted his head off his shoulders.

Then his eyes fluttered closed even though he had no intention of taking another nap.

He heard Molly's voice in the distance, added to a few others. Cheyenne, maybe. But it was such a muddle he didn't even try to figure out what they'd said. He just wished they'd be quiet so he could sleep. Yep, with the sun up and everything.

"He's passed out again." Cheyenne reached for his good shoulder. Molly grabbed her wrist before she could try to wake Wyatt up.

"Let him rest."

Cheyenne yanked against Molly's grip. Suddenly furious with her for denying her more time with her brother.

Falcon's arm came around her waist and lifted her off her feet, swinging her around. "Calm down," he said, quietly, into her right ear. "I know you're worried sick. I know you love him. And I know Molly's right. You know it, too."

Gritting her teeth, Cheyenne resisted the urge to fight, to take out her terror on all of them.

Because she did know Molly was right. Falcon was right. It was a fool's move to wake up a sick man. To shake an injured man. But for one moment she'd been desperate to see those bright eyes, the flashing sparks of gold in the brown.

She quit struggling and patted Falcon's strong arm around her belly. "I know you're right. Let me go."

He did, but he stayed where he was.

Almost as if he was blocking her way to Wyatt.

Almost as if he didn't trust her.

Almost as if he knew her pretty well.

"Uh-oh." Falcon's eyes went wide. He said a single word. "Ralston."

The crazy faded from Cheyenne's eyes, and she winced. "We left him out there, tied up."

Falcon looked around the room. "We need

to decide right here, right now, no one goes out alone again. From now on, we take a herd of cowpokes with us. Plenty of folks to return fire. These fools are vicious cowards. It's a thread through the whole business, shooting from cover, picking off people with their backs turned. We should've never let Wyatt go haring off alone but, well, but who'd'a thunk a woman'd do such a thing?"

Falcon shook his head and looked at Cheyenne. He felt so guilty for letting Wyatt ride off after Mrs. Hobart alone. He saw the regret in Cheyenne's eyes to match his. "I know Cheyenne here is a tough, knowing woman. It shames me to think I didn't worry enough about another one."

"There's a chance it wasn't Mrs. Hobart."

All eyes turned to Win.

"Did you know her at all?" Kevin asked.

With a shrug, Win said, "I've met her, of course. I wouldn't say I knew her really, not personally. She was a good cook. She kept the house tidy."

Falcon said quietly, "I got the notion there was something between her and your pa. More than a boss and his cook."

Cheyenne's head whipped around in a way that surprised Falcon. He'd've expected Win to be upset, but Cheyenne looked shocked. Win just looked worried, sad even.

Considering she didn't care much for her pa, that didn't make a lot of sense. But Falcon had more things to do than worry about women and their fussing.

"Now that Wyatt's tended, we need to get Ralston," he said.

"He'll've gotten loose by now," Kevin said.

Falcon gave his head a little sideways tilt. "When I tie a knot, it stays tied a good long while." Then he paused because, though he thought it was true, he didn't really know. "I searched him for hideout knives. If he's gone, he's either been eaten by wolves or in cahoots with someone else."

"Mrs. Hobart," Cheyenne said through a tight jaw.

"Might be, if she knew where to hunt him up. We reckoned she was running to join him when she realized we were on to Ralston's thieving. But she went a different way. Says to me she didn't know where he was. If they'd partnered up, it might be Ralston had taken off, not just from us and Hawkins, but from her, too."

He looked at Cheyenne. "Let's go bring him in if we're not too late."

She gave a tight nod of her head and went to get her gloves and hat.

"Wait a minute," Kevin said. "You just said we aren't supposed to go out alone anymore. Go get a posse from the bunk-house."

Falcon was a step behind Cheyenne, heading out. He paused to look back at Kevin, at all of them, and said, "I didn't mean Cheyenne and me. We're tougher than all of you and the bunkhouse put together. No one's gonna sneak up on us."

"You say that," Molly snapped, "just like a man who didn't recently get knocked into a river by a sneak attack. A man who now can't remember a blessed thing about himself before he came out of the water."

Falcon gave a little shrug. "True enough. But I've got Cheyenne with me now. The two of us together can handle anything."

He strode out. His moccasins silent as he left.

Someone had put all the horses up. The Hawkins hands had gone home.

Cheyenne had her horse saddled and was dropping a bridle on his when he caught up to her.

"I'm right, aren't I? Or do you want to take a crowd along?"

Cheyenne's dark eyes flashed at him. He could tell something had her extra upset. And considering she'd been furious most of the time since he met her and was half-mad with worry over her brother, he had a hard

261

time imagining what else was chewin' on her.

"Just saddle up, Falcon. I'll take care of you."

He snorted but got to work.

They were galloping out of the yard in minutes.

The two of them alone.

TWENTY-FIVE

"He's gone." Cheyenne swung down off her horse, disgusted. "Not much we could've done. We had to get Wyatt home. We left him in such a place it'd've been hard to know how to send someone out after him." But still it stuck in her craw. "I had some questions I'd've liked to ask that man."

The distant rumble of thunder told her rain was coming, and it sounded fierce. They'd lost their chance to bring Ralston in.

Falcon picked up a length of cast-aside rope. "Rope's cut. I know he wasn't armed with a knife. Someone was in it with him. Look for tracks."

They were at it for about two minutes. "Hobart." Falcon knelt. "A woman's boots here."

He looked up at the darkening sky, frowning. "Should we trail them?"

Shaking her head, Cheyenne pointed at

263

the tracks. "They even got Ralston's horse back. We didn't get the man, and we left his horse behind. We could probably find them, but it's rough country, and it looks like rain is coming. The rain will ruin any trail we might follow."

"It might not." Falcon looked at the tracks, sounding thoughtful. "I can oftentimes pick up bits of a trail left, even after rain has washed out most of it."

"I want no part of the high country in a lightning storm." She studied the sky and saw a streak of lightning brighten the dark gray, roiling clouds.

"Does this clear up any claim the man had on your land?"

Cheyenne rubbed the back of her neck. "His claim has already been overturned. But this oughta make things simple."

"Him running like he done is as good as a confession." Falcon headed for his horse.

"Reasoned like that, it makes Mrs. Hobart guilty, too." Cheyenne stormed to her horse and swung up. Furious again.

"Do you have something against the woman? I didn't think you knew much about her?"

Cheyenne gathered her reins, but instead of spurring her horse and running away from all of this, she looked Falcon in the eye. "Oliver Hawkins asked me to marry him. I was considering it."

Falcon was silent as the grave. He reined his horse down the trail they'd ridden up. But he didn't go all the way to the main trail, the place they'd split off from Wyatt earlier. Without explanation, he turned down a sharp slope that Cheyenne only recognized as a trail after they were on it.

It burned.

He was better than her, and she didn't like it. Yet at the same time, she respected it deeply.

And though she had no idea where he was going, she trailed along after him like a cattle-drive-broke cow.

He reached some place that suited whatever his purpose was, or so she imagined, and he dismounted, led his horse to a wide spot in the trail, and hitched it to a birch sapling.

Cheyenne did the same.

Finally, they stood, facing each other, and Falcon said, "Have you taken leave of your senses?"

Anger. She hadn't seen that in him.

And even so, she knew what he meant.

"He's asked, or rather suggested it as something we should talk about, several times in the last few years."

Shaking his head, Falcon said, "He never asked you to go on a buggy ride? He never told Wyatt or anyone else he was sparkin' you?"

"We hadn't, or rather, he hadn't exactly done any, um, sparkin'."

Falcon's eyes narrowed. "Haven't I heard someone say he was a lot like Clovis?"

"No," Cheyenne snapped. "That's not true. He planted himself at his ranch and stayed all this time."

"He's what? Twenty years older than you?"

"My pa was older than my ma."

"Twenty years?"

Cheyenne shrugged one shoulder and didn't answer. It'd been more like five, but that wasn't the point.

"He doesn't work the ranch. He's lazy. That's like Clovis."

"I could work the ranch."

"You'd hold no respect for him. Never, no matter how long you were married."

Cheyenne thought she saw Falcon give a faint shudder.

Odd, but she thought of Oliver and was tempted to shudder herself. Instead, she got mad.

"As women go out here, I'm old."

"Twenty-five?" Falcon snorted. "It's a

wonder you don't have a head full of gray hair."

"I'm twenty-six, and I've found a few, and it doesn't matter that he's not the perfect man. I've looked hard for a long while, and there aren't any of those. In fact, the only other man who's shown any interest in me lately is probably married." Cheyenne shoved Falcon with all the rage and confusion and jealousy one woman could possess.

He staggered back a step, but she thought he might've done it to get away from her.

"If I marry Oliver, I may not get the perfect man." Cheyenne's voice rose with every word. "But I will get a ranch."

She caught up to Falcon and jabbed him in the chest with one sharp pointer finger. "One that can't be stolen from me."

She jabbed him again. "A ranch I can run to suit myself."

Another jab.

Falcon swatted her hand aside. "Stop that."

"I'll do it because my husband will sit at a desk while I do the work I love, on land I own."

She jabbed.

He caught her hand, dragged her against his chest, and lowered his head. She slapped

267

him hard enough to knock some sense into him and herself. "You're married."

"I don't believe I am."

"You can't know for sure."

"You're right. I know you're right. Just . . . promise me you won't marry Hawkins."

"You know we can't be together."

There was too long a silence.

"You have to give me time to remember or find the truth. You have to."

Cheyenne saw the kindness in his eyes and his own confusion.

All she could manage to say was "I have to."

She cleared her throat. "Did you really think Oliver was in some way involved with Mrs. Hobart?"

"He acted mighty odd when Bud suggested Mrs. Hobart was Ralston's woman. And he acted that way with the woman he's proposed to nearby? Cheyenne, thinking you could marry a varmint like that, it's cold."

"Cold? I found him likeable. I thought we could deal well together."

"No, you were plannin' on *making* a deal. A contract as cold as signing to purchase a horse. 'You let me run your ranch, and I'll be a wife to you.' No feeling. No notion of him being likeable, only a man you could endure because you are so unhappy at home."

A strange breath of cool air washed through her. "That's what Win has been doing at our house, isn't it?"

Falcon hesitated. "Might be."

"She found her home unhappy."

"But she didn't *endure* you and Wyatt. She loves you both and considers you her best friends, and now she's joined your family."

"If she can't endure her home, why hasn't she told me why?"

"Hasn't she?"

"No, uh, well, I think . . . that is . . . she might've been going to say something once."

"And you didn't let her?"

"I was riding double with her that day we found you in the forest. I, well, I more or less pushed her off the back of my horse."

"But she's known you were considering marrying her father, and she never seemed to object?"

Cheyenne stepped away from him, crossed her arms, and said, "She'd known since about five minutes before I ran off. I announced it to her, then took off into the woods for a week."

"And within a short time of finding you again —"

269

"You say that like I was lost." Cheyenne cut him off. "I was *not* lost."

He smiled at her. "As soon as she found you, she tried to tell you something about her pa, and you wouldn't listen, made it mighty clear you weren't gonna listen."

"Maybe I should have a talk with her, huh?"

"Yep, because there's no doubt in my mind there was something personal between him and Hobart. When she ran, Hawkins didn't look like a man losing a good housekeeper. He looked like a man losing a woman he was . . . in some way of the heart . . . well, sparkin'."

Like Oliver had never done with her, Cheyenne thought bitterly. Of course, he had no public relationship with Mrs. Hobart, either. "He's carrying on with her in secret, while he's planning to marry me if I'll have him?"

" 'Bout the size of it."

"You could be a little more kind about it!"

He reared back, probably afraid she was going to slap him again, then arched one brow. Not exactly fighting back. More like, trying to figure out how to handle a loco longhorn. And none of this was his fault.

His only fault was being blunt in his honesty.

"I'm tempted to ride over to the Hawkins Ranch and use my spurs on his backside," Cheyenne said.

That must've shaken off his worry of being hit at because he laughed.

"No riding to Hawkins's today. Wyatt's hurt. Leaving for a spell was a good idea, too many worryin' folks ganged up around his sick bed — or sick table, I guess."

She wanted to laugh but thinking of Wyatt made it impossible. "Let's go home."

"Let's go home." He took her hand and walked her back to the horses. Just that, the hand-holding, the walk in the deep woods, the quiet as they mounted up, was the most romantic thing a man had ever done with her.

She was afraid that made her pathetic. It spoke of a barren sort of life.

On the other hand, she enjoyed every minute.

TWENTY-SIX

Falcon heard the whisper of cloth on cloth, so quiet out his bunkhouse window where he was just falling asleep that he had to check on it. No man walking a sentry route would be so quiet.

He slid to the window near the bunk bed he shared with Andy and the dogs. He'd left the window open on the hot night and swung a leg silently over.

"Where are you going?"

He was calm, it seemed, because he didn't yelp at that unexpected voice.

It was Andy. Who had looked like he was out cold, sleeping like a hardworking, exhausted young man. Yet silent as Falcon was, Andy had awakened.

He wondered how a youngster learned to sleep on edge like that.

For that matter, how had Falcon learned it? He'd heard that whisper of cloth and been awake instantly. Maybe the kid had

272

heard it, too. Falcon slipped to the bed, not wanting to warn whoever was out there. He whispered so softly he doubted anyone could hear him a foot away.

"Someone's sneaking around. I'm going to check. Stay here unless I call you, better chance of catching him with me alone."

He felt more than saw Andy nod his head. Not a kid to act in childish ways.

Falcon would like to talk to Kevin about their life back in Kansas.

Falcon slid out the window as quiet as a puff of smoke.

He heard the noise again. Past the bunkhouse now, heading for the house, it seemed. The window was in the back of the bunkhouse, so he slipped along the back wall, around the corner, and saw someone dressed the color of night, moving so silently he might have mistaken him for a shadow if he hadn't moved. But Falcon had eyes as sharp as a bucket full of nails.

The shadow crept past the door of the ramrod's house, where Kevin and Win stayed, easing along in the partial darkness of the moon, picking places to hide that were more in the mind than in real life. The intruder reached a gap between the ramrod's house and the main house.

Falcon closed the space between him and

the sneak, wondering if their enemy had finally decided to come straight to them with violence.

When the shadow separated from the ramrod's house, he dove and brought him down to the ground. Falcon swung back to plow his fist into this outlaw's face.

A sharp squeak of protest stayed his hand.

Not a him. Not a man.

Kevin was instantly beside him. The tackle hadn't been loud, but loud enough, it seemed. Andy was a pace back but arrived almost at once. The back door of the house swung open, and Cheyenne stood in the door with her rifle, aimed at the ground but right at hand.

Falcon couldn't make out his prisoner's face, but he had a real good idea of who it was. He frisked her and found a gun up her sleeve, another at her waist in a hidden holster reached through a slit in her dress, and a knife in her boot.

With her disarmed, he pulled her to her feet so hard he almost launched her into the air.

"Let me go."

"That's a pure waste of words, ma'am."

"Ma'am?" Kevin gasped.

A light from the ramrod's house cast its flare on her face.

"Mrs. Hobart?" Win was standing in the door, holding a lantern.

"Looks like she heard Wyatt was alive and wanted to finish things," Falcon said. "Either that or she wanted to finish off a few more from this clan."

Falcon marched her toward the house.

A light came on behind Cheyenne. Falcon sure hoped it wasn't Wyatt buying into the fight. They'd had their hands full getting him upstairs. He'd made it to his feet, and with an arm around Falcon's neck and Kevin holding him around the waist on the other side, they bore most of his weight up to his room.

No one was happy about how bad it hurt him and how stubbornly he refused to sleep downstairs.

Thankfully, it was Molly. She and Cheyenne were splitting the night sitting up with Wyatt.

It figured that everyone was sleepin' light.

Falcon sat Hobart down in a chair hard enough she'd bounced. Her eyes flashed with temper. Her cheeks were flushed. It might've been from temper, too, but if it'd been Falcon, he'd've been embarrassed at bein' caught so easy-like.

He decided she was blushing, and he liked thinking he'd shamed her.

Though he didn't intend to admit it to anyone, she'd been so good it scared him more'n a little. The only reason he'd heard her was because . . . well, honesty demanded he admit to himself, he was better. No use being humble about it.

"Why were you sneaking up on our house?" Cheyenne took charge.

The hard look in Mrs. Hobart's eyes told Falcon she wouldn't be pestered into any confession of what she intended tonight. He said, "We'll put her somewhere. The root cellar or the icehouse. Lock her in, and tomorrow we'll ride her into the sheriff and charge her with attempted murder."

She gasped. "I didn't murder anyone."

"Not for lack of trying." Falcon plunked his hands on Cheyenne's upper arms. She had her back to him because she'd scooted in betwixt him and Hobart.

He moved Cheyenne aside, got way too close to Hobart, and looked hard in the woman's eyes. "You were on your way to the house in the dead of night. Armed. That's a crime, Miz Hobart. The attempted murder is for shooting Wyatt Hunt. Now, where's Percy Ralston?"

Hobart almost collapsed backward in the chair, all the starch and most of the vinegar gone out of her.

"Wyatt's been shot?" She sounded genuinely horrified. Falcon couldn't judge it for a lie. If the woman was lying, she was mighty good at it.

"And Ralston is missing?" At this, she didn't sound overly surprised. "Will Wyatt live?"

Falcon straightened away from her. Kevin came up beside him on the right. Cheyenne on his left, the three of them faced her silently. Molly stood by the stove. That seemed to be her spot, but she wasn't cooking. Her arms were crossed, her brow furrowed with worry.

Win was watching the woman from a few paces away. She'd stare, then shake her head, open her mouth and close it, then shake her head again.

Falcon figured she'd get around by and by to whatever she had to say.

Andy was behind Hobart. He'd pulled a chair out from the table. Falcon caught himself almost smiling to think how the kid had seen or heard him. Kevin too. Then the humor faded as he wondered again what they'd lived through to be so on edge, even in their sleep.

Falcon heard a creak from overhead. "Wyatt's moving." He looked at the little cook. "Molly, get up there and tell him what's going on. Don't lie, but tell him to stay put. I'll be up soon to answer any questions. If he starts coming down the stairs, holler."

Molly rushed out.

"When did you start giving orders around here?" Cheyenne muttered.

"Don't rightly know. Don't like doing it. Doubt it'll last."

"Why did you run from Hawkins's place like you did?" Kevin asked Hobart.

"I slipped out when you got there to talk to Ralston. I realized he'd taken off, and I went after him."

"Why?" Kevin was doing better'n Falcon had been with questioning.

The woman's eyes narrowed. She was sly, planning on gettin' through this without telling the truth. Falcon wasn't gonna let that stand.

"Icehouse. You won't freeze before morning."

"There's no lock on it." Cheyenne had her arms crossed so tight Falcon hoped she didn't strangle herself around her belly. She stared at the woman.

"Figured on it. I'll stand guard. There's gotta be a lock on the jailhouse door in Bear Claw Pass." Falcon reached for Hobart.

"No, no." Hobart threw her arms in the

air, dodging Falcon's hands. "I don't want to talk to the sheriff."

"I'll just bet you don't," Kevin said. "But you shot my brother."

"I did not."

Kevin talked over her. "You think we're gonna just let you ride off? We'll take you to the sheriff and see you hanged."

"I didn't shoot him." Hobart's voice rose. She'd been coldly calm, but now the ice was cracking a little.

"Tell it to the law, lady," Falcon said.

"I can't talk to the sheriff. You can't turn me over to him."

"*Can't* is a mighty hard word, ma'am. Reckon it don't hold much water when you're comin' at us in the night. Seeing the sheriff is the nicest thing we're gonna do for you." Falcon studied her eyes, which were still calculating. The blush was higher now, but she had a chin that looked like eight days of stubborn packed into a week. But for all that stubborn, he saw someone willin' to do most anything not to talk to the law. It made her look powerful guilty.

Maybe he had the right lever to pry her open. "Kevin, grab her arm. We'll head to the icehouse, take turns standing watch, then in the morning go for Sheriff Corly —"

279

"I can't talk to the sheriff" — her words rushed out — "because I'm a Pinkerton agent."

That threw everybody into a dead silence. Watching her, Falcon saw her eyes shift between each of them, then look at the door, probably wondering at the chance she had to slip away. He clamped a hard hand on her shoulder.

"You're not going anywhere." She narrowed her eyes at him. He thought maybe he saw a speck of wisdom in the woman. But . . . "What's a Pinkerton agent?"

He didn't think this was about losing his memory. He didn't have much notion of what the words could even mean.

"It's a private lawman you can hire to investigate," Hobart explained. "I was hired to find a woman who went missing out here."

"Lots of folks go missing on the frontier," Cheyenne said grimly.

Nodding, Hobart said, "They do indeed. But her father is a state senator in Minnesota and her brother was an army general. They had the resources to find out what happened to her. A horse can buck someone off. A prairie fire or tornado can sweep through and leave the dead behind. A creek can rise and wash a wagon away. But we're living in modern times. If a tornado came through the area, we'd know it. And she didn't come out on a wagon train. She rode the train and stayed in boardinghouses. She was headed west hunting adventure. She worked in Omaha awhile, then Kearney. I tracked her as far as Bear Claw Pass. She stepped off the train, and there is only the smallest hint that she was in the area, but I can't find any indication that she boarded the train again."

Falcon still didn't know exactly what a Pinkerton agent was. It sounded like she was some kind of sheriff herself. "Why can't you tell the sheriff what you're up to?"

"I don't know for sure if I can trust him. And I want to remain a secret here."

Falcon looked at Kevin, then at Cheyenne. "Icehouse?"

"Oh yeah," Cheyenne said. "I don't like her answers. She's the most likely person to've shot Wyatt."

"I did *not* shoot Wyatt Hunt. When did that happen, where? What were you all doing at Hawkins's ranch today?"

Kevin said, "She's asking more questions than we are. I think a night in the icehouse will be good for her." He grabbed her right arm. Falcon grabbed her left.

"No." She wrenched her arms, but she

281

weren't goin' nowhere. Not with Falcon latched on tight. "I have to get back to the Hawkins place by morning. He's going to be furious that I missed making his evening meal, and that I rode off like I did. I have to be back to make breakfast."

That brought the little struggle to an end. Falcon sat her down hard on the chair. Well, not all that hard 'cuz they'd never got her much out of it.

"So a Pinkerton agent is a hired snoop?" he asked.

Hobart flushed. "That might be a good way to describe what I do. It's well-known that on the frontier the law is hard to come by outside of town. The US Marshals can get involved. A few states, like Texas, have Rangers that can provide law and order beyond the town limits. But for the most part, folks on the frontier are their own law and order."

"That's nothing but the plain truth," Cheyenne said. "And that's why this senator and his son hired you to come and hunt up the wayward girl?"

"That's exactly right."

"Then for the third and final time, why, if that's what you're doing, did you shoot" — Cheyenne shoved her hard enough the chair slid back — "my" — Cheyenne shoved her

282

again — *"brother."*

Drawing back a fist, Cheyenne swung. Hobart moved with lightning speed, faster than Falcon could have. She grabbed Cheyenne's fist with the sharp slap of flesh hitting flesh. She held that fist tight when Cheyenne yanked back.

Falcon saw Hobart's knuckles turn white with the effort to hang on, but hang on she did. He saw a toughness in the woman and something sturdy. For all her slyness, she was either the best liar he'd ever met — and since he couldn't remember much, that wasn't a hard contest to win — or she was telling the truth.

For all the rage he felt at whoever shot Wyatt, he was going to have to start asking who'd done it other than Hobart. But he'd seen her tracks letting Ralston loose. Or had he?

"I'll give you a name to send a wire. Allan Pinkerton in Chicago. Please don't send it from Bear Claw Pass. I don't trust the telegraph operator. Even if he's innocent of any wrongdoing, he might talk to the wrong people. But Casper would be all right, and you can ride there and back in a short day. Contact him. He'll verify he sent me out here."

"A telegraph can go anywhere, to anyone,"

283

Cheyenne said stubbornly. "You could give us the place to send it knowing someone back there would cover for you."

Falcon thought it'd be a pretty fancy, long, planned-out scheme for that to work. For her to have partners elsewhere who'd intercept a wire and know how to lie for her.

"Then figure out who Allan Pinkerton is and how to contact him yourself. He lives in Chicago and runs the Pinkerton Agency. I'd think that would be enough for a tele-graph office to send it for you. Tell him you met Rachel Hobart, and she told you to mention the Bishop case. That'll be enough for him to know I sent you, and he'll answer right quick."

"Bishop?" Win said the name quietly.

They all turned to look at her. The faint, rather sick tone to her voice was impossible to ignore.

Falcon saw every drop of color leach out of her face until he braced himself to jump at her and catch her when she fainted.

Kevin was at her side before Falcon moved.

"What's the matter?"

"A-Amelia Bishop was the name of F-Father's last housekeeper." Win's legs went limp, and she collapsed.

TWENTY-SEVEN

"Win!" Kevin caught her before she hit the floor, swept her up in his arms, and carried her to a chair where he then sat, holding her in his lap. Andy rushed over with a cool cloth.

Cheyenne headed for Win, so distracted she forgot all about Mrs. Hobart for far too long. When her attention snapped back, Hobart was on her feet . . . not running. She rounded the table. Not making a break for the door, but rushing to Win's side. Her eyes sharp. Taking in every word that'd been spoken.

Keen curiosity gleamed in her blue eyes.

Not like a woman who'd been sneaking in planning murder at all. More like a lawman. Law-woman in this case. One who'd just found a real big clue.

Falcon's head snapped around to keep an eye on Hobart, and Cheyenne got the idea that he'd been paying attention to Win, too.

Hobart had really missed her best chance to escape. Not that she'd've made it. But it was her best chance.

"What does it mean?" Cheyenne wanted to stand by Win. But Andy was at her head, bathing her face and neck with a cool cloth. He had a nice touch for a youngster.

Andy with the cool cloth. Kevin catching a fainting woman. Molly rushing off to calm an injured man. This whole family was too good in an emergency. They'd had a lot of practice, and it made Cheyenne want to get to know them. Want it a little.

Win's faint didn't let go easy. She was a long time limp in Kevin's arms.

"She's breathing steady." Kevin sounded solid, like a man who'd seen trouble before. But he could barely tear his eyes away from his new wife.

It struck Cheyenne's heart right to its dead center.

He loved her.

Her friend had found someone to love her.

Cheyenne and Win had shared a few girlish dreams since she'd come home from boarding school. They'd been too young for such things before she'd been sent away. And now, both mature young women, their talk had been more of work, the ranch, Win's school. They were practical women

286

after all.

But a few times they'd talked of what life they'd hoped to have one day, and of course they'd wanted fine, good-hearted, handsome men to come into their lives.

Cheyenne had a goodly number of chances; she was half owner of a fine ranch after all. But no man had stirred her heart. She hadn't seriously considered Oliver Hawkins's proposal until he'd restated it after she'd had her ranch torn away from her.

It had found a tender place in her heart to be wanted when she brought nothing to a marriage, no money, only herself.

But seeing Win held so gently in Kevin's arms. To see his fear. To see Andy's calm, competent hands. To know Molly would be here helping if she wasn't upstairs taking care of Wyatt . . . it all hit Cheyenne hard.

Joy for her friend, no matter what had caused her to collapse. And sorrow for herself, because she didn't have what Win had.

Cheyenne's eyes wandered to Falcon. There was a man she might care about.

If he remembered who he was.

And remembered he wasn't a husband.

And learned to love cattle ranching.

Yes, if not for that, he'd be a man she

287

might care about. He had given her a puppy after all.

Leaving off her strange yearnings, she tried to reason out why Win had fainted.

"Amelia Bishop." Cheyenne dropped the name into the room, pulling their attention away from Win, all but Kevin's. "Why did that name make her faint?"

Hobart straightened away from where she crouched near Win's feet, watching everyone. She came back to the chair she'd been sitting in. Put there by near force earlier, she now sat looking cool and very smart — not acting like a prisoner at all. She'd noted the same thing everyone else had, but it meant more to her.

"You tracked her movements to Bear Claw Pass?" Cheyenne asked.

"Yes, she arrived here over three years ago. It took me a while to pick up her trail. I couldn't just show a picture of her around and ask if anyone knew her. And she'd been missing for nearly a year when her family hired me. They'd waited too long to start hunting. They kept expecting to hear from her."

Cheyenne said, "The West is well-known for swallowing people whole."

"Without admitting who I was, I poked around, asked questions that might open folks to talking without them realizing I wanted more than it seemed. It worked in Omaha and Kearney, other stops along the railroad line, and what I learned sent me here.

"Amelia definitely left the train here. She'd wired her father from here as she did from nearly every stop. Once I got to town, I listened to chatter here and there and decided a woman who matched her description might be the same one who was hired as a housekeeper on the Hawkins Ranch. Her family said she was looking for adventure, a ranch would've appealed to her."

"You went out to see her, and she wasn't there." Falcon seemed to be ahead of the story.

"I found Oliver Hawkins had lost his housekeeper. He'd been without one for a while when I got there. The place was a wreck. His clothes everywhere, the whole place was in shambles. I found out he'd advertised for a new housekeeper but hadn't found one yet. There was no evidence Amelia had traveled on beyond Bear Claw Pass, and he never mentioned her by name. But I needed to look closer out there. And to do that, I needed an excuse to stay. So instead of questioning Hawkins about Amelia, I applied for the job and got hired."

"She vanished from my father's house?" Win's voice, weak and unsteady, turned them all toward her. Kevin hadn't taken his eyes off her, but everyone else was listening strictly to Hobart.

Her face was ashen. Her movements uncoordinated. But her eyes shone with a steady, intense light.

"Your father has never told me much about his last housekeeper, never mentioned her name even when I tried to get him to talk about her. His story is that she just took off. Worked for him for a while, then without telling him she was unhappy there, she rode off one day and never came back. He didn't like it, it was inconvenient, but he knew young women could be flighty."

"Not all of them," Win said, sounding grim.

"No, and though she was looking for adventure, Amelia apparently wasn't a foolish girl. She'd've contacted her father if she was able."

Hobart looked straight into Cheyenne's eyes. "I need to get back to the Hawkins Ranch before sunup. I don't want to do any more explaining to Hawkins than necessary."

"Why were you sneaking around our property?" Cheyenne hated it that she found herself believing Hobart, even trusting her. It made her feel like a gullible fool.

"I was coming in quietly, and I guess that amounts to sneaking, but I planned to come to your back door and knock. Tell you what I was looking for and see if I could get your help."

"No." Falcon shook his head. "You weren't going to tell us a thing when I caught you. You only agreed to talk when we wouldn't let up about the sheriff. You weren't going to tell us what was goin' on."

Hobart looked almost sheepish. "All right, you're not wrong about that. I was going to try and — and get information from you that might open some new leads into Amelia's disappearance. It's what I do. I'm good at it. Tricking folks into telling me more than they planned to."

Cheyenne wondered if they had all told her more than they'd planned to. Win fainting had for sure gotten Hobart's attention. And she'd learned some things about Amelia Bishop.

"What do you think happened to her?" Win's hands trembled as she rested them against her chest, her fingers entwined until her hands made one big fist. And she stayed where she was, held by Kevin.

Cheyenne knew how properly raised Win

291

had been. If she'd been thinking clearly, she'd've never sat on Kevin's lap like that in front of so many people.

"I think, Mrs. Hunt, that Amelia Bishop is dead."

Win gasped and rested her forehead on that one big fist. An attitude of prayer, Cheyenne thought.

"As I said, she was looking for adventure, but she wasn't estranged from her family. If she was somewhere settled or safe, she'd have contacted them. I have no proof, but I suspect she's dead."

"And who killed her? Isn't that part of the p-puzzle you're trying to solve?" Win raised her head, and her bright blue eyes looked hard at Hobart as if she was trying to bore into her brain.

"My job is to find her. If I find her alive, I'll take her home. If I find her dead, I'll arrest whoever did it, then tell her father where to come to visit the body. It's too dangerous to think of as a puzzle. That's a child's game. This is life and death."

Cheyenne watched Win, wondering if she'd say more. Explain what about this had knocked her off her feet.

"Cheyenne, it's your home she was fixing to invade," Falcon said. "You decide. The law or trust?"

Cheyenne's jaw tightened. Everyone in the room was dead silent, until she could hear the clock ticking.

Finally, her eyes only on Win, wishing she could read her friend's mind and understand what was going on, Cheyenne said, "Let her go back. If that's a mistake, we'll just round her up again."

Hobart's eyes narrowed, the insult hitting squarely since she'd been caught.

"And the next time we'll take her to see Sheriff Corly."

Hobart had a look in her eyes that said she'd welcome a good fight, but she just didn't have time. She jerked her chin and headed for the door at a fast clip.

Cheyenne saw Falcon's muscles bunch like he was going to make a grab for her. But he didn't.

He stood aside and watched her take off. "We never asked about her being involved with Ralston. Or about being involved with Hawkins."

Win moaned quietly. Shamed by her father, afraid.

That's what Cheyenne saw in Win: fear.

She opened her mouth to demand some answers.

Kevin stood up, Win still in his arms. "I'm taking her out of here. She needs time to recover."

He left the room, and like with Hobart, they didn't stop him. Andy followed on his heels.

Cheyenne and Falcon turned to each other. Cheyenne felt so grim she didn't think she could speak.

"We might've just let the woman who shot your brother walk out."

Cheyenne gave a tiny nod of her head. "She told a good tale."

"Truth or lies?" Falcon shook his head slowly. "I couldn't tell. But I reckon you're right. We caught her once. We can catch her again."

Cheyenne crossed her arms and looked at Falcon, trying to decide if she'd let a would-be killer walk away.

They stood there, studying each other for a long, quiet time.

Finally, Falcon said, "Tomorrow, I'm taking out after Ralston. If he can be tracked, I'll track him. But the longer we wait, the more I lose the trail."

"I'll come too."

"No, you can't. Not while Wyatt's so bad. I'd like nuthin' better'n to have you. You're a fine tracker and a likely saddle partner. But Wyatt's gonna get a fever, you know he is. Molly can do all the doctoring in the world, but he's gonna need you with him. He'll fight it off most likely if the wound doesn't fester, but for a time, he'll be helpless and confused, and you're the only one he really knows and trusts. You can't leave him."

Cheyenne knew he was right.

TWENTY-EIGHT

Falcon was wrong.

Wrong about most everything.

Wyatt was fine, tougher'n a boot and twice as feisty. Cheyenne only seemed to upset him when she fussed over him and nagged him to stay in bed.

She tended toward insults and was full of well-meaning advice, like, "If you move again, I'm gonna lasso you like a bullheaded Angus and hog-tie you to the bed."

Falcon knew this because she'd said it at the top of her lungs. Falcon had been in the bunkhouse at the time, and he, along with all the men, had heard every word.

Wyatt reacted to the threats like you'd expect. The two of them had locked horns from the minute Wyatt had awakened in the morning feeling mighty good, or so he'd shouted at his sister.

Molly had been struggling to evict Cheyenne from her own house when Wyatt showed no sign of fever. He was probably gonna be okay, but that wasn't enough to make Cheyenne leave off her fussin'.

Falcon invited her to come hunt Ralston with him to save everyone's hearing, if not their very lives. Molly had packed plenty of food. If Falcon was any judge, they had enough to be gone for a week.

Molly was a helpful little thing, but not overly subtle, although Falcon didn't think she was even trying.

They were on the trail before midmorning and back to the spot they'd left Ralston trussed up like a hog at roasting time. The rain had held off and the trail was clear as day at first.

They were only minutes figuring out which way he went, him and whoever turned him loose. A woman, but now that Falcon had studied Hobart's tracks, he was sure it wasn't her. This woman was taller, bigger all over. Her shoes were womanly, but down at the heels, one of the soles left a ragged mark like there might be holes in it.

An hour into their search, they lost what had been a faint but easily found trail. Falcon dismounted to study the rocky stretch.

"We're going to have to study the edges of this stone wherever dirt's blown in. It'll be slow going." He looked up from where he crouched, scowling at the trail's dead end.

Cheyenne nodded and swung down beside him. She tied up her horse and went ahead, leaving Falcon to study any place someone had left the rocky stretch. It was well past noon when he found the slightest trace of the horse the woman rode.

"Down this way, Cheyenne." He called her back from her own endless search.

Studying the sharp, downward slope, Cheyenne asked, "Unless he's planning to circle back, he's not headed to that valley where he had the rustled cows."

Falcon weighed it in his head. "I'm going down. See if there's more than this one mark and a for sure sign Ralston is still with her. If they split up, we'll have to pick one."

"I wonder who she is. Back at the beginning, before we'd studied the woman's tracks —"

"And before I'd studied Hobart's tracks in your ranch yard," Falcon interrupted.

"— we just guessed it'd be Hobart. Now that I'm sure it's not, it adds weight to her denial of shooting Wyatt, because it doesn't seem like she's in league with Ralston. I'm still not happy we let her go."

"Nuthin' about this makes me happy."

"I'll go get the horses." Cheyenne headed back.

"Keep a sharp eye." Falcon hesitated to let her go, just as he wondered if he oughta not go off on his own.

Suddenly, it was more than hesitation. "Cheyenne, wait."

She wheeled around, gun drawn, pointed up, mindful not to aim at him. "What?"

It startled him and satisfied him right down to the ground to see her so salty, so ready for trouble. 'Cuz he thought that was exactly what was coming.

"It's not that far to where we left the horses. I think we need to stay together better. You were out of my sight when you got ahead tracking, now you're going off again. I think we'd better not do that."

She holstered her gun as she studied him, seeming to weigh what he'd said, read the worry in his belly.

She nodded. "Come on, then. Let's get our critters and get after that low-down Ralston and whoever's in this with him."

They went together. Falcon didn't see a lick of trouble comin' from anywhere. But he felt it, and it was better knowing right where she was and her knowing right where he was. Just like her drawing that gun. Best to know where your partner was if you started in to shooting.

As they led the horses on the steep downward slope, a hidden — but not hidden enough — trail was easily followed. The varmints they were trailing were still together.

They were in heavy woods except where the trees were broken up by slabs of solid stone.

"They couldn't have come on this narrow trail by accident." Cheyenne was behind Falcon, the trail too narrow for them to walk side by side.

"Nope, they had it figured. Planned ahead. Ralston picked his getaway trail, picked his overlook to stop any pursuit. We caught him, but she, whoever she is, was waiting. He was running to her. They knew exactly what trail they'd be taking and how to slip off it and leave anyone behind that might be coming."

"Unless," Cheyenne said smugly, "those coming along behind were highly skilled trackers, better than Ralston and his woman had any hope of being."

Falcon turned to look behind him, along the length of his horse, and met her eyes, and smiled. "Yep, unless that."

She smiled back, and he moved out again.

Midafternoon, hours and hours at what

seemed to be the pace of molasses in January, he straightened from where he'd been inching along, looking for proof they'd come this way. They'd just turned off a trail more rock than dirt, a wash cut by mountain runoff in the spring but dry now.

"They're easin' up, not hidin' their trail," Falcon said. "They're not worrying about pursuit anymore."

He went down on one knee to study the tracks. He wanted to be able to find them again, find these exact horses, no matter where this trail led.

And now he looked down at hoof marks plain as day. Two horses, riders up top, no longer sweeping away a sign of their passing.

He sincerely hoped a hard job had just gotten easier.

Cheyenne gave a satisfied smile that, he had to say, was just a mite smug. "We did it. We kept after them until they let up."

"We can go faster now, but before we head out, are we anywhere you're familiar with?"

Cheyenne studied mountain peaks and the lay of the land. "Nope, we're off RHR land, and I suspect we're off Hawkins land."

"Then we won't make much better time. We need to ride careful. Before, when he was waiting to back-shoot us, you knew the land well enough to be wary. But we'll have to be ready for a sneak attack."

"They probably think they've lost any pursuers, so they won't set up to watch their back trail."

"Prob'ly." Falcon nodded and put his hand on Cheyenne's arm and gave it a gentle squeeze. "We'll keep after them as long as we've got light. But let's stop and eat some of whatever Molly sent along. We've been at this since early morning. It helps me to take a break now and then, get off the horse, stretch, eat. It keeps my attention from slipping. Even if they aren't watching, and there's a good chance of that, I ain't risking my life, nor yours, on a good chance."

"Let's look for a spring so we can water the horses."

They found a spot with some water and a little grass, then switched their horses to halters so they could graze.

They sat and ate a portion of the food Molly had packed. There were thick roast beef sandwiches and apples. She'd chopped up cold cooked potatoes and some boiled eggs and put a good dressing on it. She'd stuck in a jar of beet pickles and a few chunks of cheese. And in a small tin, she'd sent a pile of sugar cookies.

"That woman is a fine cook." Falcon was near full before they'd eaten a third of it.

"She is indeed. I should probably have her teach me, but I doubt I have the patience for it."

"All that knitting is yours, isn't it? The front room is overloaded with it."

"Yep, and all the bedrooms, blankets everywhere."

"That takes patience."

"You're right. So I have plenty of patience. That must mean I just don't want to learn to cook."

"Fair enough."

Cheyenne crunched an apple and said between bites, "There's a good chance that whoever's partnering with Ralston is the one who shot Wyatt. Ralston set up on this trail, his woman set up on the road to town. They probably planned to watch and get rid of anyone following, then meet up. She's our would-be killer."

"A pair of dry-gulching skunks. So we ride easy, and that means slow."

"Let's go." She was astride her horse before she finished talking.

Falcon mounted up, and they rode along, two abreast, each of them turned to the side of the trail, splitting the work of keeping watch. Falcon trusted her to know what to look out for, and she trusted him.

Falcon didn't know nuthin' about himself much, but trusting someone seemed risky, even stupid. He wasn't sure what he'd come from that'd make him feel such. He only knew he trusted Cheyenne.

He saw Harvey with a family, hitched up to a cart. A wave of pain tore through his head, and he grabbed hold of his saddle, a dizzy spell making him fear he'd fall.

He tried to widen that picture in his head. Harvey, his mule. Who were those folks that had him?

Patsy. Her face flashed like a bolt of lightning. Her name. What else? His head pounded like someone was inside using his skull like a drum. He was falling. He landed hard, facedown on the rocky ground, and his head bounced.

A hand gripped his shoulder and put pressure on his head.

"You're bleeding, Falcon. Stay still."

He smelled blood. Felt a hard hand just above his eyes.

"It's not serious. Just a deep scratch."

Cheyenne, she was real. The pain. He clung to the here and now as tight as a man hanging off a cliff, then pain hit again that had nothing to do with Cheyenne and bleeding.

A cabin clinging to the side of a hill.

A fist slammed in his face. No, the memory of a fist. But the pain felt as if it were pounding his flesh.

Patsy Sulky . . . a beating.

Another memory flashed, Harvey going along with someone else.

The cabin.

The beating over . . . over . . .

His head rested on the soft ground. No, the ground wasn't this soft.

The grave.

"I dug a grave."

"What?" A callused hand brushed over his forehead.

"A grave. Patsy's dead."

Warm hands, strong and steady, gentle. He felt her fiddling with his forehead and knew distantly he'd hurt himself falling from his horse. He heard soft words of prayer.

"Patsy's dead. Burying her, setting out for Wyoming was . . . it was . . ." He fumbled for more. "I just know I left because there was nothing there for me. Not anymore."

"Your wife is dead?"

Falcon felt tears burn behind his eyes. The notion that he might cry was a horror, and he fought down the need, focused on the pain in his head.

"Do you remember more?" Cheyenne pressed a kiss on his forehead. "Do you remember your mother?"

"I-I know Ma's dead. It's just a strange, deep knowing that when Patsy died, I was alone. I can't remember when or how, but I know Ma's dead." Falcon gathered himself enough to rub at the battering pain in his temples. His hands were brushed aside, and Cheyenne replaced his rubbing with her own.

It was the nicest feeling he could imagine.

"Pa, my pa is dead. And he's been dead for years." Falcon tried to sit up. A man needed to stand to face ugly things.

Cheyenne's hands were too strong in his current shape. She scooted so she held his head in her lap. He relaxed onto her, let himself be treated gently.

The pain eased. The throbbing slowed to a dull ache. He managed to open his eyes and look at her. Those black eyes, only inches above his as she cradled his head.

When their eyes met, she pulled him close into her arms until her cheek rested on the top of his head.

"Do you know what this means, Falcon?"

A swoop of pain made him wince. "Those men you and I killed, I remember them trying to kill me in Missouri."

306

"Tuttle and Ross?"

"Yes, I saw them, caught them, left them tied up." He opened his eyes again to push away from the throbbing pain. He didn't feel guilty, but he wondered if he should. "I left them with nothing, unconscious, tied up back in the woods. Figured they'd get loose eventually."

"How did they get back here so fast?"

"I-I was a few days in Omaha selling their stuff and Harvey. And I stopped in Casper to talk to the lawyer. If they got their hands on enough money —"

"Which they could have done if they knew who to send a wire to back here, and they reached someone capable of transferring funds to them."

"Maybe, but you could be thinking overly on it. They could've robbed someone, bought a train ticket. Got here fast by doin' that. They weren't no honest men, for a fact. I was long enough in Omaha that if they came on fast, they could've beaten me to the train, come out ahead of me. That's what they had to've done."

"There's more to remember," Cheyenne said. "I reckon it'll keep coming into your head."

Falcon sat up slowly. Cheyenne's care gave

307

him enough pleasure it overrode the pain. Mostly.

"I wish . . ." Cheyenne said, frowning. "I wish we could go back to the ranch. Give you a few quiet days to heal so memories wouldn't come with such pain."

"If we leave off our tracking now, we'll be hard-pressed to catch up to Ralston. Time isn't kind to a trail."

"It seems to me the pair is quitting the country. With this last turn and the clear tracks, they seem to be making fast time and going straight west."

Falcon met her eyes. Both of them silent for a stretch as they thought of what they were dealing with.

"I'd say let them go if it was just cattle rustling." Falcon watched her burr up like an angry wolf. Rustling was serious business in the West, it seemed. "But if they shot Wyatt, then we have to keep after them."

He was relieved when Cheyenne nodded without going on a shouting rampage about cattle rustlers. He figured he had some to learn on that score, but how far did a body ride to fetch around a man who'd stolen cows? Especially when they'd gotten them back.

"The sky is clear, so we should have no rain to make the trail harder to follow,"

Cheyenne said. "It's late enough in the day. Let's camp for the night."

"No, I can ride. We'll get on after 'em for now. I can rest my poor puny head when we can't see to ride. If this trail is them lighting out, then it oughta go steady for a long time. If they take to sneakin' again, we'll have to stop for the night. Right now, I wouldn't be much good on a well-hidden trail."

Nodding, Cheyenne got the horses while Falcon got to his feet. He was surprised at how hard it was.

They set out again. The tracks left by the two riders they chased were as clear as a hand-painted sign.

When the trail was narrow, Cheyenne led the way. Sometimes it was wider, and they'd ride two abreast.

They'd been an hour down the trail in silence, which was good because it was taking a lot for Falcon to hang on to his horse. New memories flashed into his head every now and then, adding to what he'd remembered.

How Patsy could skin a possum. What a woman.

How his heart had broken when she'd died. How he'd ached for that little, unknown child. The loneliness, the beauty of the Blue Ridge Mountains. On and on. His thoughts fully occupied.

His ma, memories about her popped in and out, fast, old, mixed-up with a terrible fear at being left alone.

An attacking bear.

Holding a rifle that was near as tall as he was and struggling to load the musket.

Ma, strong, work-weary, weathered skin, a kind smile.

The memories beat at him, the old and more recent. Whirling in and out of his head, bringing pain until he felt like he was more knocked out than awake.

"We'll stop here." Cheyenne's voice brought his attention to his surroundings. "I'd hoped to ride on into the night, see a campfire in the distance, but it's been a long day after a sleepless night."

Falcon thought of Wyatt and wondered how he was holding on.

"And this is a good stopping place."

He realized he'd paid no mind to their safety. It'd all been on Cheyenne since his headaches hit.

Through blurred eyes, Falcon saw the sun low in the sky, and a clearing showed plenty of grass and a solid rock wall that'd reflect the heat of a fire as the night cooled and shelter them from the mountain breeze.

Riding up to the rock wall, Falcon realized

the night was turning cool, and the wind-break was welcome. As he dismounted, he staggered. Only a hard grip on his saddle horn kept him on his feet. He hoped Cheyenne, dismounting her horse on the far side of his mount, didn't notice.

Then she led her horse forward so he could see her clearly.

"Before, when I said, 'Do you know what this means?' I wasn't talking about your memory of the attack in Independence nor any of the other things you recalled. You started speaking of it, but that wasn't what I was getting at."

"Oh, then what does it mean?"

"It means, there's no reason on this earth we can't get married." She grabbed his reins to lead his horse along with hers to stake them out to graze.

Without the saddle horn and her words swatting him in the face, Falcon's knees buckled, and he sat down on the nice soft grass. As long as he was down there, he let his eyes fall shut. He heard a distant shout of his name, then Cheyenne's strong hands helping him to lie flat.

That was the last thing he knew until morning.

TWENTY-NINE

Cheyenne gently rocked Falcon's shoulder, not wanting to jar him awake. If he didn't wake up at all, she'd be in trouble, but she'd fuss about that when she needed to and not a second sooner.

She'd watched him cling to his horse, more asleep than awake last night. When she realized how used up he was, she'd begun looking desperately for a place they could camp. She knew he didn't have long, and she admired watching a strong man go on when others would have folded up.

Finally, she'd found a place when she knew she was within minutes of simply stopping and letting him sleep flat on the trail with no good place for a fire, which would mean no way to keep warm against the cold of a high mountain summer.

She'd marveled that he had the strength to dismount, but she didn't realize how little he had left until, trying to be helpful, she'd led his horse away, planning to tend it so he didn't have to, and he collapsed.

Unless it was her talk of marriage that had knocked him to his belly.

As it turned out, he'd picked a decent spot to sleep.

She'd staked out the horses, built a fire, and fed herself but didn't bother trying to wake Falcon to feed him. She covered him with a blanket, then slept across the fire from him, getting up often to make sure he was breathing or hadn't kicked off his blanket. She fed the fire through the night to keep him warm.

The poor man. The poor, widowed man.

It was really sad his wife had died. But here he was and here she was.

All she'd learned in life was to dislike Clovis Hunt and to never marry a man like him but rather a man she respected like her grandpa or her real father, though he was only known to her through stories.

She'd hoped for a man she could respect, or in the case of Oliver Hawkins, a man she could manage.

Now here was Falcon, and she wanted to be married to him. He was no rancher and no man to be managed. But maybe, just maybe, a man she could want and respect and even, maybe someday, love.

She looked down at him as she rocked his broad shoulder. She wanted him. She meant to have him.

First, she had to wake him up. It was time to see if the night's rest was enough to revive him because they had outlaws to catch.

His eyes flickered, but they'd done that a time or two already. She rocked a little harder. "Come on out here, Falcon Hunt. See the new day."

His eyes, burning brown eyes shot with gold, blinked open and met hers. They were dazed, but this was better than he'd been up till now.

"I've got coffee boiling, and Molly packed eggs and a skillet. I found potatoes to fry, and she sent some biscuits." Cheyenne had been up awhile. She'd led the horses to a nearby spring for water. Packed up all she could. Made and eaten her own breakfast. All of this to make things easier for Falcon and let him sleep longer. And he cooperated by not moving an inch. But they needed to be on the trail. She'd cooked his meal right before she came to wake him.

"You didn't eat supper. Your belly's gotta be so empty it thinks your throat's been cut."

His lids, so heavy with sleep, faded closed.

314

She rocked a little harder. "Come along, we're burnin' daylight. Wake up, Falcon, all the way up."

He brought both hands to his face and rubbed them back and forth, then one hand brushed the ugly cut on his forehead from falling off his horse and landing on a rock.

With a groan, he sat up and faced her. "My mind is back. It's all there. Memories full bloomed and easy to hunt up."

Smiling, she said, "How about the headaches? Is the pain still as bad?"

Careful with his new cut, he slid his hands up into his hair and rubbed his head for a while. "Not so's you'd notice. Nope, the pain, it didn't make no sense. I'd long been over that pounding I took in the stream. Why keep hurting so long after?"

A quick jerk of one shoulder went with Cheyenne's words. "Reckon something in there wasn't all the way healed. Doubt many know what addled your thoughts, stole your memories. And just as few know why they cleared up. I'd imagine any doctor worth a hoot would want to talk to you and learn all you've been through. But things seem to be straightened out."

Nodding, Falcon looked around. "You set up camp, built a fire, staked out the horses." He looked down at the blanket covering him. "You did everything. All the work."

"Yep, and now I've torn most of it down so we can head out."

A smile wouldn't stay hidden when he said, "You're a mighty fine woman, Miss Cheyenne. Do I remember you asking me to marry you last night, right before I took a nap?"

She arched her brow and gave him a stern look that didn't hide the flash of humor in her eyes. "Why, I have no idea what you mean, Mr. Hunt. A fine lady like me would never do such a brazen thing as that."

Falcon pulled her close and wrapped her tight in his arms. They sat like that, there before the fire, for a long stretch of moments.

"A mighty fine woman, for a fact." He cupped her cheek with one hand. He seemed content to just look.

At last, he turned to the fire. "I find my belly to be very interested in breakfast, if you please. You've taken fine care of me. I hope you're never ailing, but I stand ready to return that care should you ever need it. And I thank you kindly."

She ran one hand through his hair. He was a terrible mess. He'd gotten a haircut since he'd come west, but his face was grizzled with a day's growth of whiskers, and his hair was next to standing on end after he ran his hands through it.

She smoothed it, noticing how heavy it was, how silky. "I like the idea of touching your hair anytime I want for the rest of our lives."

"Then I'll eat, and we'll go catch us some varmints so we can get back to Bear Claw Pass to stand in front of a preacher."

Smiling, she touched his hair one more time. "That plan runs right along in agreement with my own."

He kissed her on the forehead, one long lingering kiss, then she turned away to get his plate of eggs and biscuits.

They'd eaten a fine meal. Cheyenne had shown Falcon a spring dribbling out of a stone where she'd watered the horses. He washed the sleep away, worried the ends of a green twig until it made a likely brush, then used it to clean his teeth.

Cheyenne packed up the rest of the camp.

"I could find it insulting that you'd do work I consider a man's job," Falcon said as he mounted up on a horse she'd cared for and saddled before he could help this morning. "But I am finding myself uncommon fond of you, Cheyenne. I reckon you're about the best kind of woman there is, and I'm proud to think you're agreeable to joining your life to mine."

He looked at her solemnly, and she felt the truth of his words, the depth of his sincerity.

"I think we'll deal well together, Falcon. I think we're a good match." She smiled. "And I'm uncommon fond of you, too."

With a firm jerk of his chin, they set out to catch a low-down pair of coyotes and drag them before the law.

Molly slipped into Wyatt's bedroom to find him feverish.

Cheyenne should have stayed. Wyatt would want her here. The rest of them were strangers to him.

Molly rushed out, quietly but with no time to lose, to fetch a basin of cool water. She should have checked on him before breakfast, but it seemed sleep was the best healer. Only now no one else was around to help her with the fever. They had all eaten fast and gone with the foreman, Rubin Walsh, to check the cattle.

With the traitorous ramrod, Ross Baker, dead and no Wyatt or Cheyenne to work, there was a lot neglected around the RHR. Win might not be much help out there, but she wanted to stay at Kevin's side.

Her devotion was touching. Also a little

sickening.

Andy, of course, couldn't bear to let a ranching chore pass him by without throwing his back into the work. Admirable but annoying when Molly could have used some help around here from someone, anyone.

But they were all gone. Cheyenne and Falcon, Kevin and Win, Andy and all the hired hands. And now Wyatt had taken a bad turn.

She set the basin on the table beside his bed and wrung out a cloth. When she rested it on his head, his eyes flickered open. They had a glazed look, one that often went with a fever.

"Can you drink some water?" She'd scooped out a cup and had it ready.

Nodding, he seemed to gather his strength for a moment, then shoved himself up. The pain that lanced his face had her sliding an arm under his back.

"No, let me bear your weight. And use your right arm, rest your left."

For as groggy as he seemed, he understood and was careful with his left arm. He drank deeply from the tin cup, then she scooped up more, and he drank half again.

"Cheyenne?" Wyatt's strength seemed to teeter and threaten to vanish.

She wanted to get some broth down him

but didn't have it handy. "Can you stay awake for a bit? You should take food. Build up your strength."

"What happened? I w-was fit last night?"

"A fever's come on. We thought when you didn't take on with one the first day, you'd managed to avoid it. I'm afraid I'm the only one in the house. Cheyenne is out —" Was there a good enough reason to worry him about his sister? "Everyone is out working. Your Mr. Walsh came wanting help working cattle today and swept up everyone before him."

"E-even Win?"

"Winona doesn't seem able to let my brother out of her sight. A concept that escapes me, but there it is." Her eyes met Wyatt's with her full skeptical little-sister expression. He smiled. He was a little brother after all. He knew how she felt.

"Roundup coming. We've had some easy days after branding." Wyatt reached for the light blanket drawn over him and threw it aside with a trembling hand.

Molly jerked it right back. "You're not thinking for one split second that you're fit to herd cattle, are you?"

He gave her a frightened look. She wasn't quite sure what she'd sounded like, but he appeared to take her question as a threat.

Then stubborn defiance firmed his jaw, and he threw the blanket off again.

Careful of his injuries, she solidly held him down. He had the strength of a newborn kitten. He struggled against her hold for all of five seconds before he collapsed, looking shocked.

She rather enjoyed it. "More water?"

He nodded, and she helped him sit up again. He drank the last half of the cup.

"You're not thinking clearly because of your fever. You know you can't go herd cattle with a bullet wound in your chest, broken collarbone, and high fever. Settle down and rest. Let me —"

"Where's Cheyenne? Where's my sister?"

She got a cloth and dipped it in the cool water again and pressed it against his forehead. He gave a sigh of contentment that seemed to end his upset. She bathed his face and checked his wound, which was red and swollen but not with the look of infection. She was familiar with how that appeared.

Putting on a fresh bandage, she dabbed cool water on his brow again, and before the cloth had warmed to the temperature of his fever, he'd fallen asleep.

She wished his sister were here. Knowing full well she'd had a hand in throwing

Cheyenne out, she was still unhappy with the woman for being gone.

Cheyenne couldn't care for him as well as Molly, but it would give Wyatt comfort to have someone here he loved.

Where were Falcon and Cheyenne? How far did they plan to ride? How long would they search before they gave up, found their man, or died under the coyote's guns?

Molly had plenty to occupy her thoughts as she struggled to bring down Wyatt's fever. By herself. Like always.

At the same time she resented them all for abandoning Wyatt, she felt her chin firm as she cared for him, knowing she could handle most anything alone.

THIRTY

Falcon's hand came out, hard and fast. He snatched hold of Cheyenne's reins and dragged both mounts to a halt.

"Get down." He was on the ground before he breathed the order, and Cheyenne was a heartbeat behind him.

"The tracks here are fresh. We're close."

Cheyenne took off to the left side of the trail, the side she'd ridden on. Falcon went right. He studied the land past the edge of the woods, wishing for an easy way ahead but finding none.

He met Cheyenne coming out of the woods on her side. "We've gotta get shut of this trail. Leastwise when we're headin' around a corner like the one ahead. They could be in sight."

Cheyenne gave a jerk of her chin, saying she agreed, and it warmed a man's heart. She caught his arm and led him back to where she'd left her horse. She pointed to a rabbit trail and let him lead.

A good woman. A fine woman in all ways. And she'd said she'd marry up with him. He went forward with a smile on his face. The rabbit trail wasn't much, and there were deadfalls across it, and scrub pines lacing their scratching arms to block anyone more than rabbit high. But until Falcon saw a better option, he'd go forward best he could.

They reached past the curve of the trail and saw nothing. Went back for their critters and led them around the trail only to tie them up again at the next twist. Onward they went like that through the afternoon. They camped with no fire and had a fresh start the next day at the same crawling speed. Their sandwiches were gone and so were the eggs and biscuits. They were eating jerky from their packs and drinking from their canteens. They still had a good supply of cookies and apples, as if Molly had sent them on a picnic.

Falcon enjoyed every bite.

They'd been at it for three whole days, stopping at every curve, hitching the horses, walking through the woods until they could see what lay beyond, then going back for the horses. They moved at such a deadly slow pace Falcon was almost turned to daydreaming. Then they found someone.

This time Cheyenne grabbed his arm. "That's him."

Crouching together, side by side, they studied the man tearing down a noon camp. A woman helped him. "Have you seen her before?" Falcon asked.

Shaking her head, Cheyenne stayed silent.

Neither of them was familiar to Falcon, but then he didn't know a soul. He'd only just started knowing himself again.

Falcon urged Cheyenne to sit. They stayed there, silently watching the pair ahead of them — one who'd laid in wait to kill them, the other who most likely shot Wyatt — pack up to move.

Falcon turned to Cheyenne's ear. "Now?"

Cheyenne hesitated, then shook her head no. Falcon tried to reason out why. He'd surely agree with her if she said it out loud. Knowing he held such trust for her was enough to keep him quiet.

A skillet clanged against metal as it got slipped into a saddlebag. The pair was good at handling a campsite. They didn't talk, like they worked well as a team and didn't need to. They didn't take time to strip away any signs they'd been there, and they'd had a good-sized fire. Two folks who weren't feeling hunted.

It was a pure pleasure to know these savvy folks were making such a big mistake.

Falcon thought of how long Ralston had spent building a herd in that canyon. He had to be good in the wilderness.

Cheyenne whispered in his ear, "No limp."

That's right, this polecat had lived for years pretending to be hurt to get sympathy from Hawkins.

Watching how the two were together, the way they touched each other as they worked, Falcon saw they were more than partners. The woman would smile, then frown, all her feelings good and bad showed on her face. Including, he saw once, suspicion when she looked at Ralston. Maybe she wasn't as fully on his side as Ralston liked to think. If the woman would shoot Wyatt, she'd shoot someone else. Maybe she was tired of having a partner.

The pair rode out.

Falcon let them get on up the trail, well out of earshot, before he turned to Cheyenne. "Why'd we let them go?"

"It seems to me Ralston still has secrets. Whoever that woman is, I've never seen her. She has to be living somewhere around here. If they're making their way to a hideout, I'd like to see it. Ralston has had time to steal a powerful lot of stuff in the years since he showed up in Wyoming. Maybe there's more, maybe we can get some of it back."

"The trail they're taking don't seem like how they'd leave the country, head for California or Oregon."

Nodding, Cheyenne said, "Instead, they covered their tracks, and now they're trekking down this meandering trail. Seems to me they plan to get to their hideout, or wherever they're going, and stay around. Maybe Ralston has other crimes he's busy committing, and he thinks he can set up in his own hideout and still carry out at least some of his plans. I don't know what's going on, but I want to hang back and see if we learn anything."

"Let's see around the trail's next curve, then come back for the horses."

They followed along at a good distance, careful every time there was a curve in the trail. Falcon settled in, figuring they might be following this pair for days.

During their same careful checking of what lay ahead of another twist in the trail, Cheyenne grabbed the front of Falcon's shirt, dragging him low, hissing like a rattler.

Four men all on horseback. The woman was also mounted, but she was a few steps back from Ralston, as if she wasn't in this circle of four, at least not as an equal.

One man Falcon recognized, a tall, skinny, stoop-shouldered RHR hand with a cigarette hanging out of the corner of his mouth.

The RHR hand wasn't the foreman, not in charge at all that Falcon knew. If this group was connected to the men who'd attacked Win and Kevin, then the band had included Ross, the RHR ramrod. This man might've just gotten promoted in the gang.

Next to the RHR cowpoke was an older man, a bit of white in his overlong hair dangling beneath a tattered gray Stetson. The oldster had a scowl on his face that showed a missing tooth right up front.

Ralston sat straight across from the RHR hand with the woman near his horse's flank.

Next was a man wearing a bright red bandanna. He had a long beard. He had his broad-brimmed hat in his hands, and his head was so bald it shone in the sunlight. None of 'em was a youngster, just as Tuttle and Ross had been older. And Falcon remembered the talk he'd heard in town about those two grousing about getting older and being tired of working for someone else.

"We heard at the North Bend Ranch that Wyatt Hunt is dying." The bald man's voice echoed with satisfaction in a way that made Falcon want to stand right up and start unloading his pistol. He kept quiet, instead, and seethed.

"Not what they're saying in the house," the RHR hand said. "Pulled the bullet out, sewed him up, laid up some but not even a fever. Be back at work in a couple'a days."

"Did one of you get him?" Ralston asked.

That gave Falcon pause. If the woman had shot Wyatt, wouldn't Ralston know?

To a man they all shook their heads or said no. Even the woman shook her head, though no one paid her any mind.

Cheyenne's hand tightened on Falcon's shirtfront until he started to worry about being strangled.

"Why are we meeting clear and away out here?" Missing Tooth sounded grumpy in a way that made Falcon think he always sounded that way. A complainer, and the others so used to it they paid it little mind. But the cold glint in the man's eyes told Falcon when there was shooting trouble, this man would be one to watch.

"It's far out for you, Norm," Ralston said. "But I had to put space between me and the RHR and the Hawkins place. When the sheriff came to tell Hawkins about Tuttle, I knew I had to run, so I sent riders to you all with the message to meet here at the base of the hoot owl trail."

Cheyenne's hand clutched again, just when Falcon was breathing well again. *Hoot owl trail* must mean something to her.

"I know they'll notice you're gone from the HC, Norm, but we have to clear out the rest of the cattle, get 'em sold fast, and quit the country."

Cheyenne leaned to Falcon's ear. "Rest of the cattle?"

Their eyes met. They'd removed all the cattle from the valley they'd found. So what other cattle were there?

"We've tried to thin the herd at the Hunt place and missed every time. It's time to take our money and leave," Ralston insisted.

"Roger Hanson's an old curly wolf from the high-up hills," Norm snarled. "I haven't had a clear chance at him, but if you gave me more time —"

"Nope, for me at the Hawkins place, the time's up. It wasn't a bad plan. These four ranches looked to be easy pickin'. No crowd of family to fight for the land. Hanson, a tough man but alone in the world. Hawkins, his daughter don't care if he lives or dies and doesn't seem interested in the ranch. Judd's a mighty dangerous man. Always figured we couldn't take the North Bend, but we got some cattle. And the Hunts, just the sister and brother, but otherwise no one until that fool Clovis turns up more sons. I thought we could come away with a lot of cattle and maybe two of the ranches. Now we're done as far as the land grab, and half our cows are gone."

Falcon saw the woman looking confused and distressed, but she didn't speak up. Whoever she was to Ralston, she seemed to be no kind of partner in whatever was going on.

"We either need to make a break for it now or get back," Baldy said. "We'll be missed."

"I can't go back," the RHR hand said. "Walsh, the foreman, is too sharp-eyed, especially with the boss being shot. When I slipped away today, it was for good."

Ralston nodded. "Hope your bosses figure you for hittin' the trail, and that's that. We'll get the cattle down the road to Laramie and be there before sunup. We'll have them sold, divide the money, and hit the trail by first light."

"This wasn't the plan." Norm slapped his hat on his leg hard enough to make his horse dance sideways. "We were supposed to come out of this owning a ranch apiece."

The woman's eyes had turned bleak, but

she sat silently, lowering her head as if to cover her expression.

Falcon felt Cheyenne's fingers digging into his wrist until his hand was strangled.

She dragged Falcon back slowly. One look in her eyes told Falcon she knew something and needed to tell him.

And they had a bigger job ahead of them than rounding up Percy Ralston.

THIRTY-ONE

"Those men are from the four biggest ranches in the area." Cheyenne could barely keep from jumping out of cover and telling them all to throw down their guns or draw.

If she'd had Wyatt at her side maybe. And she didn't doubt Falcon was a tough man, but he didn't know what she was so foam-at-the-mouth mad about. He'd fight at her side, she had no doubt, but he might hesitate to just open fire. Because she knew a furious Falcon Hunt was a sight to freeze a man in his tracks, she needed him to know what she was asking him to fight for.

"Ralston is from the Hawkins place. Wells, that no-account coyote, is one of ours."

"I recognize him from the bunkhouse."

Nodding, Cheyenne said, "I'm sure he was in cahoots with Ross. The white-haired man with the missing tooth is Norm Mathers, he's a hard man. He works for Roger Hanson, a tough man but getting older with no sons to look out for him. He hired Mathers to enforce his orders."

"Looks like Mathers has plans to start givin' his own orders." Falcon's eyes were sharp and cold.

"The bald man I don't know, but Ralston mentioned the North Bend Ranch. It's along a bend in the North Platte that's south of Casper. I don't know the ranch well, but I know the man who owned it died a while back. He does have a son, Judd Black Wolf. He's a Cheyenne, not full blooded, but he's got plenty of it in him, like me. I met the old man years back, and remember his son. We were both youngsters. Judd was fierce even as a boy. And I know his reputation now. I'll promise you they'll have to kill him to steal his land. Married with a family, too. If they planned to come out of this with a ranch apiece, they've been plotting to kill each and every one of the owners. Oliver wouldn't be a hard man to get rid of. Hanson, if Norm Mathers turned on him, he'd be gone."

"It doesn't sound like Hanson was making it easy."

Cheyenne smiled to think of that tough old man. "I'd like to hear if any attempts have been made on any of them."

"Seems to me all these fools are nothing

but big-talking failures. They tried to get rid of Kevin and me before we got here. Then they went after Wyatt with notions, according to Ross and Tuttle, of marrying you and Win."

Cheyenne snorted at the thought. "And all any of them have managed to do is rustle cattle. They must have more cows somewhere. If we follow them, maybe we can get this second herd back, too, and arrest every one of these men.

"I think Ralston's been at the rustling alone for a while," she continued. "I know Mathers hasn't been here all that long. I'll bet Ralston's been cheating Hawkins for years, pretending he's had a badly broken leg that never healed. He met some complainers in the saloon in Bear Claw Pass. They realized they came from all the big ranches in the area. Ralston knows most ranchers are on their own. The sheriff doesn't come out in the country much, unless someone can show him a crime and point a finger at who committed it. They cooked up this plot. If they'd been at it, all four, very long, they'd've done some killing by now."

"What are we going to do?"

Cheyenne smiled. She saw Falcon's eyes narrow.

She knew she had a mean smile, but it didn't seem to scare him none.

"I've got a plan."

"You're lettin' them do all the work?" Falcon hadn't known he admired a woman with a twisted way of thinking, but he was finding he did.

They settled in along a trail the others followed into a canyon on another high mountainside. She and Falcon had scouted a bit, and it appeared to be a box canyon. No other way out showed itself, and Falcon could see the whole of it well enough. Not many trees and the edges of the canyon were plain to see.

Another herd of cattle and a tidy little cabin sat in this valley. From the curtains on the window and the flowers planted in the front, Falcon had a feeling they'd found where the woman lived.

The men battled to get the cattle to go where they wanted 'em to go. It was hard to watch, and Falcon was no hand at driving the critters.

He had to admit Cheyenne's plan was better than anything he could think up.

"I am letting them do the work, even though watching them be such bunglers is painful. None of them are very likely hands.

I knew Wells wasn't all that good, but I took him for a raw cowhand, or not a cowhand at all, just a man down on his luck huntin' work. I decided he could have his chance, figured we'd teach him. He was too old to be working cattle, but he was hungry and willing. Now I know he was also a traitor."

Falcon smiled at her, wishing she'd give him that mean smile again. This time he'd taste it. They had nothing much to do while those fools tried to gather the cattle. They didn't even have to be overly quiet, as the men had gone down a long, narrow-necked passage to fetch the cattle.

"Do you know how to skin a possum?" he asked.

Her brow wrinkled as she gave him a confused frown. "No. Can't recall ever having cause to do such. Are you fond of eating possum, or does it have a nice pelt?"

"Good eatin' on one, but mostly they were just plentiful where I lived back east."

"I can bring down an elk, butcher it, and haul it home to feed the whole ranch for a week. Then I can skin and tan its hide, and make a coat or a pair of chaps out of it. Is that as good as possum skinning?"

"That's good." He patted her hand. "Mighty good."

Falcon gave Cheyenne plenty of time to

study the setup and satisfy herself there wasn't a trail out of the back of the canyon, then they retreated.

And he liked her plan.

Divide and conquer.

The cattle had to string out along the narrow trail to exit the canyon, and the men would come through one at a time. A good chance they'd be spread out far enough on the winding trail that they wouldn't be able to see each other.

That's when they'd get them.

It was a long wait, and the day was fading. If they hadn't seen the men doing such poor work, Falcon might've thought they left the driving until dusk by choice.

Finally, the steady thud of approaching hooves sounded beyond the canyon opening. There were a couple of hundred head in this holding. Mainly longhorns crossed with Angus in Cheyenne's judgment. Falcon tried to remember all the names Cheyenne mentioned. The HC had Angus, she'd said. And the North Bend Ranch ran longhorns. This canyon had been a gather of rustled cattle held from the two ranches just like the valley on Mount Gilbert had been for cattle from the Hawkins Ranch and the RHR.

A patter of horse hooves sounded as they

picked up speed.

"Pay close attention, Falcon. No reason for a horse leading cattle to be galloping. Whoever it is should be plodding along, to keep the cattle on his tail. We need to take this one quietly, but something strange might be going on."

Falcon shifted as close to the trail as he could get and still stay hidden, as did Cheyenne.

Out front, before any cattle came into sight, the woman galloped, bent low over her horse. She came alongside, and Falcon launched himself out, grabbed her, and yanked her to the ground. The horse rushed on, faster now, startled by the sudden attack.

Struggling, she cried out. It was instantly cut off when Falcon clamped a hand over the woman's mouth. She looked wide-eyed at him, then turned her eyes to Cheyenne, who grabbed her kicking legs.

The fight went out of the woman, and she let them carry her into the woods without anything close to a protest.

They laid her on the ground, and Falcon, judging her calm look, cautiously eased off holding her mouth shut.

"Thank God someone's come. Thank the good Lord God in heaven." Her voice broke as Falcon let her go. Cheyenne released her legs. They both stayed close in case it was the trickery of a fast-thinking prisoner.

She grabbed Cheyenne's arm. "Hide me. You've got to help me get away from them!" The woman threw her arms around Cheyenne's neck. "You're Cheyenne from the RHR, right?"

"Yes, and you are —" Cheyenne's eyes narrowed as she looked up at Falcon. Then she took the woman by the shoulders and held her away. "I know who you are. You're the housekeeper from the Hawkins Ranch."

"Yes, I'm Amelia Bishop."

Falcon was inhaling when she said it, and he almost choked.

The woman buried her face in her hands and broke into noisy sobs.

Falcon looked up the trail. Still no one comin'. They had to quiet this woman down right quick.

"I have been looking for a chance to escape from him since we've been on the run."

Falcon's mind was tipped near upside down, and looking at Cheyenne, he thought he had a partner in his confusion.

"Amelia Bishop?" Falcon wasn't apt to trust this woman, but Cheyenne said she'd seen her before.

Was she tellin' the truth, or had the outlaws spotted Falcon and Cheyenne watching them and sent Amelia to distract them?

Falcon again looked up the trail, but it remained empty.

"What are you doing with these men?" Cheyenne asked.

"I-I'm ashamed to admit I-I am m-married to Percy Ralston."

Cheyenne's eyes went wide, and her jaw dropped. "Married? When did that happen?"

"When I took off. We didn't tell anyone. I came into this canyon to hide from Mr. Hawkins. He frightened me, and I was looking for a chance to get away from him. Percy was in the house with me and Mr. Hawkins, so we'd gotten to know each other. I finally confided my fears to Percy. He told me he'd built a cabin in a hidden canyon. He offered to take me there and protect me from Mr. Hawkins.

"I ran off with Percy, and he brought me to the cabin in there." She pointed frantically up the trail. "I lived in it while Percy stayed to work. The first chance he got to be away a few days, we rode to Laramie and got married. He'd rescued me, and he was hiding me from Mr. Hawkins. Percy told me Mr. Hawkins was hunting far and wide. I didn't dare go out of the canyon. I didn't know Percy was an outlaw then." The woman's voice rose, and she started in crying again.

"Amelia, there's a Pinkerton agent living in disguise at Oliver Hawkins's ranch. A woman. She's been there for months. And longer than that, she's been searching for you, or, more honestly, searching for your body and proof that you were killed."

"Pa." The woman's tears came faster. "I hoped he'd come, prayed that he'd somehow find me. But we went to gr-great lengths to hide. How could anyone find me?" Then her shoulders squared, and the fire of hope burned in her eyes. "But he's been searching for me. Pa." Then her voice broke, and she went back to crying.

Cheyenne looked across Amelia's bowed head and met Falcon's eyes. He shrugged. He had no idea how to handle a crying female outlaw. Cheyenne was welcome to try.

"We need to quiet her down," he said.

Cheyenne nodded. "Yep, your pa, the state senator, has been looking for a long time. The Pinkerton followed your trail to Bear Claw Pass and to the Hawkins Ranch, but there was no evidence you were here and none that you'd gone farther. Your brother, the general, has been in on the search."

Falcon narrowed his eyes. "Which side did your brother fight for?"

"He was a Union general."

Falcon didn't like it but decided not to cut up about it. "Let me round up your horse. We plan to take out your outlaw band as each man passes."

The sound of the cattle plodding toward them grew closer.

Cheyenne tugged Amelia by the arm to crouch down while Falcon hid her horse with theirs.

When he got back and hunkered down beside Cheyenne, he looked across her to Amelia. "We're planning to take these coyotes prisoner and haul them all back to the law. Maybe you can help us catch them."

He watched her and, with some doubts, judged the woman had no liking for her gang.

With a furious glint in her eyes, Amelia focused on the trail. "I can see you don't trust me. And I respect that." She drew her gun.

Falcon tensed. Before he could jump, Amelia switched her grip so she held it by the barrel. "Take this. I'm afraid I'll take the least excuse to shoot Percy dead. He's the closest behind me, but they let a lot of cattle go first. My pa had cattle back in Minnesota, and I am better with them than these four put together. Percy sent me on once the cattle finally started moving. He told me to get ahead of them. The minute I was out of sight, I spurred my horse, figuring to just keep running."

Falcon watched her closely. This was the woman they'd decided had shot Wyatt. Right now she didn't seem like the type.

"Why didn't you let your pa know you were all right?"

Shaking her head, she swiped one hand across her leaky eyes. "I should have. I had one chance, when we got married, but I still trusted Percy back then, and he convinced me I needed to stay hidden for a time. Percy said things to make me feel that I couldn't leave. He acted as if I was here for my own safety."

"Safety from what?"

"Safety from that wretched Oliver Hawkins. Why that man would —"

The first cow appeared at the mouth of the canyon.

Cheyenne grabbed her arm. "Quiet, we'll hear it all later."

Amelia shoved the gun into Cheyenne's hands. Falcon was glad she took it. He still

344

wasn't sure what exactly was going on with Amelia Bishop.

Dropping her voice to a whisper, Amelia said, "We've got one hundred eighty-six head in there. I've been tending them so I know." She crouched low. "Percy will be next."

Falcon whispered in that near-silent voice. "Let me take him off his horse."

Amelia nodded, but her jaw was so tight, Falcon hoped she could hold back from tackling Percy herself. Hoped even more he wasn't being duped and she'd throw into the fight on Percy's side. He exchanged a glance with Cheyenne and slid his eyes to Amelia. Cheyenne nodded firmly. The understanding between them was as solid as the spoken word.

He'd get Percy. Cheyenne would control Amelia should need be.

THIRTY-TWO

Falcon gathered himself, watching as the cattle marched down the trail single file. Finally, Percy Ralston came out. Riding along, looking sleepy. He didn't watch the cows particularly, nor did he look down the trail searching for his wife. He just plodded along in a single-file line of cattle, with no more sense than the cows.

He came even with Falcon. Springing like a Blue Ridge Mountain wildcat, Falcon lunged up and hit Ralston hard, carrying him over the saddle to hit the ground. Falcon had his gun out and slammed the butt against Percy's head hard enough to put the varmint into a deep sleep.

The horse he rode was as calm as Percy. Unlike Amelia's critter, who spooked and ran, Ralston's mount stopped and looked back curiously at Falcon.

Falcon hoisted the man over his shoulder, grabbed the horse's reins, and took both into the forest.

Cheyenne handled hog-tying Ralston. Amelia hitched his horse by the others. They all hurried back to the trail. The cows kept marching past.

"I was up the trail and out of sight before the others came. I can't say how spread out they are." She looked with grim satisfaction back at the place they'd hidden Ralston behind some bushes. "But if you need any help — and it doesn't look like you do — I'll throw in."

She looked around and reached over to pick up a fist-sized rock. "I can keep them quiet, too."

Then, through clenched teeth, she said, "Norm Mathers is the meanest. H-he scared me a few times."

Something about her voice made Falcon pay sharp mind to her words.

"I told Percy I never wanted to be left alone with him, but Percy was never around much, and Norm came from time to time." Amelia's hand crept to her throat.

The color faded from her cheeks, and her eyes were downcast. She didn't say more, but what she had said made Falcon want to hurt Norm bad. Made him want it right down to the bone.

Amelia cleared her throat and lifted her

347

chin, looking defiant. "Sonny Bender might be the toughest, or at least has the hardest head."

"That's the bald one?" Cheyenne asked.

"Yes. Sonny and Norm will fight given a chance. Wells, I don't know about him. I've never met him before today. There are other men in on this but only these four came today."

"Ross Baker and Bern Tuttle?" Cheyenne asked.

Amelia nodded. "I recognized Bern Tuttle from when I worked on the Hawkins Ranch. They came around pretty regular until a few weeks ago. A week or so ago, Percy said we'd be moving. He was ready to get us to a better location. Far away from Hawkins, which I wanted badly. He brought horses into the canyon — it was the first time I had one. A few days ago, after one of Norm's visits, I decided I wasn't waiting for Percy. I saddled up and followed the trail toward Hawkins's place. I was going to have it out with my husband, but I found him tied up on the trail."

"We're the ones who tied him up. Then my brother got shot, and we had to take care of him. When we came back for Percy, he was gone, and we saw a woman's footprints."

"That was me. I cut him loose, but by then, with Norm and the way a few cattle would show up in that canyon from time to time, and then finding him bound, I was ready to be done. Ready to run for home and my father. I knew I had to find an opportunity to get away from Percy and his friends. That's all that was on my mind when you dragged me off the horse."

Cows kept moving steadily down the trail. Falcon wondered where they'd go without a lead horse, and now a second driver down.

It'd be Cheyenne's job to round them up. Better yet, whoever owned them.

"The new one is Jeff Wells." Cheyenne pulled her gun, checked that it was fully loaded, then holstered it again. "I know him. He's a hand from my ranch. And these cattle are all stolen."

A hiss came from Amelia. "I didn't know. I'd begun to suspect, but I swear to you, I didn't know what I was getting into when I married Percy. I've been scheming how to leave him, and I didn't dare let him know I was planning it. But I don't even really know where I am or where Bear Claw Pass is from here. Then this meeting today, and I knew I'd fallen in with a den of thieves."

Cheyenne faced the trail, her eyes cold. "I'd say with Wells, we need to worry about him running. He might be the hardest to catch because if he's close enough to see us capture one of his gang, he'll take off, worried only about himself. That'd warn anyone who's behind him."

"It's a box canyon." Amelia hefted her rock. "He'd have to leave his horse and climb out. They won't want to be afoot."

"Wells probably won't think of that until he's over the canyon wall."

Falcon saw the nose of a horse and shushed them. Sonny Bender, the bald one. Didn't much matter which order they came in. But Falcon planned to hit and hit hard with this one and Norm Mathers.

The three of them fell silent as Bender came down the trail.

"Ralston, where are you?" Bender was alert. He was watching the cattle. Looking ahead. The trail twisted enough he wouldn't expect to see Ralston, but Ralston had oughta hear him and call back. Falcon watched the man come on, crouched even lower, hoping Cheyenne and Amelia were being mindful.

He bunched his muscles to jump, but Bender was looking all around. He'd see Falcon the second he leapt. He might get his gun drawn. Falcon held off, letting Bender draw even with him, then Bender stood up on his stirrups to look hard down the trail. Falcon was on him, had his gun butt slamming down as soon as he hit. He didn't want to give Bender any chance.

The man slumped forward, and Cheyenne was by the horse's head, holding it.

Falcon dragged Bender to the ground and out of sight, with Cheyenne leading away the horse. Amelia had a belt off her waist and tied Bender's legs as Falcon tied his hands. Then Cheyenne was there, dragging her kerchief off her neck to gag Bender.

Falcon hadn't thought of that and used Bender's neckerchief on Ralston, then frisked their prisoners. They'd only gotten back in place a few seconds before Wells popped into view.

Honestly, the man might've just come along if they'd stepped into sight with guns drawn and told him to dismount.

Falcon jumped out, grabbed him, and whacked him over the head just 'cuz the traitor had it comin'.

They had three prisoners now, one left to go, and were back in hiding with no sign yet of Norm. Falcon saw that his attack had spooked one of the calves. It'd turned off the trail into the woods and taken to grazing. A cow, maybe its mama, followed and two more cattle went after her. The next one stopped and grazed alongside the path. Several passed it and went on down.

Falcon didn't know much about cattle, but it figured they'd do this kinda thing when they weren't being pushed. Scatter when a stranger jumps in their path.

The next three cows turned off the trail toward Falcon and the women. One walked right up to Amelia and sniffed her as if it was a pet. It likely was.

"Go away." Amelia slapped it. It moved, but not back to the trail. It wandered deeper into the woods toward where the horses were tied. Falcon hoped it didn't trample their captives, but he didn't have the time nor the inclination to save them.

More cattle took to the woods, wandering, stopping. Then Norm Mathers came into sight.

He shouted, and the cattle ahead of him turned and came on down the trail. He had a lasso out and was whipping at them, pushing them. He was no great hand at herding, but the cows turned and came on down the trail, not counting the ones that had wandered completely off.

"Sonny, get back up here. We're too spread out."

There was no answer. Norm's eyes got sharp, and his hand rested on his six-gun as the cows came down again. A few more went off the trail. It was gonna be a hard chore rounding them back up.

"I need help up here." Norm fired into the air. The cows in front of him jumped and moved faster. One calf kicked up its heels, bawled, and plunged off the trail straight for Amelia.

"Ralston, Wells, where'd you get to? Bender, I need a hand."

With his gun already drawn, Falcon didn't think he could tackle Mathers and take him without firing from cover. He saw Cheyenne draw her gun and hand Amelia back hers. Falcon had a gun, but he went for his knife instead.

Barely breathing to keep from doing anything that would draw Mathers's attention, Falcon watched him continue on, furious now, shouting at the cattle. Shouting for help.

Staying low, which didn't give Falcon as much strength as he wished for throwing, he waited. Mathers came on but slowly, mighty upset, mighty alert.

Mathers was still a ways uphill when a bullet cut through the mountain air.

Mathers turned and looked at Amelia. She fired and fired again. Blood sprouted on his left arm, his left hip. Roaring, he brought his gun around, leveled it, and fired. Cheyenne got one shot off, and Mathers aimed in her direction. Bullets ripped through the brush Cheyenne hid behind. She dove, flattening herself on the ground, rolled, fired, rolled again. Her shots coming fast with her on the move.

Falcon heard a muffled cry of pain from their tied-up prisoners just as his knife whistled through the air and hit Mathers's right arm near the shoulder.

Mathers dropped his gun from the knife hit, then howled. A bullet slammed him backward off his horse. The unhappy critter bucked and kicked Mathers hard as he fell, then the horse took off galloping down the trail, scattering the cattle even more.

Falcon rushed to Cheyenne's side as she shoved herself to her hands and knees, then dragged herself to her feet.

"Are you hurt? Those bullets of his came mighty close."

Cheyenne looked herself over, then shook her head. "It was a near thing, but he missed."

Falcon scowled at Amelia. "You didn't need to shoot him."

She stood, still holding the gun. When Falcon spoke to her, she dropped the gun and clutched her stomach. He didn't see any blood, so she must just be sick from the shooting, or from her hatred of Mathers.

Sinking to the ground, she rocked herself and said with dangerous calm, "Oh, I think I did."

Falcon moved toward Mathers, not trusting him to stay down. When he was close, he saw there was no need to hurry.

Mathers was down, and down for good.

He lay on his back, gunshots in his arm and hip, a horseshoe-shaped print on his face, Falcon's knife in his shootin' arm, and a bullet right through his heart.

Amelia might've been firing wild, but Cheyenne hit what she aimed at.

Falcon jerked his knife out of Mathers's arm with cold satisfaction.

It saved the town the price of a trial, a painful testimony from Amelia that she might not be able to give well enough, and the time spent hanging him. Then Falcon remembered the cry of pain.

"I think Mathers might've hit one of his partners in crime." Falcon rushed to where they'd left their prisoners and found two of them, Wells and Sonny Bender, still unconscious, and Ralston dead from a bullet through the heart. Mathers couldn't've hit him any more square if he'd been aiming.

Falcon hesitated to tell Amelia. In her current state, she might start weeping or dancing or maybe get back to shooting again.

Cheyenne reached his side and saw Ralston. Their eyes met, then they turned to Amelia, who was still curled up on the ground, rocking.

"Amelia," Falcon said, "can you go get our horses and bring them up?"

With dazed eyes, Amelia looked at him, then, as he'd hoped, the simple chore cleared her head enough she got to her feet and headed out. By the time she got back, maybe she'd have better hold of herself.

"I could've gotten the horses and let her have another minute to get past the shock." Cheyenne holstered her gun, dusted the front of her shirt from where she'd been stretched flat out on the ground, and arched a brow at him.

He came up so close not even the air separated them. He bent down and kissed her, wrapped his arms around her waist, and pulled her even closer.

"I thought he'd shot you when you went down." He kissed her again. Her arms went around his neck. "I knew you were still in the fight, so I hoped it wasn't bad, but you went down so hard, so fast."

He left off the kissing and just held her tight, waiting for his heart to calm down.

She held him just the same.

When he was back to normal, or as near normal as a man could get with this perfect woman in his life, he eased back and said, "I love you. I have almost from the minute you walked out of the fog when Baker and Tuttle were chasing us, but I didn't know to call it love at first. And I didn't know how much until I thought you'd been hit." It was all inside him like flames, burning and growing, eating him up, a living thing, and he couldn't stop it from pouring out.

"I've already asked you to marry up with me, but know this, Cheyenne Brewster, I love you and will go on loving you for the rest of my born days."

Cheyenne's face, a little pale, a little bit messy from trail dust, turned into a smile. Her hair was flying loose from diving around but also from Falcon's fingers in it. Her lips were swollen from kissing him.

"I love you, too, Falcon. I want to spend the rest of my life with you, and I can't wait for that to begin."

Amelia came through the forest leading the horses, and Falcon sighed. She was bound to notice Ralston was dead, so he braced himself to tell her. Before she got close, he muttered to Cheyenne, "It ain't gonna begin anytime soon. Let's load these coyotes up and take 'em to meet the sheriff. And then, Cheyenne, you and I can get married and get started living."

THIRTY-THREE

"What do you mean he's dying?" Kevin rushed up the stairs behind Molly. "He was shot days ago. And yes, he had a little fever, but it was nothing serious. Why'd it go up so high today?"

"Just help me." She'd been going half-mad all day waiting for someone, anyone to come home. She wasn't in the mood to answer questions.

Win was on Kevin's heels, Andy thundering up the steps after Win.

Molly had raced for the kitchen when she'd heard them come riding in and called for help.

They gathered around Wyatt's bed as she bathed his face. "I need cool water. I need willow bark. I dosed him with the last of it. Someone needs to ride to Bear Claw Pass for more."

A movement at the door drew her attention. Rubin Walsh had followed them up.

"I've got some willow bark in the bunkhouse and a few other things." He spun away and was running downstairs.

"He needs to be packed in something cool. I got ice earlier, but I need more." She looked at Andy. "You, go fast."

Her little brother was gone, sprinting.

"Win, we'll need to pack the ice somehow. I want a lot of it. Enough to put some on his head and behind his neck. Along his sides. Anything to get his fever down."

"Pillowcases. Towels. I'll get it." And she was gone.

"I thought the fever was going down yesterday?" Kevin asked.

"It was. When I came up here to check on him, I found him like this. I had hoped he might break the low fever today but —"

Wyatt tossed his head and muttered, "Cheyenne. Chey. Where's Chey?"

"He's been saying that off and on all afternoon. He wakes up enough to drink water and have some broth, then he lapses back into this delirium."

Kevin rested a hand on Wyatt's forehead while Molly dunked her cloth to cool it and wrung it out. "He's burning up."

Pressing the cloth to Wyatt's face, his neck, his chest above his nightshirt collar, she said, "The fever came down for a time after the willow bark tea, but I used the last of it. I tried a second batch, using the willow over again, but it didn't work. I'd've ridden to town myself, but I just didn't dare leave him that long."

"I'm sorry, Molly. I should have checked before we left. I've been leaving everything in the house to you, and the doctoring, and there's been plenty of it."

"I've wanted the job. I've needed a way to help out, but Kevin . . ." Molly's eyes came up. She felt the fierce anger of being abandoned with too few supplies and a man who might well be dying.

"What?" Kevin was only kind, only always her best friend as well as her brother. But he'd betrayed her when he'd eloped with Win. Oh, not a terrible betrayal, understandable honestly, but it had shaken Molly wide awake.

This day. This long, frightening day had hit her, too. None of this was hers.

It might be that Kevin had an honest claim to it, but she didn't.

Andy had cowboying.

Kevin had Win.

Cheyenne was a rancher.

Win a married lady now.

"The school session should start up any day now. I believe I mentioned I'm going to apply for the job, and if I get it, I'll go."

"Molly, no! You can't —"

She cut him off. "I'm going to find a life of my own."

"I want you here with me. I'm building a cabin soon."

Talking over him, she said, "A cabin for you and your wife. And that's as it should be."

Something flickered in Kevin's eyes and was gone so quickly she could lie to herself and say she hadn't seen it. But she had. She did her best not to flinch. But she saw the truth in him. He did want a cabin and a life with Win. It *was* as it should be. That was only right.

"Cheyenne and Falcon haven't come back. It's been too long." She wrung out a cloth and pressed it to Wyatt's fevered brow. "I can only hope they're after Ralston and will finish this by capturing him."

Win rushed in with the pillowcases and towels.

A glance at her told Molly that Win had heard enough to know Molly was leaving. Well, Win couldn't go back to teaching. She had told Molly that when they'd talked about the teacher job. No married woman would be allowed the job. Now that they knew Clovis and her ma's marriage wasn't legal, Molly wasn't even born outside of marriage anymore. Kevin was. Her reason for being fired from teaching back in Kansas was no more.

Andy rushed in with a bucket of ice, chipped from a block. Ready to use.

"Thank you, Andy, that's just what I needed. If Wyatt gets well —"

Win's shocked gasp stopped the words.

"No!" Andy shouted.

"When," Molly corrected quickly. "I meant *when* he gets well."

She looked at Andy, sorry for scaring him. "I do mean when, Andy. I expect him to be fine."

She prayed in her deepest soul God would protect Wyatt. Protect this whole family. Protect her when she was out on her own with no one.

"*When* he gets well, I'm going to get the teaching job and move to Bear Claw Pass." She talked as she worked.

"Molly, we need you here," Andy said.

They really didn't.

But they loved her, her brothers. She knew that. She didn't bother arguing with Andy. She'd already been clear with Kevin. "When he gets well, I'll go, but I'll come out if anyone needs doctoring."

She hoped, after her bold declaration, that

she got the teaching job. But it mattered not. If the school wouldn't hire her, someone else would. She was a fine cook and kept a tidy house. She could find work in a diner or cleaning a hotel if there was one. And if not in Bear Claw Pass, then she'd go somewhere else to find work. Her family loved and wanted her, but they didn't need her anymore. She felt like a poor relation being kept around out of duty. She needed to be needed. It felt as important as life and death. Whatever she did, she was done living here.

She wrung out the cloth and rested it on Wyatt's fevered brow. She put just a thin layer of ice in one pillowcase, spread a towel under Wyatt's head, and rested his neck on the ice. Kevin was there, helping her lift Wyatt a bit so she could get the ice in place and make sure it wasn't uncomfortable and lumpy for Wyatt to rest on.

"Let's put ice in two pillowcases and —" She went back to rapping out orders, and everyone jumped to obey.

A brother who was young enough to almost think of her as his mother, but he was growing up and was even out in the bunkhouse with the men.

A brother who was once her closest companion, her partner in caring for a farm and a young boy, and who now wanted a home with his wife.

Rubin came in with several jars of medicine, and the others, all but Molly, gave way to him so she could see what he had.

Working with the medicine ended the unpleasant talk of her leaving. Yes, her time was past to live with her brothers, like some kind of child still in the family home. Or considering all the people who'd been leaving the work to her, more like an unpaid servant.

She'd been cooking for and cleaning a home that wasn't hers. She felt the self-pity well up in her, and she was disgusted with herself. She ruthlessly shoved the pathetic thoughts from her brain and focused on Wyatt. Some of these medicines she'd never used before, and she listened intently as Rubin told her how to prepare them.

It was a relief to stop talking and go back to fighting for Wyatt's life.

Cheyenne led a grim parade. A picket line of four horses, each with a man draped over the saddle. Two alive, two dead. Amelia rode after the four downed men. Falcon brought up the rear.

They were headed for Bear Claw Pass with prisoners and a story to tell.

365

Cheyenne took the lead. She figured Falcon could probably find the way home, but even she wasn't sure where they were for a while, so she wanted to take charge.

She needed to contact the other ranchers and tell them where their cattle were. By the time Mathers was done unloading his gun, along with Amelia and Cheyenne, all the ruckus had sent the cattle running wild. Since none had been left in the canyon once Mathers had appeared, who knew how far they might roam?

They reached Bear Claw Pass in another forty minutes, and the first thing she did was find two riders. One she sent to the HC to get Roger Hanson, and the other to North Bend Ranch to tell Judd Black Wolf what was going on.

She hadn't even tried to explain where those cattle were. Instead, she'd told the messengers who she was and to have the men come find her. She'd lead Hanson and Black Wolf out to the canyon and help them find the cattle, wherever they'd gotten to.

She also sent a rider to the Hawkins Ranch for Rachel Hobart to come fetch Amelia. Cheyenne figured Hobart would take charge of Amelia, but if necessary, Cheyenne would let the young woman stay at the RHR until it was decided how she'd arrange to go home.

Amelia had objected when she'd heard about the message to Hobart because any message would also be heard by Oliver.

"Stay with me, Cheyenne. I've no liking for Oliver Hawkins, and I don't want to be alone with him — ever."

Cheyenne felt her forehead furrow. Amelia had said a similar thing about Mathers and had gone on to shoot the man. She hoped Amelia had no plans to unload a gun at Oliver.

Amelia sounded like a fairly tough young woman. Somewhat lacking in common sense but bold. Cheyenne couldn't fathom being afraid of Oliver. He was just too mild mannered. So why didn't Amelia want to be alone with him? Maybe she was just generally afraid of men.

It hadn't been a long ride back to Bear Claw Pass. They'd been days on the trail following Ralston, but those had been slow, painstaking miles searching for a well-hidden trail. Cheyenne pressed hard to get to town in a fraction of the time, since the fool outlaws had squandered most of the day with their poor cattle driving.

They had ridden into Bear Claw Pass just as the sun was setting. She was weary to the bone and wanted desperately to sleep in her own bed.

She hoped the sheriff locked these prisoners in a cell and let Cheyenne, Falcon, and Amelia come back tomorrow to explain things.

She remembered she was supposed to get married the next time they were in town, but taking prisoners and killing a man had sapped all the romance out of her. Not to say she didn't fully intend to marry Falcon, she did. Oh, she surely did.

But not tonight.

It would have to wait until she'd rested and dealt with the law.

And going home reminded her of Wyatt. She thought they'd get home to find him up and about. Fussing and fuming because he was laid up with his shoulder. But well on the mend. She couldn't wait to see him.

Thirty-Four

"Get up here now!" Molly's roaring voice greeted Cheyenne when she shoved open the back door.

She'd been surprised to see so many lights on so late.

It was sheer reflex that made her turn and yell, "Falcon, get in here!"

He was leading the horses to the barn.

It was enough noise that someone came stumbling out of the bunkhouse in their longhandles with a hastily pulled on pair of pants.

The hand grabbed the horses from Falcon, and he sprinted toward the house. Cheyenne had already shed her hat and gloves.

She looked at Amelia, who was wide-eyed from the commotion.

Cheyenne jabbed her finger at a kitchen chair. "Stay."

Running for the stairs, she almost slammed into Andy running down.

Andy turned and ran back up. "Wyatt's bad. Bad."

Andy looked behind him, one lightning glance full of dread.

Cheyenne saw grief.

Running faster, she stormed into Wyatt's room. Full of people. Falcon came in hard on her heels.

Molly was frazzled. Her fine, blond hair was sticking up as if it hadn't been combed in two weeks. Two months maybe. Her pale blue eyes raging, she snapped, "Get over here, Cheyenne. Now."

Cheyenne was there before Molly could finish ordering her over.

"Cheyenne. Chey." The mumbling went on. He'd called her Chey, which sounded like *shy*. Like she was a delicate little shrinking violet. She rested one hand on his forehead and felt the fire inside him.

"Wyatt, I'm here." She leaned down, terrified at the vivid red flush to his skin, the hollow of his cheeks, as if he were fading away right before her eyes.

"Cheyenne." He grabbed her wrist so hard she thought she'd be bruised tomorrow. But she wanted the contact. She took her free hand and caught hold of his grasp.

"I'm here. Wyatt, I'm here now."

"Chey. You're all right." Then he seemed

to collapse. His muscles went slack.

"No, Wyatt! No!"

Molly grabbed her shoulders and lifted her out of the way. "That's what I needed."

"Is he — is he — is he —"

"He's sleeping." Molly took Cheyenne's hand with her own fragile one and rested it flat on Wyatt's chest. Through the panic, Cheyenne felt the steady, if rapid, beating heart.

"He's just sleeping. He wakes up from time to time and gets agitated and calls for you. He fights me, tries to get up, won't take a drink, won't lie still for the ice and cool cloths. And he doesn't have the energy to waste on whatever fevered fears he has about you."

Molly released Cheyenne and got hold of her shoulders again and pulled her tight into her arms.

Shocked, Cheyenne let herself be held. Let it push back the awful moment when Wyatt had passed out and gone limp. The moment when she thought her brother was dead.

Letting herself be held was so odd. So nice. Tears burned in her eyes. She was horrified to think she'd cry over a hug. Pressing one hand to her eyes, she let Molly hang on. Or maybe Molly was just too strong for

Cheyenne to get loose.

Which was surprising because Molly seemed fragile, fine-boned, and pale. But there was strength in her, lots of it.

Cheyenne sniffled and swiped her wrist across her eyes before straightening away from Molly and turning back to Wyatt.

Win and Kevin stood on the far side of the bed. Andy behind them. Rubin paced in the few empty spaces in the crowded room.

"What happened?" Cheyenne demanded. "He was fine when I left him."

"Well, he's not fine now," Molly snapped. "Don't waste my time with foolish questions. Win, more tea."

Win ran from the room like a lowly private being threatened by a general.

"Rubin, that's the last of the yarrow, where's my new supply?"

"I'll fetch whatever's left in the bunkhouse and send a man running to town for more of everything at first light." Rubin rushed out.

"Andy!"

"Ice — I'm going." And Andy ran like wolves were nipping at his heels.

"I'll get dry towels and pillowcases." Kevin was gone before Molly could open her mouth.

Cheyenne rushed around the bed to sit

down by Wyatt. "Tell me what to do. I want to help."

"I need you to stay here. There's not much for you to do unless he has one of those spells where he calls out for you. I've got to have you here to hand."

Molly looked at her, blinked, then looked again. "You're a filthy mess."

Cheyenne touched her hair, her face. "I am?"

Molly turned her attention back to Wyatt. "Yes, and you look like you're played out. Go clean up and get to bed. Don't expect a good night's sleep because I'll be waking you every single time I need you."

Cheyenne didn't run like the others. Instead, she studied her brother and prayed her heart out for God to touch him and heal him. Not even close to finished, she got up and left.

Falcon was waiting in the hallway when she strode out the door. She caught his hand as she walked to her room. "I guess now isn't a good time to tell them we're getting married. If Wy—Wyatt — if he, if —" Her voice broke, and she couldn't go on.

"Get in there and clean up," Falcon said. "You should sleep, but if she needs you to be with him, then you'll go be with him. We'll tell them we solved all the crimes, found Amelia —"

Cheyenne punched herself in the head. "I forgot about her. Send her up here. She can sleep in Win's old room tonight."

"Okay. And we can tell them we're getting married as soon as Wyatt can stand up for the I do's."

Cheyenne threw herself into Falcon's arms. "He looks so weak, so sick."

Falcon held her tight. She thought he might've gone on holding her, just standing there, forever. He would have if she'd needed him. Knowing that warmed her trembling, frightened heart. Finally, she let go and rushed into her room to shed her trail-worn clothes, wash up, and get back to her brother.

While she changed, she heard Falcon go back to Wyatt's room and ask what he could do to help. She met him going out while she was going in.

"I'm going to bring Amelia up," he said. "I keep forgetting we even brought her home."

Cheyenne found her first smile since she'd gotten home. "I do too." She caught his arm. Their eyes met.

He didn't hug her or draw her close. He just raised his hands to support her elbows as she rested her hands flat on his chest.

Just for a few seconds, he held her up.

Everything she'd ever wanted in a man was in that support, in that one short stretch of time.

Then he gave her a firm nod and stepped out of her way. To let her care for her brother knowing he'd take care of everything else for as long as she needed him to.

THIRTY-FIVE

Cheyenne woke with a start, sat up as if a bolt of lightning had hit her in the backside. Then she was on her feet, twisting around to see Wyatt. Still more unconscious than asleep. His face red from the fever. Wet from Molly's relentless cool bathing.

Molly worked on. She raised her eyes for a brief second to look at Cheyenne, then went to wring out her cloth. "We need more ice."

Cheyenne took one step before she realized Andy was there. He grabbed the basin he'd brought ice in before and ran.

Then Cheyenne looked more closely at Molly. "When's the last time you slept?"

Molly rested the cloth on Wyatt's forehead before she answered. "I slept some in the night."

But Cheyenne hadn't slept much, and she'd never seen Molly stop. Somewhere along the line, near morning because the sun was just barely up now, Cheyenne must have tipped over and slept beside her brother while Molly worked on.

"Let me take over. You look ready to collapse."

"There should be two people with him, and one of them has to be you. Win and Kevin finally went to bed. I'll rest when they get back and after I've made breakfast." The look Molly gave Cheyenne was strange. Calm, but something more, something deeply buried. Cheyenne was just too worried and too tired to figure out what it was, but Molly had a fire tamped down inside, and like a pot boiling with the lid on too tight, Cheyenne thought this hardworking woman needed to let off a little steam before she exploded.

Sleep might be a good place to start.

"Amelia used to be the housekeeper at the Hawkins Ranch. She can cook while you sleep."

Molly sniffed but didn't say anything, just went back to fighting Wyatt's fever.

He stirred. "Cheyenne, Chey!"

He'd said that so many times. Cheyenne sat beside him, took his hand, and talked to him. It calmed him to know, in his confused state, that she was there. His big sister who had always been there was with him still.

He was agitated, which was as close as he got to being awake. While Cheyenne soothed, Molly got more herbed drink into him, more water. She even got him to swallow a few spoons of broth. Then Molly made up fresh ice packs and put one behind his neck. One over top of his head. She set one on each side of his belly and chest. By the time she finished, the willow bark and yarrow seemed to calm him.

"He's going to get well, isn't he?" Cheyenne hated how weak she sounded, like a child asking an adult for comforting lies.

"I think he will, Cheyenne." Molly reached across Wyatt's still body and clutched Cheyenne's wrist. "A fever is normal for a wound like this. The wonder is it didn't come up that first night before you and Falcon left. I rebandaged the wound while you were sleeping. There's no sign of infection. And the tea works to fight off the fever. If it was going too high and we couldn't bring it down, I'd be more worried."

"We caught the bad guys. I haven't even told anybody. And that woman downstairs is Amelia Bishop, the woman Mrs. Hobart, the Pinkerton agent, was looking for."

"And where are these bad men you caught?"

Molly sounded almost like she was being

378

sarcastic.

Cheyenne decided to ignore that. "We hauled four men into Bear Claw Pass, then brought Amelia home with us. We sent a message to the Hawkins Ranch for Hobart as well as messages to two other area ranches that we'd arrested four of their men. Well, not four of *their* men. Two of the men are dead, and one of those still alive is from the RHR. No matter, the ranchers need to come in. There are cattle to round up. We need to ride to town to talk to the sheriff, and Falcon and I decided we'd get married."

"What?" Molly squeaked.

Cheyenne felt her face heat up at the same time she took some satisfaction in surprising snippy Molly.

"I reckon we'll get hitched when we get to town. But we aren't going to town until I'm sure Wyatt is out of the woods."

A movement brought her eyes to the doorway.

Falcon stood there, his usual rumpled self with messy hair, homespun clothes, and scruffy face. She was so in love with him.

He smiled at her as if he knew her thoughts. "Rachel Hobart is here, and she headed straight for the room with your ma's painting. That's where Amelia is. I think

379

she's kinda tryin' to hide. You want to come down and talk to them? We can't let Amelia go until we've talked to the sheriff, and Hobart's got a look in her eye that makes me wonder if she might just swipe her away, head east for Amelia's family."

Cheyenne surged to her feet, then looked back at Wyatt. "I can't leave him."

Molly sounded weary when she said, "Go on. I'll call you if he gets upset again."

Someone really needed to take over and let Molly sleep. Maybe Hobart knew some doctoring. She'd probably had a solid night's sleep.

"I won't be long."

Molly snorted.

Cheyenne would have lost her temper and said a few things to remind Molly of whose house this was and that she was an intruder, but Cheyenne was afraid she'd stop wringing every ounce of her skill out to save Wyatt's life, and besides, Cheyenne was too busy running for the stairs.

"I told you to wait, consarn it!" Falcon rushed for the back door and slammed it shut just as Hobart was pulling it open, with Amelia firmly in hand.

Rachel Hobart turned back, rolled her eyes, and, still with a firm grip on Amelia, led her captive — or her partner in the escape, Falcon wasn't sure which — to the kitchen table. They sat down.

Cheyenne asked Amelia, "Do you know how to cook?"

"Yes, I'm a very good cook, why?"

"Just asking. We'll discuss it more later." Cheyenne sat at the head of the table.

"I told you we needed Amelia to explain what went on out there to the sheriff." Falcon stomped around the table and sat down to face the pair. Amelia had a faint pink blush on her cheeks. She knew she'd been caught.

Hobart looked as steady as stone. She only narrowed her eyes at Falcon. "You don't need her. The sheriff will believe the story you and Cheyenne tell. We can catch the train if we hurry. Otherwise it might be a week. And I don't want any trouble with Hawkins. He won't be happy to have me quit, and he'll be furious about Amelia."

Falcon slammed the side of his fist down hard on the table. "You're staying. If it's a week, then so be it. She's staying." Then he turned to look at Amelia. "We rescued you. We probably saved your life 'cuz you were gettin' ready to light out, and those men might've killed you, fearin' you'd talk, tell their secrets. We need you to tell your story to the sheriff before you go, and that's that."

Amelia shrugged and slumped into her chair. "I just want to go home. I'm sure I've broken my mother's heart, and my father has spent a fortune searching for me. My brother and father would never stop searching. I want to go home, end their grieving."

"Send a wire," Cheyenne snapped.

"Hobart, you can just ride on into town and wire her father with the good news," Falcon said. "Tell him you'll bring her home as soon as possible. He doesn't know when the train comes through. Today or a week from today."

Then to Amelia, he said, "Are you trying to hide something? Are you going to end up locked up right alongside your husband's outlaw friends? Seems strange to me you'd be so het up to leave, knowing there'll be a lot of questions asked by the law. That's a betrayal to my way of thinking, and we don't deserve that. We might even have trouble making our case stand without you. Cheyenne and I might stand trial for murder if you leave."

Amelia straightened up and rested her elbows on the table. "I'm sorry. I just want to go home. Hobart wants this to be over. And I feel like the danger is still around. We shouldn't have tried to run."

"You're right about that." Cheyenne shoved her chair back and stood up. "Amelia, we've got a lot of folks to feed, and my brother is upstairs fighting for his life. Make breakfast for about ten people. Falcon, stay and watch them so they don't run off." She strode toward the stairs. "And Hobart, whatever a Pinkerton is, for the last few months you've been a housekeeper, which should mean you can cook, too. Help Amelia. I've gotta take care of my brother."

Her feet pounding up the stairs drowned out any reply the two women might've had.

THIRTY-SIX

By midmorning Wyatt's fever had gone down enough that he was lucid. He wasn't happy, but he was awake and making sense — mostly.

"They were planning to steal all four of the biggest ranches in the area?"

"Yep. There was at least one man from each ranch in on it, but they might have partners. No one's admitted that yet." Cheyenne had told him twice, sitting on his bedside, holding the hand that wasn't strapped down. She wasn't sure if he was a bit addled from the fever or just stunned beyond belief.

Falcon had left Andy downstairs to guard the women, who were cleaning up after the noon meal. Amelia Bishop and Rachel Hobart seemed to accept that they weren't going anywhere. They'd also sent Rubin to keep an eye on the horses in case Andy wasn't wily enough.

Now Kevin and Win stood at the foot of Wyatt's bed. Falcon leaned in the doorway behind them. Cheyenne was on Wyatt's left and Molly on his right, still urging water into her patient and warm herb teas and broth, then bathing him with cool cloths.

"I guess I can see how they'd think they could take over the Hawkins Ranch." Wyatt swatted at the cloth Molly pressed to his forehead.

Cheyenne controlled a flinch when she heard the easy acceptance of Oliver Hawkins's weakness.

"But how could they think they'd get their hands on this place? We're not gonna just be run off."

"I think the rustling was the main crime all these years," Falcon said.

Nodding, Cheyenne said, "I think Ralston was doing it slow and steady, skimming off only a few so we'd never notice. I wonder how many he's herded to town and sold over the years?"

"We know that's been going on a long time 'cuz of finding your bull in there," Falcon went on. "Add in Ross and Tuttle and their grousing in town, and a little quiet rustling suddenly bloomed into a bigger plan."

"Hawkins they could kill easy." Wyatt

lifted his one working hand and held out his index finger. Then he held out a second finger. "Hanson was getting old on the HC with no heirs to deal with. But he's a known man with strong connections. They'd've needed to make it look like an accident, and he's a savvy old man. If they used the chaos of Pa's will to take the RHR, that still marks them as fools for thinking Judd Black Wolf could be killed. That man's tough and fierce."

"They said they'd hoped to get at least two of the ranches. I suspect they'd given up on Judd's place." Cheyenne squeezed Wyatt's hand, so glad he seemed to be past the worst of it. But the fever had come down once, then gone back up. She hoped this time it was down for good.

"He's got a reputation as a dangerous man," Wyatt said. "But we don't really know what's going on over there. Maybe his cowhands are all in on it. Maybe he has enough traitors on his ranch they figured to win a fight against him."

They all fell silent for a time.

Wyatt rubbed his shoulder gently. "Which one of them shot me?"

"If they're smart," Falcon said, "they'll blame it on one of the dead guys."

Molly eased Wyatt into a sitting position,

and Cheyenne helped to hold him up.

Molly brought a tin cup of water to his lips.

Falcon said quietly, "Cheyenne and me're gettin' hitched today."

Wyatt spit water half the length of his bed. "You're what?"

He inhaled wrong or something and started choking.

Cheyenne glared at Falcon. "Not the right time."

Molly patted Wyatt's back until he started breathing right again.

"You're marrying my sister?"

Falcon rubbed his forehead in a befuddled way. "Your brother's marrying your sister." He looked at Cheyenne. "We're gonna have'ta explain this just right to the preacher, or he'll kick up a fuss about the vows."

"It'll be fine." She hoped.

"I thought we'd do it in town when we go talk to the sheriff. Cheyenne, maybe we had oughta go while Wyatt's feeling good."

"You can't marry him," Wyatt said. "You've only known him a few days, and for most of it, he didn't know his own name."

"I liked him real well without his memory,

and now that he's got it back, I like him still."

"Especially now that we're sure I'm not a married man."

Wyatt shot straight up in bed. Then he grabbed at his shoulder with a yelp of pain.

"You need to either shut up or get out of here." Molly tried to get Wyatt to lie down again.

"Ready, Cheyenne?" Falcon made a gesture to the hall as if he'd let her go first.

"You thought he might be married, and you were already —" Wyatt batted Molly's hands aside with his arm that wasn't pinned tight to his body, and groaned in pain.

"We were not already anything." Cheyenne talked before he could say more. "Leastways, not exactly." Cheyenne wanted to look at Falcon, but he wasn't helping.

"Get out, all of you." Molly stepped back from Wyatt's agitated motions, scowling, hands on her hips as she seemed to be considering what to do to get him to be still.

"They're not going anywhere. Over my dead body."

"Well, considering your dead body was almost upon us last night" — Cheyenne patted him on his good shoulder — "I take that threat seriously. But we're getting married. I admire Falcon's woodland skills. He's a strong man I can respect and who'll work hard at my side and be good protection for me and any children we may have. I want to marry him, and I'm going to."

It was quite a little speech.

"You're just doing it to get a third of the ranch back. And Kevin already gave you his third." Wyatt was reminding her he was a pesky little brother.

"I think his bullet wound has started bleeding again." Molly leaned so her face was right in front of Wyatt's. "You need to be still."

"I do think, if my figurin' is correct," Falcon said, "that my ma might've still been alive when Clovis married your ma, Wyatt. I would need to think on it some, try and pin down the year she died, and I don't know what year your ma hitched up with Pa. If they had you right away and you're six or eight years younger'n me . . . ."

Falcon stopped and scratched his head. "I don't rightly know just how old I am. But I know how old I was when she died. I think Pa's marriage to your ma isn't legal, which means Pa's will isn't legal. So you go back to the original will your ma left, and this ranch is divided between you and Cheyenne. She won't get my third. I'll get her half. And anyway, I have no interest in being a rancher, so it don't matter to me how much of a ranch I own."

Molly looked at Kevin. "If the will isn't legal, then we're out." She sounded chipper about that.

Cheyenne couldn't believe how many people didn't want her ranch.

"I'll get packed up just as soon as we're sure Wyatt is going to live." Molly looked ready to start filling up her satchel right now. "I'll get the job at the school. Kevin, you get a job in town. I'll live with the parson, and you and Win can find a place to live until you can afford some farmland. Andy can either come with you or stay here and be a cowpoke. Unless, Win, you want to go to your home and take Kevin there. Live on your pa's land. It's bound to be yours one day."

"Kevin and I are going to be farmers on a corner of this ranch." She met Cheyenne's eyes. "If we don't own a piece of it, we'll buy a few acres just off the RHR. I'd like to stay close to you all, and Kevin would like to stay close to Molly if she's teaching in town. I have my schoolteacher money. I never spent much of it, so we can afford to buy a few acres."

"Now, Win." Kevin sounded embarrassed. "A man hadn't oughta let his wife —"

"Out." Molly shooed her hands at them. "Except I need more ice. And Win, can you mix up more herbs? And —" The general was back in command of her patient.

Falcon grabbed Cheyenne's hand and dragged her out of the room. "Let's go to town before Sheriff Corly lets the prisoners go."

"He wouldn't do that." Cheyenne wasn't absolutely sure though. "And we need Amelia and probably Rachel."

They rounded them up and lit out for Bear Claw Pass.

THIRTY-SEVEN

"I'm a married man." Falcon was having a hard time not just beaming down at Cheyenne as they rode back to the RHR.

The prisoners were locked up tight. Sheriff Corly was satisfied with Cheyenne's story, backed up by Falcon and Amelia. And Jeff Wells had confessed to everything, as a man who'd just gotten in on a plot in recent days often does. He'd pointed the finger at his cell mate and named off a few other traitors. None on the RHR, but a few on the other ranches. It sounded like half the men on the Hawkins Ranch were in on this. Oliver Hawkins was a poor judge of cowhands.

Sonny Bender was mad as a rabid polecat. They had to move Wells to the second cell in fear for his life. Both Bender and Wells denied shooting Wyatt. That left Mathers and Ralston. The sheriff decided to blame them since no one could prove otherwise.

Amelia had sent her wire home. The

sheriff said she and Rachel could catch the train to Minnesota when it came through, and then Oliver Hawkins showed up and threw everything into chaos.

Finally, Oliver went along with the posse to arrest a bunch of his hands while the deputy stayed to watch the prisoners.

Enough men came around to join the posse that they were able to hold a trial right off, and the sheriff sent a wire to get a transport to take the men they rounded up to Laramie for the hanging.

And tucked into all of that, Falcon had married the most beautiful, smartest, toughest woman he'd ever heard tell of.

"We need a cabin." Falcon found himself wanting time alone with his wife. He wanted it something fierce.

"I've got to make sure Wyatt is all right, b-but —" Cheyenne looked at him. She was deeply tanned, but under it she was blushing.

"But what?" He thought he knew. He might've felt a little heat in his own face.

"Well, it's just, well, it seems to me . . . it's . . ." In a rush she said, "You can stay in my room. With me."

She blinked at him. Those black eyes almost burning into his. The color running high under her tan.

"I don't want to do that. Stay in that house with folks all over everywhere."

"There's really only two. Wyatt and Molly."

"That's two too many."

"Haven't you been sleeping in the bunkhouse?"

"Yep, and we're not staying there." They rode in silence for a while. He said, "We could camp out?"

Cheyenne didn't answer right away. "Do you think we've caught everyone who was trying to kill us?"

"Stands to reason Norm shot Wyatt, but there's no proof of that. If it wasn't him, it was Bender, I suppose. No surprise he'd blame it on someone else. It wasn't Rachel, like we thought, nor Ralston, nor Amelia."

Cheyenne reached from her horse to his. "I don't feel like I can go off just yet. Not until I'm sure Wyatt's all right. I suspect I'll spend the night tending to him, so we won't have what you'd think of as a proper wedding night."

Her hand tightened on his arm until he flinched. Then she turned those beautiful black eyes on him. "But if I do get a few hours' sleep, I'd like to have you beside me, Falcon. Can you please stay in the house with me?"

"There ain't much I'd say no to you about, Mrs. Hunt."

"I'm a Hunt." Cheyenne shook her head almost violently. "Well, at least it's only by a roundabout way that it's because of Clovis."

Falcon laughed. He shifted so she was torn loose of his arm, and he held her hand as they rode along.

"I'm a man who's never had much family, Cheyenne. My ma and me alone until I was barely old enough to fend for myself in the wilderness. Then once I was growed up, Patsy for a short while. But more than anything, I've lived my life alone."

She squeezed his hand tight.

"For a time, I didn't even have a past I could remember. But now, I'm a man with a past, and a future with you. More important, I've got right now. I believe myself to be the luckiest, most blessed man alive to be mixed up in the Hunt clan."

"Losing my ranch, losing what I saw as my future, led me to you, or better to say led you to me." She looked at him, enjoying those brown eyes streaked with gold.

"People fail, Cheyenne. All people fail, that's why we need a Savior. That's why we need forgiveness. I reckon we'll both need forgiveness many times before we're done with this life." He nodded silently, a tiny movement, thinking it all over. "But we'll both try and remember to trust."

They rode on. Hands joined, heading home.

"We need to try and reason out when my ma died. So we can make right what Clovis made wrong with that thievin' will. My past is a little murky."

"We'll get to it, Falcon. We'll get to everything. But for these few blessed minutes while we're headed home alone, to a hurting brother and the confusion of our unexpected family, let's just enjoy the ride."

He bent across from his horse to hers and kissed her.

She returned the kiss, then smiled. Her eyes twinkled. "I've never ridden a horse holding hands before, and I've sure as certain never been kissed while I was riding."

"Neither have I, but I think I could learn to like it."

They rode on.

Falcon wondered if their troubles were finally at an end.

He wondered if they'd ever know who shot Wyatt.

He wondered if he owned a third of a ranch or nuthin'.

But he didn't wonder about love. He had Cheyenne.

ABOUT THE AUTHOR

Mary Connealy writes romantic comedies about cowboys. She's the author of the Brides of Hope Mountain; High Sierra Sweethearts; Kincaid Brides; Trouble in Texas; Wild at Heart; and Cimarron Legacy series, as well as several other acclaimed series. Mary has been nominated for a Christy Award, was a finalist for a RITA Award, and is a two-time winner of the Carol Award. She lives on a ranch in eastern Nebraska with her very own romantic cowboy hero. They have four grown daughters — Joslyn, married to Matt; Wendy; Shelly, married to Aaron; and Katy, married to Max — and six precious grandchildren. Learn more about Mary and her books at

maryconnealy.com
facebook.com/maryconnealy
seekerville.blogspot.com
petticoatsandpistols.com